FADE

Yolanda Brown

Mary Schmich wrote,

"The real troubles in your life are apt to be things that never crossed your worried mind, the kind that blindside you at 4 p.m. on some idle Tuesday."

CONTENTS

Hi, Cecile!
I hope that your
ninety eigth birthday
is SUPERB!! Thank
you so much for
your love of reading!!
I hope you **FADE**
enjoy!! ☺
Yolanda Brown

MONDAY MORNING

For most of my twenty-two years I'd convinced myself that nothing would ever bring me back to Savannah, Georgia, save an act of God, but in the summer of two thousand seven I came home. The hot night air made my sweat stained t-shirt cling fiercely to the back of my neck and arms as I drove. The blue gray dusk of early morning was coming, and I felt the draw and warmth of southern comforts luring me in. Every scant breeze that flooded in through the car windows chilled my skin to the point of numbness and long after I had climbed into the drivers' seat I'd watched the scenery change from the bustling social circles and brilliant neon that lit the bars of downtown Raleigh, to darkened two lane roads that could only be illuminated by the headlights of my car.

I glanced over at the passenger seat and marveled at how few articles and possessions I'd brought along tonight. I tried to stay focused on the road ahead, on the distance that I'd already put between myself and my life back home. I might as well have been floating toward a new destiny, the unknown coursing hot and thick like a thousand volts of electricity passing through me. My car inched onward into the darkness, the hum of my '67 Ford Mustangs' engine relaxing me into a sort of limbo. I flipped open my phone. 4:30 a.m.

The sun would be rising in a few hours' time, but a rampant sort of fatigue kept my arms and legs stiff and heavy.

Every attempt I made to wake my limbs had failed and I felt them sink deeper into exhaustion. I desperately needed a shower and some sleep (maybe just a few hours), but I kept on driving. Just outside of Fayetteville, Tennessee I found the Cumberland rest stop and eagerly greeted the approach of sleep. The car rolled to a stop at the curb before I shut off the engine. The keys swung back and forth in the ignition like wind chimes rushing past each other and when I could not fight off sleep any longer I slid down in my seat, locked the doors and let my eyelids sink like heavy stones in a body of water. I'd been having the same dream for the past few months, the one where I was four and at play in the backyard. I found that even when it rained I almost always hated being indoors. I ran beneath linens and sheets and pieces of our clothing trying to bring them to a standstill. I loved the way things outside felt and smelled so differently: The laundry soap, freshly cut grass, the warmth of the sun.

I'd lie on the lawn for hours and stare up at the clouds as they slowly drifted by without ever seeming to move. The wind rustled my hair and my shadow kept in close step beside me no matter how many times I jumped or spun around. I heard my mother call me in to wash up for supper, but the sky had never seemed so blue. I watched my white cotton dress move and flare as I ran. She called out to me again and I trampled the soft grass beneath bare feet and up the back steps as the screen door slammed behind me...

I opened my eyes a little wider, letting the sunlight in and fumbling with my limbs. My red beads hung motionless on the rearview mirror and I pulled myself up and tried to get back my bearings.

My paper-thin t-shirt still held traces of yesterday's deodorant, my jeans were horribly wrinkled, and the dirty canvas and once white laces of my Chuck Taylors were all like the histories of every road trip I'd ever taken, worn and tattered in some places yet completely comfortable in others. I rubbed away the fog of sleep from my eyes and started the car. I'd often thought about the house where I'd spent the first ten years of my life and how much I'd grown away from it, from the very idea of what home itself was to me now.

I could smell the stale earthy scent of rain and the gathering clouds told of it. The first few drops grew heavier until they crashed into my windshield. Hundreds, thousands and then millions of tiny drops that merged into sheets and fell. My car surged forward, wipers on full blast as I passed a 'Savannah Welcomes You!' sign. In the eight and a half hours that I'd been driving on I-95 I'd only thought about what could happen on Monday morning just once, knowing I'd sworn off the notions of heartfelt apologies and tearful reunions with my mother. I was sure by now that we both had. My grandparent's words were a fresh reminder that had awakened me from a sleep and hung in the space around my head. Their voices held a familiar lull as they rose and fell like an ocean's tide sweeping in not even two nights ago.

"Go see your mother."

I sat up in bed, unsure of whether I'd been dreaming just then, covers sliding over unseen bed edges. I bit my bottom lip, an involuntary response to nervousness that I'd had since childhood, something I hadn't been able to shake. The rain had all but subsided to a steady drizzle and the horizon line reminded me of a painting I'd done a few months ago.

It had taken a lot out of me, left me in emotional tatters. I hadn't left my apartment in two or three days and outside of showering and this nothing else seemed worth doing. Traces of paint had stained the crevices beneath my nails for a long time afterwards and I was reminded of that skyline and distant scenery formed by paint stretched across canvas each time that I looked at my hands. The only thing that made sense to me was my art, though I hadn't had the courage to display most of it. I still thank God for the scholarship that got me into The University of North Carolina.

Only after I'd rounded the corner of the old neighborhood did I feel my chest tightening. The Craftsman style house stood exactly as I remembered it, as best I could. There were daffodils around the trees and the lawn was a perfectly manicured green. I parked my car at the curb then sat for a while, unsure of what should follow. Eventually I got out, pulled on my sweater and flung my bag over my shoulder then began the long walk up the driveway, counting the steps in my head. By the time I reached the front porch, my shirt was splattered with rain and my hair was beginning to frizz. I pulled down my sleeves and exhaled roughly.

Before I could stop myself I'd already reached out and rang the doorbell. I drew back my hand and let it fall stiffly at my side. It's funny how the things that drive you away from a situation can sometimes wind up dragging you back when everything else is said and done. I don't know how many seconds lapsed, but before the door swung open I'd debated running. Instead I stood.

The woman that emerged from the house was a familiar mystery to me. Her deep mahogany skin had lost its glow and become sallow and pale and her long dark hair hung loosely about her shoulders in soft waves that framed her oval shaped face.

At forty-six my mother Angelia was still every bit the fiery southern beauty she'd always been. In an instant I knew that my words would sound empty and hollow, though nothing would come to me. Finally, she spoke, and I was ashamed that I couldn't recall how soft her voice was, barely above a whisper, range and tone that told of her carefully guarded keys and codes.

"What are you doing here?"

"I came to see you, mama."

She pressed her lips together and stood staring at me as if I was the tidal wave of destruction that had just caused her world to collapse. A long silence threatened to ruin what had taken all of fifteen minutes to build up. I hadn't noticed that the rain had stopped until a faint breeze blew. I thought her next words might be, 'What do you want?' and I had been ready to run as I slowly backed away from the door and felt myself inching off the porch. I was about to turn and leave when she stepped forward.

"There's a spare room upstairs. Put your things there," she said as she set down her cup and took a key from her ring, handed it to me. I looked at the key for a long while.

"I have to go. I'm gonna be late for work."

"Okay."

She picked up her cup again but didn't take her eyes away from my face until she turned and walked to her car. I gripped the key tightly then turned toward the door. Framed photos in every size and shape lined the wall that ascended the staircase, each one a memory of something good but long gone in my life.

At the end of the foyer there was a photograph of me standing on the front porch, beaming. My hair had been braided into two pigtails tied with grosgrain ribbons and I wore my favorite hoodie (the one with the white stripes down the arms). I carried my backpack and lunchbox and an unshakable confidence in my five-year-old self. It was my first day of grade school and I waved 'Goodbye' to my mother and boarded the bus a few moments after that picture was taken. Even then I knew no fear of teachers, of making friends, or of recesses and lunches. I shook myself free from the daydream and set about exploring the rest of the house.

The brown leather armchair and ottoman were still in the corner near the bay windows. The coffee table, media cabinet, the pale flax colored walls, the thin silk curtains, the den, great room, linen closets, bathrooms, the kitchen-all the same, but somehow grander. I dropped my bag at the foot of the stairs and slowly climbed upward to my old room. (Third door on the right). The doorknob was cold to the touch and it gave way easily when I pushed.

Dust and light flooded into the room as I drew back the curtains and stood there taking it all in. Surrounding the stark white walls were a dresser with a lamp on top, a small yellow chair, the twin bed, all dust laden. I sat down on the chair and thought of my mother's face at the sight of me. Not quite disappointment or anger, but something different like despondency had seemed to overtake her for a moment.

Now there were new subtleties, like the way the corners of her mouth held tiny laugh lines, though I didn't know what made her happy, though I didn't know when she'd smiled last or how the brilliance in her eyes was like Ruysch's *'Flower Still Life'* to me. Everything was quiet and I was lost in the instance of being here again.

My room remained unchanged, as if I didn't exist for my mother past the third grade. I slumped over, my eyes closed, rubbing my hand across my forehead and when my phone rang I was jolted upright again. The dimly lit screen hurt my eyes.

"Hello?"

"Samarra?"

"Hey Jason! How're you?"

"Why haven't you called me? I haven't heard from you since Friday."

"I know. I just got here."

"So, when are you coming back? What about your finals?"

"I don't know."

"Call me when you find out."

I sighed, hoped that he'd understand how tired I was, maybe hear it in my voice.

"Okay. I have to go. I'll call you later."

The line went dead, but I could still hear his voice ringing in my ears.

HOME

I stood under the shower head and felt the stress from the long drive finally leaving me as hot water coursed over my shoulders and down my back. The sound of running water soon gave way to the frantic buzz of tattoo needles and a memory, when at seventeen I'd sat for my first tattoo. I closed my eyes and relived the way that the scenes in the shop merged seamlessly between small talk between artists and their clients, cherry blossom soap and punk bands playing on the radio. I can still hear my artist Ollie's voice during our session as he spurred me on:

"We're almost done. Hang in there!"

I could almost feel myself sinking back down into the cushions of the chair, giving up about an hour and supreme trust, the sharp sensation of the needles as shading was added in heavy strokes. It was as if the moments of pain were the beginnings of my independence. I stretched out my arms in front of me and rinsed away the suds. The markings, stars I'd had inked onto my wrists a few months ago, gleamed on my skin. I always suspected that each time my mother saw me I became more diminished as a person, like I'd always be a pariah, some shameful secret to be whispered about amongst family members and neighbors only in the light of day. She would want to know why I was here and what I wanted, but now I was finding it hard to give myself any real answers.

...I smelled coffee in the air and heard my mother stirring around downstairs. I laid there on my bed looking up at the ceiling and wondering which course the day would take. The stairs creaked beneath me as I slowly ambled down into the kitchen then took a seat at the table. She'd already fixed me a breakfast plate and she glared at me over her cup although her eyes had wandered over the walls and across the table before finally resting on me. Her spindly looking fingers were locked around her coffee cup. We sat in silence for a long while (perhaps steeping in our own thoughts), forks scraping over half eaten remnants of toast and bits of egg before I got up and cleared the table. Although I didn't turn away from the sink, I could feel her eyes on my back.

I'd only gotten a few hours' sleep last night and I couldn't keep my mind from turning over.

"Why are you here?"

I held my breath and hoped if I didn't answer she wouldn't ask again, but she did.

"I talked to Grandma Camille and she thought it might be a good idea for me to go to the family reunion, since it's been a while."

"You haven't bothered before now."

"I know. I thought that--"

"You show up unannounced and expect things to just be okay?!"

"No! I expected you to be more, I thought we could talk--"

"Talk about what Samarra," she said, "You let your grandmother run your life, but you won't bat an eye at me! What about your father?"

I dried my hands on the dishtowel and fully turned toward her.

"What about him?!"

She shook her head as she spoke.

"You'll never know what he sacrificed for you!"

"Oh, I was wondering when we'd get around to that! He chose to walk out on us! He never gave me a second thought! My name's not brandy or whiskey or vodka--"

I felt the sting of her hand across my face and even with the dishtowel pressed against my cheek the pain could not be dulled.

"Don't talk about your father that way!"

She stared at me with an anger that was palpable, but I couldn't look away, even as she turned and walked out of the kitchen. She slammed the front door so hard there was an echo left in her wake. I stepped outside and felt cool grass beneath my feet, still wet with dew. It's strange how you can never take words back once they've escaped your lips. I thought of how many words I'd spoken in vain. I was sure that she couldn't be concerned with such things. If I left now I could be back in North Carolina in time for dinner with my friends. It would be like I went for a drive. Then I wouldn't have to explain anything else and we could live guilt-free lives. No more questions or awkward silences or empty stares.

I went back up to my room and gathered up my belongings and stuffed them clumsily into my bag, snatched my keys from the dresser and bounded down the stairs.

My face was throbbing from the deepening heat that was rising up from the inside as I sat down on the bottom step and let my bag and keys fall beside me. My phone was ringing.

"Sunny?" (His nickname for me)

"Hey Jason!"

"What're you up to?"

"Nothing, really. I don't know if I'm even staying for the reunion. I guess I'm trying to convince myself that coming here wasn't a mistake."

"Mmm Hmm."

"Jason--?"

"You've got your art thing coming up, huh?"

"My 'art thing'?"

That showing had been almost a week ago. I knew that he'd never taken anything I'd done seriously, least of all my painting, but I tried to completely ignore the fact that he'd just evaded my struggle with loneliness and my pervasive need to see him. A thickness permeated the line.

"What's wrong?"

"I just feel like we're not on the same page. Do you even care?"

"Of course, I care! How could you say that to me?!"

"Well, I--"

"Look, I'll call you later."

Just as I stood up and breathed deeply the line went dead. I snapped the phone shut and threw it in my bag. The last time we'd seen each other before I left for Savannah was when we'd met at Elmo's early one morning just before finals. I'd slipped into a booth near the window, quickly scanned around the diner, but he wasn't there. Two and a half hours later he sauntered over to the table wearing a neatly pressed black blazer, dark denim jeans, a crisp white shirt and newsboy cap. My order had arrived and I'd already finished my blueberry pancakes. The tea in my cup had gone cold long ago. Jason stared out the window, watching raindrops fall onto the slick sidewalk, as I too had done only a short while before.

"Hey Jason?"

"What?!"

He looked at me, his honey colored eyes and full lips set hard against his face.

"Maybe I should go."

"Maybe you should!"

"I waited for you for two hours! You could've called me. It's not like--"

He sighed deeply, sat back in his chair, and stared at me.

"I think it's really easy to be without you lately."

I pulled my sweater around my shoulders as I fought back tears, tried to counteract the hurt that had just descended upon me. He'd acted like our situation was tenuous, like I only sought him out when I was wanting, but it wasn't that way.

"What's wrong?"

"I don't wanna talk about it, okay?!"

"Okay."

I felt a coldness settle over my heart as I watched him get up and walk away, the way he'd done so many times before. As the memory evaporated, I dried my eyes, got up from the stairs and got in my car......

The Magnolia tree in the yard had been standing long before my grandparents Jamison and Camille bought the house. The soft ambrosial scent of its blossoms would drift through the house and linger there for hours 'til the wind finally carried it away. I'd often dreamed of scaling its tallest branches, of jumping through its giant canopy like a free runner through London, but a million days had passed between those summers and now. My fondness for my grandparents was something that had never diminished even in my long absences from them. The retired Marine Corps Master Sergeant and the former registered nurse were my lifeline until I left for college. They made sure that I never broke nine o'clock curfew, that I knew I was a child of God, and that (according to Grandma Camille) a girl should always uphold two things: Her intelligence and her reputation.

They'd been supportive when I'd decided to leave for college just weeks after high school graduation. They'd known about Jason, my grades, my tattoos and I'd visited my heartaches and joys on their doorstep as many times as summer vacations had allowed, without fear of judgment. I pulled up to the house and saw my grandmother working in her flowerbed, out among the yarrow and coneflowers. She glowed, almost radiated a peacefulness as she hugged me. We gravitated to the porch swing as the afternoon came to a draw.

"It's good to see that you made it alright," she said as she took off her gloves, revealing bright pink nail polish.

"It took me almost a night and a half to get here. Where's grandpa?"

"He's running some errands."

I nodded and noticed she was staring at me.

"What?"

"You look like you're not getting enough to eat. Are you eating?"

"Yeah. I've been eating."

"How's your mama?"

I shrugged.

"I dunno."

"Hmm. Did she ask you about your trip?"

"Not really, no."

She poured me a glass of lemonade.

"Are you staying at home?"

"Yeah, but I think I'm going back to Raleigh tomorrow."

"I know you're doubtful, but just give it some time and see what happens."

I inhaled and caught the subtleness of magnolia surging on the air. Even in the waning light I could see the heathery highlights in her already silver hair.

"You are still coming to the reunion?"

I nodded.

"Mmm Hmm."

"Well, good. How's Jason?"

I shook my head and I knew she'd already read my invisible words. She'd always been the sort of woman that could see deep into a person's rough intricacies, within the parts that were most often tied down, fettered by impossibly heavy chains of expectation.

"You know you have to leave everything in the hands of the Lord, Samarra. Everything."

"Yes ma'am. I know."

I still thought of Jason as I pretended to brush away the imaginary dust that had settled in my eye suddenly.

"Are you staying for supper?"

"I can't, maybe later."

"Alright, then."

"How's grandpa?"

"He just passed his yearly physical. He taped his health screening to the refrigerator door!"

We both laughed then sat quietly for a moment. I cleared my throat.

"I should probably get going."

We rose from our seats and hugged each other. As I was walking to the car she stopped me. She went inside and reappeared with a cardboard box: A care package filled with granola bars, pretzels, bottled water, cookies, lemonade mix and the like. I started on the drive back home knowing that I couldn't be the first to break, not this time. I rolled down the window and let the wind catch my hair up in a furious mass of tangles...

THE LIGHT

I unlocked the front door and rambled upstairs to my room. I closed the door and set down my box on the floor then stood in the darkness waiting and listening for some sign of life across the hallway from my mother's room, but it was quiet. The tiny backlit screen on my cell phone served as a flashlight as I flopped down on the bed and tossed the contents of my bag to one side, rifling past my sketchpad, pencils, a hairbrush, a pack of gum, stamps, my wallet, lip balm, scraps of paper, tampons and an apple to get to my iPod at the bottom. I curled up on the bed and switched on the music. The sounds of The Fray drifted in through the earbuds: *"It's always have and never hold, you've began to feel at home. What is mine is yours to leave or take, What's mine is yours to make your own..."* I slipped into an uneasy sleep to dream of Jason and me lying in a field of tall grass. He was different, or I had changed. He smiled and held my hand and things just felt better at least for a little while.

I awoke to the sound of my Bible crashing to the floor. I peered over the side of the bed to find it sprawled out in either direction, pages worn and folded, spine upturned. I gripped it tightly and held it close to my chest. After a long absence it had found its way back into my bag. I hadn't been to church in a month of Sundays and almost every prayer I'd ever said and every sermon I'd ever sat through came to mind, rapid fire.

I closed my eyes. What should I ask God for this time? Wisdom like Solomon, understanding or knowledge like Peter, courage like Ruth or Esther? If I had confessed even to myself at that moment I would've been convicted wholly of complete selfishness. He already knew that what I wanted more than anything was for Jason to marry me. I prayed, felt out of practice, like my words were chafing the ceiling and I was grasping for the light. I got down on my knees, bowed my head and prayed from the depths of my heart...

PARTING GIFTS

When my mother walked into the kitchen I was eating a granola bar from the care package. She began putting away groceries, continued ignoring me. The brown paper bags crunched together as she folded them and stacked them on the counter. In her pencil skirt, with her hair pulled back the resemblance to Grandma Camille was strong. She'd worked at the same small law firm for eight years as a secretary. The offices of Carter, Sims and Dixon were the only ones in town that handled medical malpractice cases.

For the longest time her routine remained unchanged. She would come home from work and cook dinner, do the laundry twice a week and repetitiously clean. My parents barely spoke sometimes, never touched each other it seemed. Now she was alone in this huge house. I thought that during those months that I was out of school on summer vacation she'd have asked me to visit, but she never did, and our association remained dormant.

"Don't you wanna know how things are going at school?"

She smiled, a fleeting grin at best, but she didn't answer.

"Mama?"

She shook her head and, in an instant, she was gone, treading the stairs up to her bedroom where the door abruptly closed, and I was left in silence alone. I needed some air. I walked outside onto the porch. I thought that she would rush out and stop me, that she would say, 'Wait Samarra! Don't go! Let's come back inside so we can talk.' I've always been good at fooling myself right into an infinite fallacy, though.

...I was pretending to be directionally dysfunctional as I drove past all my old haunts: Ellis Elementary School, the community center, St. Peters Missionary Baptist Church or Saint Pete's as we called it in youth group. I flipped on the CD player. A mix tape that I'd put together one Saturday night. Listening to something I'd made was always satisfying. I missed my 'besties', Crystal and Dorian, whom I'd known since junior high school. They would have been laughing at me because I couldn't have been unintentional if I'd tried.

They'd dated each other, briefly broken up, Crystal had proposed to Dorian and they'd finally gotten married last year. She'd left a picture of herself on my phone as she stood in profile, her large round belly jutting over her maternity pants, a broad smile on her face. I'd thought of Dorian and Crystal as the couple that Jason and I should have been: Committed, married, real. I wanted to call Jason just to hear his voice, to see where we stood, to hear what he wouldn't or would say. His number was first on the speed dial, but I pressed the buttons anyway as I sat in a gas station parking lot.

"Hey Sunny!"

"Hi! Are you busy?"

"Not too busy. What are you doing?"

"Nothing much."

I heard glasses clinking together and conversations in the background and knew he was at work bartending.

"Mmm. How's your mom?"

"She's okay, I guess."

"You know, if you don't feel comfortable being there you shouldn't stay."

"I have to try to make it work."

He took a few orders, made some drinks. I wanted to tell him about the altercation, but I hesitated.

"I might be coming down there. I was thinking we should see each other before I get tied down with studying."

"That's great!"

"I'll work out the details, okay?"

"Okay."

"I'll call you later."

We said 'Goodbye' to each other and hung up. I guess that I was just glad that he was talking to me. It was late, around eleven thirty, when I got home. I felt like a teenager trying to sneak back into the house. I made a beeline for the stairs, but my mother was waiting in the kitchen.

"Samarra?"

I turned toward her as my heart beat wildly. My fists were clenched so tightly that my fingernails left deep impressions in my palms. I fixed my expression before I faced her completely.

"Hmm?"

"How long do you intend on staying here?"

"Not long. Just 'til the reunion's over. Is that okay?"

Her eyes narrowed as she looked at my arm, at my tattoos. She didn't respond.

"Why are you mad at me?"

"You know why!"

"No, I don't! I know that we don't see the same situations the same way. I don't wanna get a nursing degree mama! I don't!"

"You'll always be this way if you keep making the same choices!"

"You don't like my decisions because they're not yours to make!"

We were both breathing heavily, staring each other down. I sat in the armchair. She stood at the door.

"Samarra, I just wish you could understand how hard you make things. Your father would never have allowed you to--"

"He never cared about anything that I did!"

"That's not fair! It's not his fault he had a disease!"

I quickly got to my feet.

"Let's talk about what's not fair: Being sent away when you're a kid 'cause neither of the people that're supposed to care about you and love you want to be bothered!

"Nobody sent you away, Samarra! You--"

28

"Or watching your mother trying to compete with your father's mistresses! Or being too young to understand why you just kept ignoring me--that's not fair, mama! I don't wanna talk about him anymore, please!" I turned away from her, "I'm going to bed now."

"I want you to leave!"

"If you didn't want me here you wouldn't have let me eat and shower!"

"I made a mistake! Consider them your parting gifts."

"That's okay, mama. I make it a point not to accept gifts from strangers."

I walked upstairs to my room. My bag was packed and waiting beside the door, just in case. I flopped down on the bed and sighed. My bottom lip was raw where I'd bitten down with such force that it bled. I didn't cry, didn't even feel like I had to. Deep down I was tired of running away instead of having it out with her. She'd made me feel a deep, enduring regret about having come here. It was as if she saw me as that nine-year-old girl again, vacant and void of any real opinion. I could never be that person for her...

BATTLE SCARS AND WAR WOUNDS

In those few fleeting moments between dusk and twilight everything in the world feels softer, slower, simpler. On a morning just like this one I'd held my first art showing at a local gallery or Jason asked me out for the first time or I'd completed my first semester of school. I felt like the events of the last few days were spoiling my beautiful moments, turning them dark and ruinous, clouding my perfect view. The last forty-eight hours had gone by in one long blur and I'd almost forgotten what true spontaneity was like, to go swimming late at night or dance around the apartment fast and hard or to show my sketches to a stranger. Grandma Camille had said that I should wait it out, but waiting was hard, especially with an unanswered outcome.

Jason was the remedy for what ailed my burdened mind. I lay in bed on my back, listening to music and thinking about the first day we ever met: I'd stood in a corner of the Alpha Phi Alpha fraternity house at the annual fundraiser party cradling my drink until it was watery and useless. When he approached me with a group of his friends, I pretended to ignore him. He wasn't going to quit staring at me until I acknowledged him, so I spoke up, albeit softly.

"Hi."

"Hey."

I anticipated some grand one liner, but there wasn't one.

"My name's Jason."

"I'm Samarra."

"Can I take you out sometime?"

About two weeks later, he'd insisted on paying for dinner and ended up spending most of his three hundred dollars in one night on sushi, sparkling cider, later ice cream. He'd held the door open for me and I'd laughed at his corny jokes. I'd scribbled down my number on a napkin. He'd talked about his family, his fraternity, his roles in SGA and the golf team, his college major, his future and the ways he'd seen me in it with him and I'd adored him almost instantly. I loved him for his ambitiousness, his drive, his caramel colored skin, his attention to detail and the way he could level me with just a touch or a smile or the right words.

I turned over and heard my mother walking down the hallway, down the stairs, the pillow crumpled underneath my head. I looked at the clock on my phone. It was six thirty and I knew she was preparing to leave for the day to go to work. In real life the daily grind was inescapable, even for her. I laughed to myself. 'Real life'. In reality, my mother had been tickled fuchsia when I'd brought Jason home to meet her, back when we were saying more than just a few words at a time to one another. I knew that she saw him as a way for me to better myself the instant she spotted him. He was this athletic, gallant, clean-cut, all American sort who would settle me down and normalize me.

He had a certain kind of pedigree that for her, meant that with me he should have complete rights and privileges. In no way, shape or form was I to let him go, no matter how I had to ransom my heart; no matter how often; no matter what the cost. Sometimes I couldn't separate our lives, didn't know where his began and mine ended or who I was just by myself. It seemed to me that our odyssey was becoming less and less about how much we loved each other and more about whether or not we cared anymore. I picked up the phone to call him when the doorbell rang. I ran downstairs and opened the door wide. He stood there with a half a smile on his face and a small bunch of my favorite lilies in his hand.

"Jason!"

"Hey Sunny! How're you?"

We hugged each other tightly and he kissed my cheek and handed me the flowers.

"It's so good to see you!"

"Thank you!"

"Do you want to go get some coffee?"

His shiny, five speed, dark blue performance machine sat in the driveway, gleaming in the sun. We ended up stopping at a coffeehouse, sitting in a corner talking.

"I missed you."

"You, too."

I sipped my warm tea, set down my cup. He smiled faintly, noticed that I was admiring his fresh new haircut. We stared at each other and as he took my hand and squeezed it, I thought that in that moment everything would be okay.

"What?"

I heard what sounded like my disembodied voice begin to speak words that were not my own:

"What's gonna happen when you start school?"

"What's supposed to happen Sunny?"

"I don't want you to forget about me in the lean times. Do you know what I'm trying to say? I mean--"

"No, but I do get that you're insecure, though."

He let go of my hand and frowned a little as he sat back in his chair with his arm draped over the side. I tried again:

"I just don't want things to change, okay?"

"Okay."

We both fell silent. His phone rang and he looked right at me as he pressed it to his ear and left the table in search of seclusion. I watched him walk outside and prop himself up next to the door. A few moments later he came back to the table and pushed his chair back underneath.

"Are you ready to go?"

In my mind I blurted out some elaborate responses, but I said nothing as he paid for my tea. The trip home felt uneasily silent and small talk seemed necessary, so I volunteered.

"Crystal e-mailed me a couple days ago. She's seven months now."

"'Ya know, Dorian and I made a bet. I say it's gonna be a girl, he says a boy. One hundred bucks!"

"I guess we'll see!"

"Yeah!"

Jason looked over at me and grinned. I imagined him as a child and how he must have made his parents breathless from all his activities and achievements. Alton and Cora Henson enrolled their son in karate, French lessons, accelerated reading, cello lessons, boy scouts and swimming and art classes growing up.

Doctor and Mrs. Henson actively held several board of director seats, were chair and co-chair of the African-American historical chapter in their community and gave to their church and charitable organizations, never anonymously or without some epic fanfare or publicity. Their penchant for success and gain had branded itself onto Jason early on and he'd never let me forget that he would do whatever was necessary to graduate from medical school. They'd be proud, I was sure. I only met his parents once, when they'd invited me to dinner one evening, though their dinners weren't like everyone else's.

As I sat in their dining room in my thirty dollar 'fancy' dress, I knew the kinds of assumptions they'd made about me: 'What was someone on a scholarship doing with their son?' or 'Why was I majoring in something as paltry as art?'

They'd barely looked at me during the five-course dinner, let alone talked to me. It was one of the few times that I'd felt relief and dejection at the same time. The former because I knew this night would end eventually. The latter because no matter what I did they would never care. My appearance looked 'ragtag' to his mother he'd told me much later. Our first argument had been about his mother and father and that dinner, how she'd scrubbed, disinfected and air dried the silverware, glass and plate that I'd eaten and drank from that evening and how they'd talked about my inadequacies.

He defended me against the onslaught, he'd said. I thought of him as charming and chivalrous. In my three hundred and sixty degree world he'd have never told me that I was too poor for him. This always made me laugh because of its transparent absurdity and how I knew better.

His parents' reality was of another nature entirely. I was too dark and ethnic looking, my lips were too full, my hair was not straight enough nor my skin light enough. They'd mentally given me the paper bag test and I'd failed miserably. Ever since the dinner incident I'd managed to push away their commentary and completely sidestep his parents. To them I could be nothing more to their son than an acquaintance from school, though we were much more by comparison, he'd been my beau for the past four years.

The car stopped and when I looked up again we were in the driveway. As we stood in the foyer together he swept my hair away from my face and laid his hands on my back. He leaned in and our lips met with an intensity that was ardent.

"Jason?"

"Hmm?"

I knew that there had to be some sort of bridge between our next words and his ever-tightening grip.

"I'm glad you came."

"Me too. Um, I'd hoped that you'd come back to Raleigh with me Sunny."

The grandfather clock in the hallway ticked off the minutes. I thought of spontaneity, the now or never.

"What's going on with us?"

He looked away, as if I'd brazenly blindsided him and he needed to catch his breath. He took a seat.

"What're you talking about? I don't -"

"Monday was the first time we'd talked in weeks. We can't just ignore that!"

Jason continued staring off into the distance, said nothing.

"If you feel like you're making a mistake, then you should say so! I think I have the right to know!"

His phone rang again and I felt like an unraveling thread that had once been too tightly wound.

"Just talk to me please!"

He stood up and continued his conversation with his back towards me, mumbled a quick explanation then hung up. A few seconds later he turned on me.

"Why are you acting so grabby? I thought you missed me! I can't even remember the last time we were together!"

"You are being so selfish right now!"

"How am I selfish?! How am I selfish when you're the one I'm doing this for?"

"You're doing this for yourself! It's no secret where your loyalties lie!"

"Do you think this is easy for me? Do you think I want to have you on my case all the time Sunny?"

We stood close enough to touch, but staring in silence. I'd wanted to take his hand. I've replayed what happened next in my head wondering what, if anything, I could have done differently.

"Why can't you just be honest with me?"

"What do you want me to say Sunny? Huh?! Do you want me to cop a plea or somethin'?"

"No! I want you to--"

"I can't do this without you Samarra."

"Do you love me?"

"You know that I do."

"Do I?"

He was clenching his fists.

"What do you want from me?!"

"I want you to want the same things I want! I want you to be sure about us. I--"

Jason glanced down at his phone before he stashed it in his pocket.

"Who just called you?"

I felt like I was struggling to keep my head above water, like he was watching me fail, sinking slowly.

"Where's all this coming from?"

"You know from where!"

He scoffed, rolled his eyes at me.

"I don't know what you're talking about! I don't think YOU even know what you're talking about!"

"Who is she?!"

Jason walked toward the front door.

"So, it's okay as long as we don't talk about her, huh?"

He turned, rushed toward me, grabbed my wrists, and pushed me up against a wall. His eyes radiated with rage as he stood only a few inches away from my face yelling and swearing. The battle scars and war wounds deepened. He'd pinned me so tightly that I felt myself slowly losing air, panicking at the harshness in his tone, the umbrage in his eyes.

"I'm done! Do you hear me?! I'm sick of you!"

"Please don't," I screamed out in pain, "STOP IT!"

He shook me so hard that the back of my head hit the wall. I'd never pictured us ending this way, but I could feel the icy chill of ruin seeping in ever since last April, perhaps even before then. I could barely stand and when he finally released me I felt my entire body crashing itself, against the turbulence, and I soon sank to my knees, sobbing. I heard the screen door slam open. He was on the phone, speaking quickly, deliberately as his voice drifted and grew fainter. I saw things through a blur of tears and knew that I wouldn't be able to keep myself from falling apart or feeling like I was crashing headlong into something I could neither control nor fully understand, but that I blamed myself for. I heard his tires scream as they pulled away from the curb and not ten minutes later I heard the front door open again...

...The cop reached up and turned off the radio clipped to the epaulet on his shoulder as he joined the second, older officer. They both stood hovering over me.

I'd already been asked my name once, but his words were like static in my ears. The younger officer helped me to my feet.

"Are you", he referred to his notepad, "Samarra Wells?"

I slowly lifted my head.

"Uh huh."

"Turn around, please," the older cop said.

"Why?! For what?"

He put his hand on my shoulder and spun me around and I went manic when I heard the steely ratcheting of the handcuffs closing around my wrists.

"Why are you doing this?"

"Just calm down, okay? We--"

"I didn't do anything!"

The second officer nudged me forward to the door, stopped on the threshold.

"We received a call from this location saying you were trying to hurt yourself."

"No! No! That's not true!"

"You weren't restrained to keep from hurting yourself?"

"No! I don't understand--"

"You didn't try to commit suicide because of a breakup?"

"NO!"

"Why don't you tell us what happened, in your own words then."

"My boyfriend was just here and we, we~"

I rambled off and stopped talking. They were both observing me. The bruises had already started forming over my arms and wrists.

The older cop called in an incident report number.

"I'm sorry. We have to take you in. It's for your own protection, Miss Wells."

ALL MY TOMMORROWS

Every half an hour someone walked past the door, shined in a flashlight and peered in at me, as if I were an animal on exhibit before they dashed away. In all the hours that I'd been at the Haven Harbor Treatment Center I'd gone hoarse from all the shouting I'd done. In that time, too, my heart had been pounded to dust and hadn't beat in quite the same way since. The look in Jason's eyes, the unimpeachable smugness, the satisfaction on his face infuriated me. In the dark five by eight room I tried to guess what time it was, what my grandparents were doing right now. The thin mattress I'd been lashed to creaked violently as I attempted to free myself. The worn leather straps were tight on my ankles and already swollen wrists and the ill-fitting gray smock that replaced my regular clothes bunched around my waist from the restraints.

Sleep had proven elusive, worry a near constant, but prayer unceasing. There were few comforts in the sparse space beyond the bed, a tiny table that was bolted down to the floor, a window with metal grates over it. I tried to concentrate on anything else outside of the present, pretended that there was some great masterwork painted on the ceiling tiles overhead, like in The Sistine Chapel. I'd studied it so closely during my required reading and course work that I could picture every square inch of it, each detail, until my head lolled over against my shoulder and I slept...

...The light snapped on and I immediately turned away. I heard someone approaching and I struggled to open my eyes. They felt swollen, full of grit.

A man in a white doctor's coat stood at the foot of the bed reading from a chart.

"Could you loosen these straps, please? They're really tight."

He didn't respond, but instead walked around to the side of the bed. I rolled my head into the pillow as he jabbed his index and middle fingers against my neck, waited, jotted something down on a form. He shined a pen light into my eyes as he held them open with this hand then kept writing.

"Please!"

He looked down at me. His eyes were a pale icy blue, the kind of eyes that could cleave someone in two whenever he wanted. His nametag was simple: Doctor Antonoff. He suddenly put down the clipboard. His voice was husky, never rose above a few octaves short of a monotone, kept a composure that instantly made me apprehensive.

"Have you used any drugs or alcohol in the past twenty-four hours?"

"No!"

"What caused you to want to take your own life?"

"I didn't try to kill myself! You're not listening to me!"

"Do you think you'd be in here right now if you hadn't?"

He picked up the clipboard and flipped a few pages before reading aloud.

"You're twenty-two years old and you've been admitted, how many times before?"

He took another step forward and leaned over me and I quickly turned my face away from him.

"You go to hell! You don't know anything about me!"

"Oh, I know just about enough, Miss Wells."

He produced a syringe filled with a cloudy liquid and thumped at the plastic cylinder. He pushed down the plunger with his thumb and sent up a stream of the solution into the air.

"What is that?!"

"Tell me what else I want to know, and you won't ever have to find out."

My heart was slamming against my chest. I knew that I'd find no quarter, no sanctuary as he moved closer to the bed.

"You only get three chances. Do you understand?"

I nodded.

"Do you want to live?"

Without thinking, I looked at the needle.

"Yes."

"No, you don't!"

"Why are you doing this?"

He grabbed my arm and pushed up my sleeve. I closed my eyes.

"You should have said it like you meant it! Two chances left."

I squirmed around as his grip tightened.

"Do you think that there's something wrong with you?"

"I don't know!"

"Last chance!"

He was looking at my arm, maybe thinking of arcane things I could never know when an unseen voice roared through the speakers:

"Code Three to the ICU! Code Three!"

The doctor put the syringe back in his coat pocket and switched off the light before exiting the room and locking the door behind him. I felt my breath escaping me as I turned away sobbing...

"Hey! Hey, wake up!"

Someone was shaking my foot. I opened my eyes and tried as best I could to lift my head. The man standing there put a finger to his lips.

"Shhh! You have to be quiet!"

He said this, even as he was loosening my ankle restraints then my wrist bindings. He helped me to my feet, set my bag on the bed and stood waiting as I got dressed.

"What's going on?"

"Hurry!"

He turned away as I pulled on my jeans and shirt, then picked up one of my shoes to put on.

"No, they'll make too much noise."

"Okay."

47

He opened the door and we scurried from the room, down the hallway. At the corner, near the check-in desk, we stopped and waited while he made sure that we were safe.

"Who are you?"

"My name's Bobby. I went to high school with you. Second period biology, remember? Mrs. Prescott's class? I remember you used to sit in the very back."

I looked down at his badge, back up at his face again. He'd been a star athlete: A wrestler, a football player, a weight lifter. His crooked smile was still the same. I struggled to keep my voice beneath a whisper.

"Why are you helping me?"

"I read your paperwork", he craned his neck to see around a corner, "There's nothing wrong with you Samarra."

I looked over his shoulder, down the hallway at the maze of corridors and breezeways, at the inescapable entries and exits and cringed.

"C'mon."

We ran down the hallway and ducked down behind a serving cart at the approach of footsteps. After two orderlies had passed by, we made a dash to the door. He took his key card from around his neck and swiped it and we stepped outside. Bobby looked down at his watch, scanned the parking lot.

"Won't you get into trouble?"

"It doesn't matter. I already put in my notice. Too many crazy people in here."

We looked at each other. He laughed.

"I'm not talking about the patients."

"Oh."

I grinned.

"By the time anyone realizes that you're gone, it'll be late enough."

"Okay."

"There's a cab out there on the other side of the parking lot. If you go now, you can make it. Just--"

I threw my arms around him and hugged his neck. By God's grace, he'd given me all of my tomorrows back.

"Thank you!"

"Okay."

He grinned a minute.

"Three, two, one-Run!"

Bobby gave me a little shove. I sprinted to the other side of the lot, shoes in hand. The taxicab driver was waiting with the engine idling. I stood at the car with my hand outstretched toward the door, daring to believe that this moment was somehow real. I turned around. He was still there, waving and ushering me away. As I jumped into the cab, I waved at him. Bobby nodded and walked back inside. I pressed my hand against the window as the taxi lurched away into the night...

SAFETY NETS

While most of his friends were day laborers or Pullman Porters, my grandfather, by necessity made another choice and enlisted in the United States Marine Corps at the callow age of eighteen. He'd not been searching for anything in particular on a balmy afternoon in May of 1932 until he saw a young woman with an infectious laugh and a lovely face looking at a window display with some friends in downtown New Orleans. The rest was tempered, fated.

She, in turn, was thinking perhaps of nothing other than finishing school, her nurse's certification, home. She'd pretended not to see him at first until, according to her re-telling, he was standing on the sidewalk in front of her 'gawking'.

Her friends hadn't known what to make of him, but she'd already felt the earth shifting beneath her feet and had seen it as a sign that the Lord in His generosity had caused this to be so. The rest was tempered, fated. To me they were the model, the most caring and unpretentious people that I knew.

They were the Ossie and Ruby of the Owens clan, the forebears of a capable, brilliant, but genuine propagation that would see them honored and carried on forever. I owed them a debt that I could never repay. I thought of them now as I sat at the counter in a diner on Lucas Street and Seventh Avenue and felt a jolt of terror rush through me at the thought of my being an as yet unaccounted for fugitive.

What would they think? I thought of Jason and how easily someone like him could make promises that would always turn out to be as empty as his heart was. What kind of life could I really have expected to have with him? It was deeper than face value: I'd been asleep and dreaming a fools' vagary until the very end, the immensity of who I thought I'd been, smashed and muddled, waiting to be reawakened and put back together.

I looked up into the face of a man with a heavy jaw and a deep drawl. He wore an apron tightly knotted around his broad waist and a backwards baseball cap. The man glanced down at my hands and waited, leaned back against the counter. He hadn't said anything about my being here for three hours and only having ordered coffee.

"Can I get you somethin' else?"

I picked up a menu and thumbed through it as he looked on. I took my time, glanced at each picture, read each description before deciding.

"Can I get a BLT with extra bacon, please?"

He smiled a little, refilled my coffee.

"Sure."

When he was gone I looked around the diner. The two men sitting to my left, truck drivers I'd guessed, were chatting quietly. On the other side at the booths a family of four were eating and talking. It was a quiet Sunday, non-descript, perfect to blend into. I turned over the menu and started doodling on the back.

Before my order had come almost half of the menu was covered in everything from lightning bolts and roses to banners and small imaginary creatures from my own inner ramblings. The cook set down my plate, admired my handiwork.

"Hey, that's pretty good."

"Thank you."

He slid some napkins under my plate.

"It keeps my mind busy."

When I looked up he'd already gone. I settled down into my seat, said grace and ate...

...The rubber soles of my shoes made a blunt static noise against the sidewalk. I was only a few blocks from my mothers' house. I wondered if she'd noticed anything different, worried about me or where I was. I pushed my hair out of my face. I hadn't seen my reflection in nine or so hours and I wasn't overjoyed at the possibilities. My face felt dry, as if it was covered in a fine layer of brick dust. I kept on walking until one last block separated me from home. I passed a Spanish-style house with a beautiful tiered fountain in the front yard. Water cascaded down from the top tier, the spray evaporating into the air.

I approached for a closer look. Another step and I was next to it, my hands wrapped around the basin. The water looked so cool and refreshing and I leaned forward and stuck my hands in the reservoir, cupped them together, filled them with water and wet my face until I felt better.

I was still rinsing my face when a black and white police cruiser stopped in front of the house and one of Savannah's finest got out. I quickly turned around, water still streaming from my face and hands. The cop stepped up onto the curb.

"Miss, what're you doing?"

"It's really hot. I was--"

"What's your name?"

"Samarra."

"Samarra what?"

"Samarra Wells."

"Do you have identification on you?"

I handed him my license and as he stood there looking at it I dried my face on my sleeve.

"This is an out of state license. Do you live around here?"

I looked him over. The shiny silver nameplate pinned to the pocket of his uniform shirt glinted in the sun. His last name, Edwards, was carved into it. His face was round and soft and with his lack of facial hair and his unadorned ring finger he looked young enough to have just stepped out of the academy.

"Hmm?"

"My mom lives in this neighborhood on McCarthy."

He stared at me.

"Where are you coming from?"

"The hospital."

There seemed to be a marked difference in the way that he looked at me as his eyes narrowed and he seemed to step away from me, his neck craning back.

"Are you alright?"

I'd read someplace that it was illegal to lie to a cop, but I wasn't sure how to answer yet. Would he have an adverse reaction to the truth if I said, 'No'? Would I be back in custody if I couldn't answer correctly?

"I, almost."

"Excuse me?"

"Yes."

He handed me back my license.

"Have a good day Miss Wells."

"Thank you, officer."

I continued my trek home, knew myself to be stronger than I looked from the outside...

...It was almost dark when I got home and my surroundings were quiet as I dashed upstairs. In my room I reached up for the light switch.

Everything was as I'd left it. I folded up my jacket and stuffed it against the door bottom to keep the light from filtering underneath. I took off my shoes and threw my keys on the dresser. I reached down into my bag and yanked out the large manila folder with the hospitals' seal, my name etched onto the tab in thick, obtrusive black marker: **Wells, S.L…6-23 -07#3597228**.

Bobby had pushed it into my bag perhaps to help me re-write my own personal history that had been distorted and misrepresented by others. I turned it over. There was a grid on the back, a sort of chart with names and dates, intake information. Only three signatures were on the folder. Two were nurses and the last one belonged to R. Antonoff. I sat up on my knees and spread the papers out around me on the floor. The files were extensive, my entire history laid out in detail, but for everything they said there were other things they did not promulgate: I'd kept up a 3.8 GPA, written numerous papers and interned all through my alleged histrionic depression and intermittent emotional instability. I pulled up a piece of paper from the bottom of a small stack. It was the incident report from my arrest on Saturday. I sat down and stretched my legs out in front of me. Past the letterhead of the Chatham county police department dated 6-23-07 at 13:10 pm, it began:

Officers Campbell and Fisher dispatched to residence located at 6210 McCarthy Avenue on a suspected 10-56 A call. Upon entering the residence black female, early twenties was found in a seated position on the living room floor. Female subject was initially unresponsive when asked to identify herself by officers. Subject was then advised that the purpose of said stop was a welfare check. Subject showed signs of trauma to arms and wrists. Bruising had occurred; due to subject's highly volatile emotional state she was unable to clearly communicate the origins of said markings. Subject responded to Wells, Samarra. Miss Wells was placed under custody for her own protection on a 10-56 order, twenty-four hour hold for observation. Release of subject dependent upon doctor recommendation and approval.

I turned it over, sighed aloud, and rubbed my eyes. After I'd shuffled through a few more pages I found a medical release form that wasn't complete yet. I read it, re-read it. If I had stayed Doctor Antonoff would have had permission to pump me full of drugs, do whatever he wanted. It wouldn't have mattered if I could prove that I wasn't suicidal, no one beyond Bobby had seemed to care. I put away the release. There were photographs of my wrists, my arms, my hands. There was one last picture of me. I turned it over and felt my hand fly up against my mouth in a way that was almost involuntary.

I almost couldn't recognize myself. My hair was messy. There were leftover tear streaks on my face and my thick lips were parted slightly, like I'd been breathing through my mouth. I'd had a foggy, listless, faraway look in my eyes, but I'd been recusant when I stood to lose everything because of a lie. I turned over the pictures and at the bottom there was one last page, an affidavit from complainant, Henson, J. Jason. I rubbed my eyes and turned the page. The type-written one paragraph statement was curt:

He'd ended our relationship and I'd become upset. I'd started acting strangely in the car on the way home. I'd threatened to 'cut myself' and he'd grabbed me to keep me from hurting myself and gotten to the phone to call the police because he feared for my safety.

They'd believed him and not me. I rolled my eyes. I wasn't about to falsely condemn myself just so that he could escape. I gathered all the pages together and sat, thinking of how I'd been saved. I said a prayer of thanks that He was greater than my problems, my fears, my trauma, my issues, my insecurities (big and small) and my failures. My thoughts were staccato, shaded in browns and grays crossing and cutting into each other like stalagmites, interrupting nearly every word on the page in front of me. I closed my eyes again and laughed to myself as exhaustion set in and I knew that I would never need another's safety net again, except the Lords'.

FEAR

The year that I turned eight I'd started taking dance classes. My grandparents enrolled me, I partly suspect to keep me focused on anything other than home. My mother and father had been arguing more, until one day she packed my clothes, toiletries, and my stuffed rabbit one morning during summer vacation with the subterfuge of a visit. Grandpa James would make me grilled cheese sandwiches and sometimes after church we would go out for ice cream. My favorite things were there at my grandparents': The steady supply of fresh peaches, the best books, and grandpa's chess set, so at first, I was happy, but after a couple of days I knew something was wrong.

She'd said she'd come back for me and I held on to that for so long that it became a sort of mantra for me, one that I would repeat whenever I was anxious or nervous or sad. My mother would tell me that my father loved us so much that when he'd have to leave on one of his work trips he'd miss us until it would hurt and although my few memories of him had been laced with an irresolute sternness, whenever my father smiled at me I felt like I'd been bathed in light and a feeling of complete love and fealty would cover me. I would secretly defend him in my head whenever they argued. As a kid, I'd looked at him so differently, as if he was immune from anyone's scrutiny.

He'd only come to see me once after they'd divorced. In fourth grade he'd come to my school during recess. He'd lifted me up and said that he was happy to see me, that he loved me as he hugged me. I couldn't comprehend that something about him was different or that it was the last time we would see each other, even as the sweet, sharp redolence of alcohol lingered on his breath. He'd repeated himself a lot and promised that he would stop by and see me after school. I'd believed him. I'd held on so desperately to the things he'd said that nothing else was possible.

But the older I got I slowly began to unravel his aura of mystery bit by bit until my only recollection of my father was of that day on the playground all those years ago and not the things I'd made him up to be in my head. Maybe they were the only minutes of honesty between us. Neither of my parents had tried to dispel the fear and guilt that I felt because I thought that I was the reason my father chose not to be sober or why my mother stopped talking to me because if she was the Great Wall of China, with her intricate twists and turns, then my father was Mount Kilimanjaro-- impossible, insurmountable.

By the time I was permanently sent to live with my grandparents I could already do the dishes, cook for myself and do laundry. The adjustments became gradual until I didn't feel homesick at all anymore. They were astounded by my self-reliance, but for me it was just a routine that worked well. I swallowed hard as I stood at my bedroom window. The phone only rang twice before my grandmother picked up.

"Hey nana."

"Samarra! How're you, hon?"

"I'm okay, um, are you and grandpa going to be home later?"

"Sure, we'd love to have you over for supper! See you at seven?"

"Okay."

I rubbed my hands over my wrists. The bruises were still there. I went into the bathroom and ran cold water over my hands. I'd wanted to rush into my mother's room and tell her about what had happened, but I didn't dare. Even as I stood in front of the mirror examining my face, I wasn't sure what I should feel for Jason~ absolution, joy, hatred? I showered and got dressed then headed out the door. Was it lasagna night? Thai? Creole? The drive took longer than usual in the heavy evening traffic. I pondered whether to tell them about what had happened between Jason and me or to remain tight lipped and let it pass.

The modest bungalow where my grandparents lived was comforting. They'd left the porch light on for me and when I rang the doorbell I was ushered into the dining room where the aroma of chicken parmesan circulated through the air. Grandpa James smiled and beckoned me over where he pulled a quarter from my ear just like when I was six. We hugged each other then sat, said grace, and ate. I didn't have any idea how long I'd missed the taste of real food 'til now. Over the course of the meal and several hours we talked about people from church that we knew, their vegetable garden, which things to get rid of at their yard sale next weekend. I drifted into and out of their conversations without really focusing.

I looked down at my wrists and thought about the Doctor and the needle. I made up some sort of excuse about having to go to the restroom and quickly retreated down the hallway. I sat on the edge of the bathtub and cried as quietly as I could. My heart was throbbing at a pace that forced me to steady myself. I figured that these beats would grow closer together until it was normal again. I blew my nose, straightened my dress, and got myself together. I hadn't gone longer than forty-eight hours without talking to my grandparents, but this just felt hard.

I returned to the table and helped clear the dishes. My grandparents were working together scraping and rinsing plates and I found myself staring at them. Fifty-two years of marriage and they were still enamored with one another. They'd survived so much, especially being separated by nearly five thousand miles all while they were still so very young. I could tell them about yesterday and lay it all out, but I was tired. I was quiet. They noticed.

"Are you alright, Samarra?"

"Mmm. I guess so."

They looked at me, eyes wide, as they sat at the table.

"Just tired."

I felt fear lurking closer. My grandparents walked over to the table and took seats.

"Uh huh," she said, "What's really wrong?"

"What's going on?"

I breathed deeply partly because I was glad that there was only truth between us, but partly because I was ready to cut away the wrecked places, because the bitterness was ubiquitous, burdensome. I looked at them both and began to bring the last few day's events to the light...

COMPLICATIONS

In seventy-two hours I would return home to a man I was sure did not love me, had betrayed me forever. It had been as if the deep miasma was gone and I could see myself for the first time as helpless and weak and watered down. No matter how many times I closed my eyes I could still see his face or remember the warmth of his skin or the way he smelled.

Back at my mother's house, I looked around my darkened room and missed it, missed being here. I walked over to the window. The moon was full and magnified in the starless night and the curtains swayed as the wind wandered in. At the apartment it never seemed as quiet. Just as my eyes were adjusting to the darkness a light came on from across the way next door. A man came into view a moment later shirtless and barefoot. He stood in front of his fridge drinking from a milk carton. His skin was clean and tanned beneath the light, shoulders strong and defined by hard work.

I found myself studying him, his easy movements. His physicality lured me in and I switched on the lamp and grabbed for my sketchpad and pencil. In sweeping motions, I drew his features, free handing and shading all a blur: His back, the space between his shoulder blades, dark hair that skimmed the back of his neck, his hands.

For the first time since I'd arrived back here I was calm, without any reservation. I wasn't lost. This wasn't complicated.

My heart beat in a salient rhythm, my eyes capable of nothing else beyond the sight of this captivating stranger until he shut off the light and was gone. I stood at the window, wondered what his name was until the mess in my head clarified itself. I cautiously wound my way down the hallway to the bathroom and left the light off as I washed my face. The sun was just beginning to peek over the tree tops when I contemplated leaving. While my mother slept I could get away. She'd been a sound sleeper even after my father had left.

Not long after she'd been served the divorce papers it was as if something within her began to fall away. I could never understand the depths of her sadness or the kind of insatiable depression that lingered and made her want to check out or why she'd allowed the shadow of melancholy to cast its long shade over her life as she meandered through long periods of inactivity that left her virtually bed-ridden and reclusive.

I used to hear her crying at night from across the hallway as I lay awake listening and unable to move, helpless. I kept my teachers at bay by shrugging and saying, 'She's not feeling well'. She'd come to pick me up from school one afternoon still dressed in her bathrobe, her hair soaked with water and on the ride home she was strangely silent and wouldn't look at me. I was never able to ignore the way she'd lock herself away in their bedroom and surround herself with his pictures, the clothes he'd worn, his old vinyl LPs.

I wanted to feel exonerated from it all and I vowed to myself after the reunion on Friday, Raleigh or bust. Something was picking away at the discord that was growing inside me, magnifying it, as I walked across the hallway into her room. I took the house key from my pocket and held it in my hand.

It was cold. She stirred in her sleep and the last of my resolve eroded away. I walked over to her dresser and slammed down the key. It sounded loud enough to wake the dead in the enclosed space. She opened her eyes and sat up in bed.

"What're you doing?"

"Can I talk to you?"

"Samarra, it's late."

"I really need to talk to you."

She sighed and switched on the lamp on her nightstand.

"Um, something happened to me last night."

The way that her eyes, somewhere between hazel and a coffee brown and not unlike my own, focused so unflinchingly made me fidget and I hesitated, reduced to around the age of seven again.

"I was, I was put somewhere. In a place where~"

The words felt like cotton in my mouth.

"I couldn't tell you straight away, but--"

"What are you talking about?"

"Jason was here and we had a fight and he, he um, "I bit my lip and turned away from her, toward the door, "He had me put in a mental hospital on a twenty four hour hold."

"Samarra, what did you do?"

"What?"

"You must've made him do it! Jason would never do a thing like that unless he was trying to help you!"

"Mama, do you think there's something wrong with me? Is that what you're saying?"

"I'm saying that he's the best thing that ever happened to you and now~"

She shook her head, threw up her hands. I stood there staring at her for so long that her response startled me. I swallowed hard.

"Are you done?"

I nodded.

"Yeah, I'm done. I'll see you at the reunion."

FAR AND FEW

Each memory that I had my senior year of high school would resurface in different ways, at unplanned times and remind me of the way I'd used my art to get me through and my inability to blend in. The motorcycle boots, Chuck Taylors and dark fitted clothing I wore and the right side of my head I'd shaved made me the object of vague crushes among the boys in my class and the accessible target of most of the girls.

As my classmates floated in a sea of sameness I was far and few between them as I drew inwardly. I can still hear the two girls sitting in front of me in calculus class gossiping about me, how they'd turn around gawking at me over their shoulders, how quickly the lies had spewed from their lips and circulated around the classroom, how other people would turn around and ogle. I'd gathered my books together and quietly ducked out of class one Thursday, through the back exit, around the side of the building then across the front grounds onto the commons. There, just beyond the chain link fence was my day's redemption. I threw my backpack over and hoisted myself up and across. There was no one to stop me, no one to scold me or lecture me about how I should stop and think before I made the wrong choice. It was just about noon when I walked through the door of the house. Grandma Camille came out of the kitchen drying her hands on a dishtowel.

"What are you doing cutting class?"

"I couldn't stay there today. I'm sorry."

She walked toward me. I threw my backpack on the floor and she stood where she was, her eyes widening.

"What's wrong?"

"I think I'm going crazy! Something's not right with me! I can't~"

After she'd offered me a seat at the kitchen table and a cup of tea I'd told her about what happened. Steam billowed up from our cups as we talked.

"Could you call mama for me?"

Grandma Camille looked at me for a long while before she spoke.

"Samarra that might not be the best idea."

"Why not?!"

"It's just better that you don't see her. Your mama's not doing so well right now."

"I just want to see her!"

"I know you do! I know."

"Why can't I help her?"

"I want you to listen to me. None of this is your fault. You have to try and understand that, alright? Sometimes we can't help the people we love when we want to most."

She grasped my hands and I instinctively bowed my head, kept asking Him if I wasn't meant for something else, something better than this. I prayed for Him to mold me, to make me strong for what I was yet to face.

The words paralleled even now, years later as I stood at the back door in my grandparents' kitchen. Her absence tampered with the very fabric of who I was, perhaps. In many ways, too, it honed and shaped me into a person that I would come to love as an adult. I couldn't let any of it distort or destroy me, never that.

SECOND GUESSES

I pulled into a parking lot and cut off the engine. It was deserted and dark outside. The sun had set long ago. I leaned against the steering wheel and rested my head on my arms. I thought about the way some fish conserve energy by settling at the bottom of the ocean and remaining perfectly still. I was in a weightless freefall, too, plummeting toward the end as I clenched my teeth and waited...

My eyes jerked open. I knew that if I just breathed slowly, in and out, that soon enough I could stop the panic that I felt from invading my body and my hands wouldn't shake and I could finally regain control. My nerves were uneven, and my mind was scattered over a million distant acres. I opened the car door to get some air, but the whole world was collapsing inward. I picked up my phone, but my eyes felt weak and I leaned back against the headrest, my fingers gripping either side of the seat. I put a hand to my mouth but could not contain the torrent in time.

I tried to think, to ignore the darkness coming at me from all sides, to focus on something else like the sacred heart of Jesus, when another influx came. I leaned forward dry retching and heaving as my lips bore the bitter, noxious remnants of vomit. I looked down at my shirt and felt my body stiffen at the vertical stripe of puke down the front. The warlike banter in my head began again as I fought between being disgusted and agitated and barmy.

I slowly slid out of the seat and stood up, walked to the passenger side and pulled my emergency box up onto the seat and rummaged around in it. There were all kinds of things in that wooden produce crate that had helped me out at one time or another: A blanket, a flashlight and batteries, a change of clothes and an extra pair of socks, a few snacks and non-perishables and a toiletry bag with some personal stuff.

A cold sweat had formed across my forehead and neck. In the darkness I pulled my shirt up over my head and once I had it off I used it to wipe my mouth and face and threw it on the seat. I grabbed for the gallon jug of water and turned it up. Rinsed and spit; again, until the foul taste was almost gone from the back of my throat and tongue. I found another shirt in the box and although it was a few sizes too big and gaped at the neck, it was dry and smelled good, clean.

After I'd pulled back my hair I sat back down and put my feet up. The night seemed long, but fragmented. The heat index had topped out at seventy-five degrees most nights, though it felt much hotter. I don't know how long I sat there before I grew restless, but soon I was back out of the car and standing at the guardrail near the edge of the bluff overlooking the city. The trees bent and bowed in the wind, dark outlines driven by an invisible air. The hundreds of lights that were shining from below reminded me of the glowing yellow pegs scattered across a Lite Brite board. They were so distant. Each one of those lights led someplace or belonged to someone because they feared the dark or loved the light and I wondered what waited on the other side of the bluff.

The railing was cold to the touch and I ran my hands back and forth across the steel. I thought about the drop and how long it would take me to meet the bottom, about the last words that Jason had said to me before we'd lost our equanimity, before I spent most of my waking hours trying to mollify him, knowing that the same hands that could hold me tightly had left plenty of bruises and left me with few choices other than walking away.

I thought of the grace of Jesus as I silently asked for His help. I thought of the way that I'd lost all my reasons to keep on believing in love, about the way I could either alter things now or perish in the quondam and what was. I thought of why I'd really come back here. If it was only because of a dream, then surely, I would never have ventured away from my life in progress. There had to be something else, some tangible beacon that bade me to be still and wait, though I couldn't see it now. I took one last look at the lights then I walked back to my car.

I found a spare key beneath the doormat and just as I put it into the lock, the handle turned, and my mother opened the front door. I hastily dropped the key into my bag and followed her into the kitchen where she sat on a stool next to the island. Her petal pink top and dark slacks made her look distinguished. I set down the bags of Chinese takeout I'd brought with me and walked over to the sink. As I washed my hands, the scent of lighter fluid filled my nose. I sniffled then wheeled around and searched through the bags, never fully looking at her.

"How was work?"

"I didn't go to work today. I had to take care of some things."

I opened the lid of my Styrofoam container and broke apart my wooden chopsticks as I sat down across from her.

"Sorry about yesterday."

"Yesterday?"

"Yeah. Sorry."

I slid the second container across the counter toward her.

"I got you a number one. It's got beef in it."

"Thank you."

Some of the color had come back into her cheeks and her face was a little fuller, a little healthier. She looked pretty. Her hair was pulled back into a fishtail braid that hit at the middle of her back. She crossed one of her legs over the other but didn't speak. I wanted to ask her about the smell emanating from the backyard, but I did not dare. She was watching me eat as if I was some new and undiscovered specimen underneath a glass atrium to be meticulously studied or recorded, as if she was trying to remember my face, preserve the memory.

"Aren't you going to eat yours?"

"Later. Did you get your exam grades back?"

I shook my head as I looked up from my food, continued chewing.

"Not all of them."

I carefully opened a packet of soy sauce and spread it around. With the loathsome undercurrent in the air I wondered how someone could be sitting in the same room and still be a trillion miles away. The bitter taste in my mouth was returning, couldn't be washed out easily with water, and I knew that it would be there as long as I stayed. Her words from the night before gamboled their way into my head again. Only one thing came to mind: Miscalculation. Both hers and mine and the unrequited truth in us waiting to spill out.

"Are you going to the reunion?"

She nodded.

"More than likely."

"I heard that Gramma Owens is coming."

"You've never met her. She's held this family together for a long time. It would be completely different without her."

"I can't wait to meet her."

My mother smiled to herself and brushed her hand across her eyebrow. Just as I finished my lunch the phone rang. She looked away toward the other room. I tentatively watched as she rose from her seat and went upstairs to answer the phone. When she was well enough away from me I gathered up the trash on the counter and put everything into the kitchen bag. I picked up the trash and walked toward the door, listening for her return. Once I was out of the house I slipped out of the gate that encircled a portion of the yard.

In the eastern corner the smell of lighter fluid flared as I got closer and saw a small plume of smoke tickling its way up into the air and the still smoldering remnants of something burning down to its foundation. I stood over the ashes, nudged at the unburned bits of paper with my foot. I picked up a piece and tucked it into my pocket before I grabbed the trash bag and tossed it into the big bin at the back of the house. As I came around the side I heard the back door open and my mother met me halfway between the gate and the door.

"Where were you?"

"I just went to take out the trash."

"Mmm."

The light in her eyes had been replaced with a dismissive, lengthy stare and she kept her arms close to her sides.

"Who was that on the phone?"

"Your grandmother."

"Oh. Is everything okay?"

"Why wouldn't it be?"

I shrugged.

"Just asking."

"Everything's fine."

The question about the lighter fluid and the fire danced a pirouette at the tip of my tongue, but I was silent. She saw me looking at the gold charm bracelet on her left wrist and she lifted her arm up. I could recall each of the six charms almost photographically: The silver key, the red dimensional heart, the shiny horseshoe, the clear diamond, the little blue bird and the lock and the way they would clink together whenever she walked or moved her arm, the prismatic rainbow that would appear when the sun would hit the diamond.

"You still have that?"

A fat grin spread over her face.

"Of course, your father gave it to me."

"I know. Why are you wearing it?"

Until I truly studied her face, I hadn't realized what my own expression might be outwardly portraying, and I quickly looked away. She turned around and went back into the house, but I didn't follow. I walked out through the gate and onto the driveway, back to my car. All these years later, he still held sway over her, still controlled the rising and setting of her sun.

I sat in the passenger seat and looked down the street and out into the distance. I wished that I was back at home sitting near the window sketching or at the art supply store or doing laundry or anywhere except here. At the house next door, a man came outside carrying a small boy in his arms. After a few minutes the kid was placed in the backseat of their SUV and they were gone.

Without looking back toward the door, I pulled the charred sliver of paper from my pocket and tried to make sense of what seemed like every other letter, perhaps a name-her name. There were numbers and words that I did not understand: Sample size, fine needle aspiration, hormone receptor negative. I let the wind snatch it from my hand and I watched as it fluttered away down the street in sweeping arcs and loops. When I walked back through the door she was standing at the sink and I took a bottle of water from the refrigerator. In many ways I was testing the waters that we swam in as well.

"I got a B on my psychology exam."

"That's fine Samarra, but that's not what this is about!"

"Then what is it about?"

For every word I'd thought of saying on my way into the kitchen there were at least three of four more I'd dismissed from my mind. She turned and faced me.

"I was okay until you came back!"

"What? What are you talking about?"

I could see that her wrist was bare again. I thought of my own secrets, oddly enough, and which ones she would never know about.

"I can't do this anymore!"

"Mama--"

"That's enough!"

She closed her eyes and sighed.

"Samarra?"

"What!?"

I felt my heart beating riotously.

"The only reason that I'm so hard on you is because I know that you're not living up to what you could be! I don't want you to squander your potential!"

"Yeah!? What do you even know about me?"

My grip tightened around the bottle. At any moment either of us could have ended the self-induced torture that we nefariously handed to one another, but it was not to be.

"What about when I called you last semester and invited you to come see my sculpture?"

"I had to work!"

"It was a Saturday!"

She turned away and looked out the window as I stared her down.

"All you had to say was that you couldn't make it! That's all you ever had to say. Just tell me that you can't be there for me mama!"

"Why does everything have to be about YOU Samarra?"

"It doesn't! It's not!"

"Well it seems like it to me!"

"You're supposed to be my family! If nobody else cares, you should."

"Maybe it's about time you started caring for yourself."

"What's that supposed to mean?"

"You're a smart girl, you'll figure it out soon enough."

Her ability to just cancel out everything else around her, including her feelings, was the thing that bothered me most about her. She turned around rather abruptly and walked away, was halfway up the stairs when I called up after her:

"What's wrong with you? What did you burn?"

She bolted downstairs to where I stood in the doorway that separated the kitchen and dining room. She tried to regroup as she clenched her teeth. I looked over her face and felt a sudden pang of sadness in my heart, perhaps because I couldn't reach her.

"It would've been better if you hadn't come here."

"What was it?"

"That is NONE of your business!"

"Look, if you're not going to tell me what's going on with you, fine, but don't treat me like I'm stupid!"

She spoke slowly.

"I don't want you here! You need to leave!"

I walked over to the counter and picked up my bag.

"Don't hate me, mama."

"It's too late for that now."

I heard myself gasp and saw her frown slowly morph into a wry smile. I wiped my eyes and looked out the door.

"You're mad at me because of a stupid bracelet. None of it matters! Can't you see that?"

She picked up a glass from the counter and threw it at me, where it broke against the wall next to my head and shattered into pieces. I put a hand to my mouth but stood unmoved as I looked down at the crystal fragments.

"Get out! Now!"

I walked to the door and pushed it with such force that it banged against the side of the house. The arrows of animosity had been loosed by thousands of archers at once and I hoped that they found their marks...

A HISTORY OF INERTIA

I'd driven around in a manner befitting a tourist last night. It scarcely felt like I inhabited the land of the living when the sun came up and I was forced to choose between fight and flight again. I'd told myself that I'd been doing my mother a favor by keeping my distance, though I'd agonized, ate less, and stayed up late some nights dismantling my relationship with her, that somehow it was the right thing--the mature thing to do. I was pulling myself apart at the seams just trying to get her to acknowledge me again and it felt infinitely better that she shouldn't worry about me. People moved on every day, why couldn't I?

On Friday it rained outside, and I was exiled to the inside of my grandparents' house. When I walked into the kitchen Grandma Camille directed me to some peppers on the counter that needed dicing. As I stood at the sink washing my hands I listened to them discussing a young

Senator from Hawaii with a unique name who'd be throwing his bid in to become the forty fourth President of the United States, a man named Barack Obama. The hopeful tone of their conversation made me smile.

"I think that he can make some definite changes for the better."

My grandmother nodded.

"He has a good chance, I think."

I cut up the peppers and I felt my hands working. I missed the rhythmic motions that accompanied painting, as well. I wanted to feel the brush between my fingers again and watch the canvas spring back as I applied the paint. I'd salted away one hundred dollars and as I made a mental note of supplies to buy a stream of color quickly saturated my conscious thoughts and I imagined the peppers as blue, black and white polka dotted, tartan plaid, gold foil starred and peppermint striped. I rubbed my eyes against my sleeve, shook my head. When I looked up again my grandmother had crossed the kitchen and was next to me with her hand on my shoulder.

"Samarra, are you okay?"

"Hmm?"

"Are you okay? You had the strangest look on your face."

"Did I?"

She took the knife from my hand and set it down on the counter.

"Maybe you should go sit down."

I pulled up a chair at the table and sat down.

"Is it Jason?"

"No!"

Grandpa Jamison stopped what he was doing at the refrigerator, listening intently. She took up my face in her hands and looked at me directly.

"Samarra you don't need a man to validate who you are!"

"I know."

"It doesn't matter who he is! You deserve to be treated with respect!"

"I know."

I was the one who studied psychology, but I barely knew it by the direction this conversation was taking.

"What's on your mind?"

"Everything and nothing."

I knew that I had to learn to self-soothe without always burdening them down with my problems. Grandpa Jamison folded his arms across his chest.

"It's your mama, isn't it?"

"What?"

"You've barely been home and when you are it's only for a few hours at a time."

"It's because I can't talk to her."

"You have to be able to see where she's coming from, too."

I sighed.

"Why?! All she ever talks about is dad. We can't even have a conversation unless we talk about him!"

My grandparents looked at one another, then at me.

"Why do you think that she feels that way about him?"

Until he asked me I hadn't considered that my father may not be completely responsible for my mother's history of inertia, that the edifices that they occupied had crumbled a long time ago, before I'd even been born. We could never move forward until God granted us permission . I shook my head as I spoke.

"I don't know."

He leaned forward in his seat.

"Samarra, your father and I didn't see things exactly alike."

"Like what?"

He scratched his eyebrow, sighed.

"Like your mother."

I got up from the table.

"I have to finish the peppers!"

"Wait!"

His eyes were wide, and I eased back down into my seat. I felt my lips part, but I couldn't say anything. I'd wanted to ask where I fit in, if it was wrong for me to be angry with her, if I should go home.

"You didn't like him?"

"No."

"Did you ever?"

His chin jutted out stiffly and his eyes narrowed.

"Not really."

The severity of his disdain had never seemed as obvious before, but knowing Grandpa Jamison it wasn't hard to guess why he'd kept his peace: He'd done his best to protect his only daughter, no matter how much she believed in Anderson, the then nineteen year old architectural student with lofty ideas and strong opinions that trumped everyone else's, including her own most of the time. I sat back in my seat.

"It's not that he was a bad person. I just don't think he was right for her."

"What if she really saw something different in him?"

"I think that his differences were what made her want to stay away once she left."

My grandmother glanced over at my grandfather. She placed her hand over his and I saw the subtle nod of her head and we were maintaining radio silence again. She left the room then returned cradling a pale blue photo album in her arms. She sat down again and opened the cover with my grandfather and me looking on. My eyes fell to the page. The photos were neatly arranged, a brief caption beneath each one. There were pictures of church picnics, family vacations, informal snapshots of my mother and her older brother, Uncle Mike, birthday parties. She pointed to one photo in the bottom left corner of a young woman in a tea length patterned dress and gloves and a wide brimmed hat.

I read the caption: 'Angelia, 16. c. 1977'. I'd never seen a picture of my mother as a teenager before. I looked up at my grandmother, disbelieving. She smiled.

"You're more like her than you know."

I'd all but forgotten lately that my mother was young once, perhaps filled with dreams and possibilities that were fresh and attainable, easy for her. While the rest of the world had moved on she'd stayed exactly where she was, unchanged, even as I moved away, became a junior then a senior at UNC, grew in other ways, too. She rested her hand on a picture on the last page.

"This is the only copy that we have. She gave this to me after they were married."

Grandma Camille carefully removed the photo and handed it to me. It was my parents' wedding photo. The authenticity of youth and love had melded together in them as my father held my mothers' hand and she clenched her bouquet in the other and he kissed her cheek.

"Wow!"

"You keep it."

Grandpa James took the picture from me and looked at it then at me.

"You alright, kid?"

"I think so."

In time he spoke again, still looking at the photograph.

"I shouldn't have tried to change her mind. I should have given them a chance. What I mistook for arrogance was confidence, maybe. I can't tell him that now, but you can still talk to your mama Samarra."

"Do you think that if I try talking now she'll listen?"

"There's only one way to find out, 'ya know?"

...I snuck around to the side of the house until I'd worked my way to the gate. After I'd pushed open the latch and walked through to the back of the house I stood and peered through the window, but the kitchen was dark. I popped the door lock with a deconstructed paper clip and walked into the house. I found my mother sound asleep on the sofa in front of the television, as if she'd been waiting up for me some late night. I took off my shoes and went upstairs to collect the few things I'd left behind: A book, a couple CDs and a scarf.

When I returned she hadn't moved. I could only wonder what was going on with her, why she'd been so resistant to my being here. The clock in the hallway was ticking, as always. I'd thought of the conversation with my grandparent's non-stop on the drive here, but now that I stood before her the words would not unwind and dislodge themselves and all I could think to whisper was, 'I love you, mama'. I opened my bag and took out the photo Grandma Camille had given me and put it next to her pillow. This vestige of what she coveted most could speak volumes, say things that I could never be able to verbalize, at least not right now. I turned and walked through the back door and into the cool night air, back to my car.

SEARCHING FOR PERFECTION

Across the way a door opened, and someone ran for shelter from the rain at a parked car. Once inside he tousled his hair and settled into the drivers' seat. I reached over and cranked up my car, but there was no turnover. I tried again--nothing. Twice more, but it wouldn't start. I yelled out and sank my head into my hands. I tried again and again, but there was no response from the car. I turned off the ignition and clutched the keys in my hand. I thought only for a moment about how the osmanthus would be in bloom and the tiny white flowers would be visible from the north window of the apartment by now.

My paternal grandmother called them tea olives. In the only existing photo of her, she'd posed behind a hedge of tea olives in her flowing white gown. I'd never seen someone look so genuinely happy. I'd always like to think that my mother had that same kind of smile right after she'd given birth to me and that it had lingered for a long time afterwards or come during the day as she busied herself with tasks and I invaded her thoughts. It was the most random of thoughts that had crossed my mind since I'd gotten here. Before long I was in tears and I couldn't stop myself. I was instantly taken aback by someone standing at my car door and I dried my eyes. The car across the street sat empty.

I looked up at him as he motioned for me to roll down the window. I only cracked it a few inches as he leaned over, but quickly recoiled knowing that he'd startled me.

"I'm sorry. I didn't mean to scare you. Do you need help?"

He pronounced every word with a sharp fidelity that gave away an accent that was neither southern nor American. There was an acuteness in his stare and with raised brows he laconically questioned my next move. I hesitated, nodded slowly.

"It won't start."

I had taken for granted that he was standing out in the rain being soaked through and through.

"You can get in if you want."

He lingered for a moment then walked around the back and got in on the passenger side. The sleeves of his dark blue oxford shirt were rolled up to his elbows and he shuddered from the cold night air.

"Thank you."

I could feel a warmness growing in my face, like my junior high crush had just been revealed to the entire world.

"My name's Damon Marsden, by the way. I live next door."

He extended his hand.

"I'm Samarra Wells."

He shook my hand. His were soft and clean. On the ring finger of his left hand there was a single band of gold. We were both quiet.

"So, what happened?"

"Hmm?"

"What happened to your car?"

"I don't know. It was fine yesterday."

After Damon had asked me a bunch of questions about oil changes and fan belts and tune ups, none of which I knew anything about, he asked to see my owner's manual, quickly leafed through it.

"We should move your car away from the curb, so you don't get a citation."

He got out and came back around to the driver's side again. He leaned over and shifted into neutral, angled in through the window and used his upper body to guide the car into his driveway.

"I'm going to need you to steer Samarra."

I'd never heard my name spoken by someone with an accent and I found myself listening carefully to understand him. He glanced down at my hands, wrapped around the steering wheel, then pushed it along until it was secure.

"You live next door?"

I shook my head.

"No. I'm not from here. Not really."

I took my phone from my pocket and dialed the number of a taxicab company that I'd committed to memory. He cupped his hands together and blew warm air into them. I pretended not to see him looking up into the sky quietly observing the stars, searching for perfection, perhaps.

"Beautiful, aren't they?"

He smiled and tugged at his earlobe. I got out of the car and stood beside him, leaned against the door, stargazing.

"You're right."

After a moment he turned and looked at me. He spoke softly.

"If you're not in a hurry you can wait inside."

I'd forgotten that southerners, even transplanted ones, were used to hospitality and kindness. The five months I'd spent interning in New York for my fellowship had caused me to deeply miss my roots, but as a kid I always wanted to be a native of some other place, some exotic faraway island, had never wanted to admit that I was from the south because of the stories my grandparents would tell me about the Movement of the sixties and seventies. Now I found myself feeling like there was something about Savannah that I'd truly missed.

"Do you usually invite women home so soon?"

Almost suddenly his eyes gravitated downward and a slight blush was followed by a smile.

"No. No, I don't."

In time a set of headlights peeked through the darkness and the taxi stopped in front of us. He opened the door for me.

"Thank you, Damon."

"You're welcome."

He held up my car manual.

"I'll get this back to you."

Damon smiled faintly and tapped the top of the cab as it pulled away. I made a mental list of things that awaited me when I got home. I called Grandpa and Grandma to see if they would put me up for the night. I could imagine their excitement when they'd see me...

FIREFLIES FOR SEARCHLIGHTS

I opened my eyes and felt a stagnant heat encompassing the room. The calendar on my phone said that it was July fifteenth. I silently wished that I could go back in time and change bits and pieces of this week. I'd wanted to travel this summer, go to the museum, learn to cook a formal five course dinner, take more dance lessons. I turned over on my side, could still hear my mother's voice echoing in my head, as I attempted to give myself a small measure of solace so that I could stay afloat. I got up and got dressed, left my grandparents sleeping...

...I pulled up in my grandparent's sedan to find Damon already at work on my car. I got out and slowly approached him, noticed a tricycle lying on the lawn.

"Good morning."

He looked up from his work.

"Good morning."

He was quiet and I stood watching as he moved around the sides, wrench in hand. I tried to follow along, but all the parts were perplexing.

"So, what's wrong with it?"

"Your carburetor needed replacing."

I shook my head.

"Your carburetor is what gets the petrol to your engine, see?"

I nodded.

"You do this for work then?"

"No, I'm a photographer. I work freelance mostly."

"Do you ever go? To work I mean?"

He looked up at me and laughed.

"I'm on a sabbatical this summer."

"All summer?"

"Yep."

"Oh. Must be nice."

"Yeah, it is. I get to spend time with Nate."

"Oh. So how much is it going to cost?"

"Don't worry about it, okay?"

"I can pay you."

"It's okay, really."

"Alright."

Damon didn't say anything else and I sat on the lawn and waited. Eventually he wiped his hands on a towel and looked over at me.

"Would you like to join me for a drink?"

"A drink?"

"...Orange or apple?"

I took in my surroundings: There were what must have been hundreds of records stacked against a wall. There were African masks hung along one wall, a large armchair against the other, black and white photos scattered everywhere. Overhead, exposed beams. Beneath our feet there were soft rugs with bold patterns. There was a fireplace. It was something reminiscent of a *Pottery Barn* catalog. His walls were the color of a simmering spice and I instantly felt welcome. As he stood scrutinizing the contents of his refrigerator, from my seat on his couch, I could see that he was so different from Jason in just about every way: He wore worn in jeans and a faded t-shirt and Chuck Taylor All-Stars. (Jason would never wear 'Chucks' and had never owned a pair in his life). His hair was unruly and wayward, his ears pierced.

"Sorry, all we've got is tea. Is that okay?"

"Yeah, that's fine."

Ice cubes clinked against the glass as he sat down and placed a large glass of tea in front of me.

"Thank you."

He nodded as he sipped his drink. I took a swig of tea. It was perfect and another spoonful of sugar or a wedge of lemon would have ruined it. He looked at his watch as he set down his glass and got up.

"Excuse me for a minute."

"Sure."

He walked down the hallway, his wallet chain rattling as he moved along. I got up and looked at the pictures on the mantle. It seemed that everyone's family pictures were indistinguishable, singular moments captured on film. Damon's were no exception. The smiling faces of friends and family, a very large Great Dane, a few children scattered throughout, at the park or the beach. Soon enough he returned.

"I'm sorry about your wait. I had to take my insulin shot."

He scratched his head and checked out my glass.

"Do you want more?"

"No, thanks."

"So, where are you from Samarra?"

"I was born here, but I live in Raleigh."

"North Carolina?"

"Uh huh."

"Do you miss it here?"

I shook my head, a blatant lie. Already I'd lied, perhaps from nothing more than nervousness, an uncertainty.

"Were you born with diabetes?"

"Nah. I was diagnosed when I was around fourteen," he rubbed his hand passively over his arm, "The shots don't hurt like they used to. I just have to remember to check my blood sugar every day."

"I can't imagine it's an easy thing."

Damon nodded in agreement, smiled as the corners of his mouth turned upward. His eyes brightened, eyes that had seemed darker in the glare of the street lamp last night were now clearly green underneath his long lashes.

"'Ya know, I haven't seen a car like yours in a long time. How long've you had it?"

"Since I was sixteen."

"Mmm. It's in excellent condition."

"My grandfather gave it to me. None of his other grandkids wanted it."

I sat back on the couch.

"Yeah, well not everyone has the guts to drive a classic."

"I just needed some wheels."

We sat quietly for a moment and I felt an electricity in the air, a simple absoluteness. Somewhere in the distance a door opened and a small boy with earth colored hair and large, beautifully curious eyes wandered into the living room. He stood at Damon's knee. Damon placed his hands on his shoulders and I looked on as they talked.

"Did you sleep well?"

"Mmm Hmm."

"Do you want some banana later?"

"Yeah."

"Okay. We'll get you some later."

The boy crawled up into Damon's lap.

"Samarra, this is my son. This is Nathaniel Addison Marsden."

He looked at me and hesitated a little, but when I smiled at him it was returned. He was so small and helpless and his hands gripped his fathers' pant leg as Damon stroked his hair. He slowly eased away from Damon and crept toward me.

"Hi Nathan. My name's Samarra."

"Hi!"

I could see his father's resemblance in him, the commonality with them.

"How old is he?"

"He's three and a half."

"Cute."

"Thanks."

He hadn't seemed to notice that Nathan was playing a few feet away. I felt like I was sleepwalking, coasting along without moving and when I looked back at him, his gaze hadn't changed, his train of thought seemingly unaltered. He got up to put away the glasses then turned toward me. An eternity ticked away before his eyes finally moved away from mine.

"Can I ask you something?"

"I guess so."

"What happened to your wrists?"

I looked down and realized that I'd been negligent in covering them and a sickening feeling made my head swim as I hastily pulled down my sleeves.

"It's kind of a long story, okay? Let's just leave it at that!"

"I'm sorry. I just thought--"

"What?"

"I thought maybe you were down, like someone hurt you."

I got up, intent on leaving. He did the same.

"Did I say something wrong? I didn't mean to..."

His voice trailed off as if he'd forgotten what he'd meant to say. We both stood in the middle of his living room as my mind constantly ran marathons in search of some motive or reason for his actions.

"Are you going to stare at me all evening or should I go?"

"Just, I want to start over with you. I didn't mean to make you uncomfortable."

"I should go."

I walked over to Nathan and stooped down.

"Bye, Nathan. It was nice to meet you."

I picked up my bag from the ottoman and headed for the door.

"Samarra, you don't have to -"

"It's okay. I'll be back tomorrow for my manual."

Something strange seemed to come over me as I wiped away the tears that had begun falling only moments ago. I walked back to my grandparents' car, stood next to the drivers' side door watching as fireflies began to glow in synchronization with some tune that only they could hear. Their tiny green beacons were my searchlights...

NATHAN'S CURIO

"Samarra!"

The quaver in Crystal's voice was deepening but rising to the surface.

"My water just broke and Dorian's taking me to the hospital!"

"Just be calm, okay? It's gonna be okay!"

Being so far away from my friends was quelling my heart. I'd always told them that I'd be there for this moment, that I wouldn't have missed it for anything.

"Just breathe!"

I could hear her quickly drawing in and releasing shortened breaths. It took a few minutes, but when Dorian came to the phone he sounded winded.

"We're going in now Samarra. I'll call you in a few hours. Pray for us, okay?"

"Okay."

We both hung up the phone and I closed my eyes and entrusted them all to prayer...

...Grandpa Jamison was reading from *The Savannah Tribune* about the escalating tensions surrounding more American troop deployments to Iraq and Afghanistan.

He shook his head, fluffed his paper, and turned the page. He looked up from his reading and glanced over at me where I sat in the alcove of the window seat. Eight of the voicemails that Jason had sent me had gone unanswered. There weren't going to be any more games of apology by phone, no more confiding in him or holding his hand, nothing tangible between us now. He had never spared my feelings or truly shielded my heart. He'd never stood for me or held me up to his parents. My thick skin was more like tissue paper and I sighed aloud.

"Something bothering you, kid? You haven't said two words all evening."

"Sorry."

"Your grandmother and I are going to see your mama tomorrow. Would you like to come with us?"

I wanted no part of it and in my heart, I knew things probably wouldn't be any different. Grandpa James folded up his paper. I shrugged.

"Now we both know that you're here for a reason. Just tell her what you need to. Get it off your mind, okay?!"

"Okay."

He picked up the sports section. I watched him for a moment. For as long as I can remember he always read his newspaper in the same order: Events, comics, front page then sports. I began to rummage through my bag in search of my iPod when my hand brushed against something small and hard. I gripped it and tugged until I held a child's action figure in my hand.

When I pushed a tiny button in its back its arms moved up and down, his fierce grimace unchanging.

"Karate chop action. Genius."

Grandpa looked up from his periodical.

"Hmm?"

"Just thinking out loud."

I smiled to myself.

"Can I borrow the car?"

FINDERS KEEPERS

The scent of barbecue saturated the air and began dampening my senses as I walked up his driveway. It wasn't just sapid, but the sort that left a piquant ripe aftertaste that tended to stay on your mind days after you'd eaten it, the kind of barbecue that food critics and writers devoted entire columns to, or at least it smelled that way. I hadn't peeked over the hedges on the walk to the door to see if my mother was home, but I knew that it was midday and that she was still at work. I rang the doorbell and waited. Damon opened the front door and looked almost startled to see me standing before him again.

"Samarra."

"Hey Damon."

"What's up?"

I reached into my bag and brought the superhero back up. He looked at it and grinned. He was growing a serious five o'clock shadow.

"Nate will be thrilled! We tore the house apart looking for this. Thank you!"

"You're welcome."

When it seemed that we'd both run out of things to say he looked down at his feet. It all felt like a situational test that only one of us could pass.

"Look, I apologize if I made you feel uncomfortable the other day. It wasn't my intention."

"It's okay."

"Oh, your car's ready. I'll get your keys. You can come inside if you like."

"Thanks."

I stood in his foyer trying to decide if the kindness of this almost stranger was as sacred as the seconds that ticked away, and I plotted what I'd say to him next. He walked back into the room and handed me my keys. I felt embarrassed by the way I'd talked to him before.

"Thank you again. I really appreciate this."

He nodded. I was about to apologize just as he began.

"So, you're leaving?"

"Yeah."

My response sounded like a small, contained whisper; hopeless as any attempt I'd found to make penance for my wrongs so far this year. He mentioned something about having a few friends over for a small get together, that he wouldn't want me driving all that way on an empty stomach and that Nathan would be there, too.

"Samarra?"

"Hmm?"

He offered me his arm and then waited while I stood deciding if I should take a chance...

...Zara Lee West was born at 9:04 in the morning after her mother stayed in labor for twenty-seven hours and her father held his wife's hand while he tried to balance a camcorder in the other. She was four pounds two ounces with a head full of hair and eyes that resembled tiny marbles as she slept. She would still be sleeping when Dorian called and I spoke to them for the first time since Zara was introduced to the world. I wanted to see them so badly that I felt like I'd choke on the tears before we'd meet each other again...

I took a step forward and let my arm interlock with Damon's. I'd never stood so close to anyone besides Jason before and I felt like molten lava had been poured into my stomach. As we walked outside I wondered what his wife would think of this situation or if she was waiting nearby to ambush me. For a moment I wished that my chosen profession would have been as an escape artist. His backyard was festive. Strings of lights were all around. There were a fire pit and a grill and people scattered and talking, a few kicking around a soccer ball. There was soft grass, a cooler and a long table with chairs around it, cushions, and a table runner.

"I didn't bring anything."

"It's okay."

"I can't stay long. I have to--"

"Samarra, you don't have to be so defensive. None of my friends bite and neither do I. It'll be fun!"

"Okay."

He stopped walking and turned toward me, a sudden look of seriousness hovering.

"You're not a vegetarian, are you?"

"No."

We both laughed and I felt the jitters easing up. One of the partygoers produced a camera and soon there were dozens of flashes. As the photographer circulated around taking candid shots of everyone it felt like I was about to be thrown back into senior class picture day, practicing my smile in the bathroom mirror. He stood next to Damon and me and fired off a few shots before moving on to the dog. Damon flushed a little as he sipped from the soda can. Nathan ran toward us and looked thrilled to be up so late.

"Hi dah!"

Damon crouched down at his level.

"Hey son! Do you remember Miss Wells? She's the nice lady that came over the other day."

The little boy nodded.

"Hi!"

"Hey Nathan!"

Damon lingered for a moment then went to attend to his other guests. I turned back to Nathan.

"Hey guess what? I can count to twenty and I can read some and my dah says when I go to school I'll be way ahead!"

"That's wonderful!"

"Do you want to see my dog? Her name's Roxy."

He reached for my hand and pulled me along with little resistance to a corner of the yard where the same dog from the picture was sitting lackadaisically on the grass. As he showed me one of her favorite tricks I glanced up to see Damon admiring the two of us, a half grin covering his face.

"Guess what?"

"What?"

He cupped his small hand over my ear and whispered:

"My dah thinks you're pretty."

"Oh, really?"

He sat down on the grass.

"Uh huh, but don't tell."

"Okay, I won't."

"Okay."

His childish simplicity made me want to beckon back the days when I was a kid, but only for a moment, a temporary flash of sentimentality. Some other children approached Nate and he soon abandoned his dog and me to go play with his friends. I walked over to Damon, who was drinking another diet soda.

"Can I get you something?"

"No, I'm fine."

He reached around into the cooler and handed me a soda.

"Thanks."

My phone rang and I let the voicemail catch the incoming call.

"Are you ready for dinner?"

"Okay."

"Great!"

We walked over to the table and were joined by his other guests. I was eagerly introduced to everyone: Micah (more commonly known as 'Mic') a tall clean-cut guy and his wife Natalie, a stylishly dressed woman with long brown hair and Jeremy, (of Japanese ancestry) and his wife Anna, (whose beautiful complexion floored me) and their assorted children. Both Mic and Jeremy I learned were involved in church ministry, one as a youth pastor the other as a praise and worship member. Damon leaned over and whispered:

"Could you help me in the kitchen for a second, please?"

"Sure."

Once we were in the kitchen he began gathering up the place settings.

"I'm glad you decided to stay."

I smiled, but I couldn't help but think that at some point the line between friendship and unfamiliarity would have to be blurred, that we could play finders keepers with fragments of information as he handed me a covered dish wrapped in a tea towel.

"Do you mind?"

"Not at all."

"Thanks."

He continued counting silverware, didn't look up and for a moment neither of us said anything else. Then he held the door open for me and followed behind as we approached the table. We remained standing as everyone else stood up. We all bowed our heads and closed our eyes. He began:

"Father God, we come before you tonight thanking you for giving us strength in our bodies, for being Jehovah jireh, our provider, always. We ask you to bless our guest Samarra and her family and keep them. We thank you for the gifts of fellowship and friendship. Amen."

Everyone at the table was smiling so I dropped my guard and picked up my fork. Conversations and laughter crossed and intersected the table and it was easy to feel welcome. After the ribs and burgers were eaten and the seafood salad, green beans, rolls and corn on the cobb were gone, along with the peach cobbler and vanilla ice cream, and when all the guests had left and only Nathan, Damon and I remained the evening was giving up and deepening to a mellow ending. As he and I gathered the dinner dishes together Nate played nearby. Soon enough we were all back inside and standing in the kitchen. He scraped and washed the dishes and I rinsed and dried them.

"Thanks for helping me with these."

He was up to his forearms in suds scrubbing the plates, concentrating fixedly.

"You're welcome."

"Did you have a good time?"

"I did."

"I'm glad."

He grabbed for a nearby dishtowel and dried his hands then handed it to me. We gravitated to the living room.

"We should grab a coffee sometimes."

"I don't think your wife would appreciate that. Besides, I don't think I'm your type."

"I'm not attached to anyone anymore."

"Why are you wearing a wedding band then?"

He looked down at his hand then back up at me.

"I guess after all this time I just got used to it being there."

He frowned a little, plunged his hands down into his pockets and I stole the opportunity to change the subject.

"What're you doing with the rest of your summer?"

Damon shrugged.

"I haven't really thought about it that much. How about you?"

"Mmm, I'm going to try to get my portfolio together, hang out some. I dunno."

He put a hand over his mouth and cleared his throat.

"Why does it seem like you don't ever trust anyone?"

"I have my reasons."

"You can't go through life as a pessimist, it's no fun."

" Well, everything happens exactly like it's supposed to."

"You sound like you're trying to convince us both."

I looked daggers at him, then away toward the window.

"Look, it's obvious that somebody hurt more than just your feelings. The taller the wall, the harder it is to tear down, that's all I'm saying."

I couldn't help but laugh at myself for being so naive to think that no one else could ever understand the depth and gravity of what is was like to be me before tonight.

"You don't know me Damon."

"Just listen, alright?! I know that you shouldn't sell yourself short, not for anyone. You're very talented."

He held up a stack of papers, stood grinning at me. I instantly recognized them: A dahlia I'd done in pencil and ink, the watercolor landscape, still lives and various stages of hands up close. At the top of the pile was the pencil sketch I'd done of him.

"Where did you get those?!"

"They were on the backseat of your car."

I tried to snatch them away, but he held them high over his head forcing me to come closer until I could feel the warmth exuding from his skin and smell the leftover scent from his soap. Our game of keep away continued until the burst of sirens outside tore through the stillness and we ran out onto the porch. I felt stunned, as if I'd been dredged through icy waters when I saw my grandparents next door on the front porch and the EMTs going inside the house. I began to come apart.

"Damon, I have to go! Thank you for everything. Good night."

Before he could ask me any questions I bolted off the porch and ran next door as fast as my legs would carry me...

BEAUTY FOR ASHES

There were so many thoughts in my head that it was like a View Master on high speed while I waited in the emergency room visitor's lounge with my grandparents. Somehow, I wanted my mother to be who she sometimes was before: Happy, playful, affectionate. The floors smelled like ammonia and despite the cheery primary yellow on the walls, this place belied the real reason anyone came here. It felt eerily quiet with hardly any doctors being paged or foot traffic or elevators opening or phones ringing. My grandparents both sat staring out into space as he held her hand. I stood away from them at the window. Grandma Camille called me over.

"We waited for you Samarra. Where were you?"

Nathan and Damon came to mind.

"I was visiting someone."

I felt so small that I couldn't lift my eyes to meet hers. I waited, unsure if I even wanted to know. Finally--

"What's wrong with her?"

"When we got over there she was unconscious. She knew we were coming. We tried to wake her up. There were pill bottles everywhere."

"What do you mean?"

"Samarra, sit down."

I looked at both of them and sat where grandpa had been.

"She has stage four breast cancer. It's metastasized. She'd already been to see a specialist. She knew about it weeks ago."

I sank back in the chair, barely able to say the word to myself: CANCER.

"What?! Why didn't she tell me?"

"We only found out tonight. About an hour ago."

I couldn't be touched by the fact that I was crying or that my face was even now saturated with tears.

"I have to go!"

I got up to leave, turned to walk away, but soon enough I discovered that my legs couldn't support me when I crumpled to the floor. They helped me back into the chair.

"Do you remember Isaiah sixty-one; three Samarra?"

I couldn't think. In my selfishness I hadn't thought of any words fitting enough to pray to my God, wouldn't know where to begin, considered only my own feelings.

"No."

They both held my hands and recited:

"To all who mourn in Israel, He will give beauty for ashes, joy instead of mourning, and praise instead of despair. For the Lord has planted them like strong and graceful oaks for His own glory. Amen."

More than I ever had before I missed Jason. I missed him so badly, in fact, that the very core of my heart ached feverishly, and I wanted him to be here now and hold me and tell me that it would all be okay. I couldn't stay in the room a moment more and I scrambled out into the hallway. After I'd dialed his number and it rang twice I snapped the phone shut. He didn't deserve to hear my voice, would never realize all that he had done for me, who he would make me...

FREE BULLETS

I walked back into the waiting room where my mother's parents were standing. As I turned the corner I saw someone else with them. His back was toward me, but I could see that he held a small child in his arms. His hair showed from beneath his toque. He turned around. It was Damon.

"Hello Samarra."

"Hi."

I took him in: He wore a V-neck t-shirt and jeans that were torn at the knee, a red and black Buffalo check jacket, black Chuck Taylors. Grandma Camille looked over at me.

"This young man lives next door to your mother."

"I know. We've met."

She slowly nodded, raised her eyebrows. Damon chimed in breaking the silence up into a thousand little pieces.

"We came to see if you all needed anything."

He turned to me.

"Are you okay?"

I didn't answer him right away. I felt my eyes narrow as I thought about what must be going through his mind and what had caused his wife to possibly abandon him and Nate in the same way my father had my mother and me.

"I'm fine."

"Let me take you home."

"I'm fine."

Grandma Camille put her hand on my shoulder.

"Samarra, the doctor said there's nothing we can do right now. She's resting. We'll stay here with her. Go ahead."

...As Damon strapped Nathan into his car seat I stood on the curb. He shut the rear passenger door then turned toward me but froze in his tracks.

"You're shaking."

He took off his jacket and draped it around my shoulders. The lining was soft and smelled like him, like Yardley soap and I slipped my arms into the sleeves.

"C'mon."

We walked around to the passenger side and he opened the door and helped me in. We were traveling eastbound away from the medical district. I could close my eyes and see the scrap of paper that I'd found and in a second, I realized that it was a part of her biopsy results and that she'd not wanted me to know.

She'd tried to burn away the truth as if it were some real, physical thing that she could touch or hold. I felt my head sinking and time elapsed before I opened my eyes again. When I couldn't hold on any longer I began blurting out things to him. He kept glancing at me.

"I haven't seen my mother in almost three years. It's not that I don't love her, I just couldn't deal with all the conditions she put on everything. I should have just done what she wanted. Now--"

"This isn't your fault. You know that, right?"

"We never really got along with each other. Nothing I could ever do was good enough for her!"

He looked straight ahead, eyes on the road as he clenched his jaw.

"Did you talk to her about the way you felt today?"

I shook my head, but felt my eyes welling. We stopped at a red light. The glow of the city lights was positively beautiful as it stretched out into the dark emptiness. The last thing I'd said to her was that she was a stranger to me. I hadn't known how much I may have hurt her.

"Let's talk about something else, Samarra, okay?"

"Okay."

He was right, a subject change was perfect.

"Did I tell you that I'm teaching Nate to play piano?"

I looked back at the tiny moppet who was asleep and oblivious to the world.

"Really?"

"Yup," he looked over at me and smiled, the proud papa, "He can play chopsticks."

"Chopsticks?"

"You know, like in the movie *BIG* when they're on the giant keyboard? In the toy store?"

"Oh, yeah. That sounds like fun."

"Where are you from Damon?"

"Kensington. In South Africa, Cape Town."

"What else?"

His eyes inquisitively poured over my face.

"My parents still live there in the house we grew up in. My dah Richard is a newspaper man and my mum is a teacher. I have an older brother named Aaron. I know it's prosaic, but that's it. That's all."

"How often do you see them?"

"Maybe twice a year. We speak on the phone a lot, though."

"So, what did they do about the Apartheid laws?"

"My dah, my father~"

"Uh huh?"

"My father worked at a small local paper. He was up for editor one year and he was really hoping that he'd get the job, but his boss found out that he'd been staging these anti-government demonstrations, and they busted him down to copier. I think he felt like he had to get these stories out, 'ya know?"

"Mmm Hmm."

"His best friend at the paper was named Daniel Ademe. He was the only person of color that worked there. His family would eat dinner at our house sometimes. His son, Adewalye would play soccer with my brother and me. It was a long time ago, but I still remember them."

"It's hard to believe you're so~"

"What?"

"Normal."

He put the car in park and amid the laughter that followed I put any thoughts of my mother to rest for a short while. After he'd unstrapped Nate from his car seat and opened the door for me we all went inside. We stood in his living room.

"I'll be back in a minute."

I sat on the sofa and waited for him to return. It wasn't long before he was back.

"You've had quite a night, huh?"

He looked over at his clock. It was almost three in the morning. He sighed.

"So, what now?"

"May I have a drink?"

"A drink?"

"Oh, I forgot you have a child. You might not keep alcohol in your house. I apologize."

He walked over to what looked like a chest and opened the doors. It turned out to be a fully stocked bar complete with clear and dark liquors, wine and shot glasses, a martini shaker, decanters, highball glasses and a bar tool set and ice bucket.

"I never said I didn't drink Samarra."

I laughed as he set out two glasses.

"Pick your poison."

I pointed to a dark colored something with a black and gold label.

"Mmm. Johnnie Walker. Good choice. On the rocks?"

"Yes, please."

He dropped a few ice cubes in each glass and poured a bit of scotch-whiskey into both, palmed napkins around each glass. He handed me one.

"Do you want some music?"

"Sure."

He walked over to the entertainment nook and opened an old school record player. He put on a record and we were revisited by Otis Redding edifying us with the strength of his love via song. He closed his eyes and listened as he sipped his drink. There was a picture of Nate dressed as a pea pod sitting on the coffee table. I picked it up and took a closer look. Damon sat next to me on the sofa.

"Where's his mother Damon?"

"I don't want to talk about her right now."

"Sorry."

"It's okay. It's just a sore subject. I can't go there without some really bad flashbacks, so..."

"I get it."

I took a sip of the whiskey and swallowed hard, almost coughed.

"It's good, huh?"

The ice cubes in my glass were beginning to slowly melt as he refilled both glasses.

"Mmm Hmm."

"I love this song."

"Me, too."

He swirled his glass around, took a sip.

"I think it's safe to say that we're both alone Damon."

"Oh, it's absurd how safe we are together, you and I right now."

The record turned over and another song soon began.

"I like talking to you."

"I'll take any complement I can get. Thank you."

"You're welcome. Do you want a refill?"

I nodded and he obliged. I felt as if I was floating high above this couch, above this house. A warmth that was all but indescribable was drowning out my senses along with most of the bad things that had happened today.

"Can I ask you a question Damon?"

"Yup."

"Do you think that love is a male or a female?"

He sat back in his seat.

"Definitely female."

"How do you know?"

"'Cause love is too beautiful to be a man. She's sweet like candy, but she can sting, too. Plus, she's too emotional not to be a woman."

"Well, if love were depressed and then turned suicidal?"

"Uh huh?"

"Then Jason would be cruel enough to give away free bullets."

He winced as if he was in pain.

"Oooh!"

"Yeah, it's true."

"He's a love murderer."

We both laughed. After a few moments he got up and took our glasses, set them on the kitchen counter.

"You can sleep in my room if you like."

"Excuse me?"

"I'll take the couch."

"I can't sleep here!"

"I'm not going to do anything to you!"

"I know you're not!"

The record was still playing. I tried to get up, but it was useless. I picked up my bag, dropped it.

"I think you should stay here Samarra."

137

"I'm going home!"

Damon walked over to the record player and shut it off. He turned off the light, leaving the room barely lit before he headed upstairs.

"You can let yourself out then!"

...Waking up in an unfamiliar place startled me back to the realities of last night: My mother was in the hospital, I hadn't called my grandparents yet, I really needed to see my friends and I had shared a drink with (and probably insulted) someone I didn't quite know. I moved aside the blanket that covered me and sat up. My surroundings looked the same as they had last night. It took a minute to process it~ I was lying, I had been lying on Damon's couch, had even stayed here overnight! I got ready to leave when I heard someone coming downstairs. Damon stood next to the couch.

"Good morning."

He looked at me and grinned...

TAKE BACKS

Having the steering wheel beneath my hands again made me feel safe and sturdy. I put my foot on the accelerator and revved the engine before I put the car in drive. As I drove down Lincoln Avenue to get to my grandparents' house I couldn't help but follow my thoughts back to my mother. Somewhere in the deep hiding places of my heart I hated her for not telling me that she'd have to spend the next few months being shuttled between chemotherapy treatments and appointments and taking a cocktail of medications that were too substantial to even conceive of and that she may have to wind up less than whole after difficult surgeries. Maybe being sick had hardened her to the point of apathy and she just couldn't bring herself to say the words.

In the rearview I could see myself getting further away from unfamiliarity and closer to home. My stomach growled, and I remembered that I'd last eaten some twenty-four hours ago. I pulled into my grandparent's driveway. Of all the things that they'd ever told me about my mother, in the years that she'd been an absentee parent Grandpa and Grandma had never said that she was selfish or given to her own wanderlust. I thought of her face as the paramedics brought her in and the old black and white photo of my mother that my father kept in his wallet. She'd stared at the camera head on, a look of defiance and strength, but also something else, like sagacity emblazoned on her face.

She'd taught me to read when I was very young (around three) and her patience was legendary my grandparents had said. I remembered our talks about her study abroad trips to Spain and Greece and how she and my father shared a mutual love of the arts. She'd always say that it brought them together. I was unable to recall anything my mother had done to deserve his neglect or lack of communication or trust or love. Still, I just hadn't been able to see that when it came to the equation of her life, unlike my father, I didn't factor in.

I thought of little Nate and how he must have surely felt the absence of his mother and the way her warmth and love could have swaddled him like a security blanket. On that night in the emergency room Grandpa James had said that they'd found pill bottles everywhere. She'd tried to end it. She hadn't thought of me. I watched the sun begin to take its place in the sky and I thought back to the evening of my second-grade play and its aftermath. On that night in 1989, our play was about the weather and I was a raindrop. (Cara Delaney had beaten me for the coveted role of the rainbow). I was dressed in my blue papier- mache raindrop suit. My role was simple, my lines epic:

"I make green grass grow strong and high. I'm a raindrop from the sky! You can use me to wash, to bathe and to cook. If you're really not sure, then just take a look: I'm made for more than you may think, I'm something good for you to drink!"

I'd been proud of myself for not forgetting my lines. When I rejoined my mother and father after the play was over there was no commentary on how I'd done. Approval was a funny thing to me, always sought after never gained.

As a kid I thought that I needed theirs more than strawberry ice cream or watching my favorite television show or playing outside. In the car on the way home my parents had argued back and forth in raised tones and words I couldn't yet comprehend. Once my father had dropped us off, he was gone, never pausing to even say 'Goodbye'.

The look in my mother's eyes was telling; it spoke of disbelief at the turn of tonight's events, of wondering who he was meeting this time, of how long he would be gone. I went to her room and knocked softly at her door. When she didn't answer I'd pushed it open. She'd been crying, and her mascara was in disarray on her face, her emotional balancing act undone. She cursed at me, grabbed my arm, and pushed me out into the hallway.

"I don't want to look at you! This is your fault!"

She slammed the door in my face and I ran to my room in tears, stunned, holding my arm and shouldering misplaced blame. I needed her to know that she didn't get a take back, that I'd always be her child whether she wanted me or not. I finally got out of the car and made my way to the front door. Grandma Camille answered.

"Samarra! It's so good to see you! We wondered--"

"I'm sorry."

We stepped into the kitchen. I was about to ask if she and grandpa were upset with me.

"It's alright, child. We love you. No one's angry with you."

"Okay."

"Are you hungry?"

I nodded and watched as she set to work scrambling eggs and making toast and grits. I sat down at the table.

"Don't you have some cereal?"

"You can't survive on cereal Samarra."

I grinned. Things had been put back together and the conversation didn't turn to hospitals or cancer or my mother, thankfully. I couldn't keep drawing conclusions on the sidewalk in chalk only to have the rain wash them away. I also couldn't leave though until I thanked Damon for giving me back my wheels or Nate for cheering me up when I thought of his sweet face. I couldn't leave without thanking my grandparents for stability again...

ESCAPE

My first day back at the house was equal parts caution and routine as I worked on cleaning in my mother's absence. As I watched suds engulf the bathroom sink I realized that the sheer silence in this house was making my nerves raw and ragged. The yellow rubber gloves I was wearing squeaked mercilessly as I scrubbed the shower door. I opened the window to let in some air and heard the soft ramblings of Billie Holiday from some not too distant corner.

I shut my eyes and listened as her voice plunged into the depthless sorrows that we were both too familiar with. I was almost done when the doorbell rang. I ran downstairs only to stand hesitantly for a moment, my hand stranded on the doorknob. The last time I'd opened this door to someone he'd tried to hurt me, break me. I opened it anyway. Damon was there, sheepishly grinning.

"You still here?"

I nodded.

"Yep."

"Can I show you something then?"

"Okay."

...Dust inundated the still air as he threw off the tarp that had covered the large thing in the dimly lit corner of the garage. The Indian-like motorcycle gleamed. Damon stared at it head on, a glint of speculation filling his eyes.

"I had this a long time before I ever met Kirsten."

It was the first time I'd heard him call her by name, but by now he wasn't fazed about talking about his ex-wife. The easy tone of our conversations was far more commonplace.

"She hated this bike, but she couldn't stop me, at least not until after Nate was born."

His line of sight was unwavering.

"Do you miss her?"

I felt like I'd started a fire of consequence that would burn verity to its outer edges and there was nothing to extinguish it with now. I hadn't meant to ask the question with such deliberate sounding disregard. He took a deep breath, a pause perhaps before the plunge into the truth from which he could never return with me.

"Sometimes."

We were quiet for a moment just before he looked over at me.

"Do you know that you do this thing where you bite your lip when you seem nervous? You're doing it right now, actually."

I stopped immediately and tried to be 'normal'. He smirked.

"I can't believe you have a motorcycle!"

"We all have our pursuits Samarra. This just happens to be one of mine."

These days I was beginning to feel as if I'd been searching for everything except happiness. Maybe I didn't want it to find me because I was trying to be emotionally incognito.

"Wanna go for a ride?"

"Okay."

He handed me a helmet.

"I think all of your hair will fit."

We both laughed. He put on a pair of Ray Ban shades then reached in his shirt pocket and handed me a pair, too.

"Standard equipment."

Damon opened the garage door and slowly backed the bike out onto the driveway. The wind blew, and my hair whipped around my face as I put on the helmet and fastened it.

"Have you ever been on a bike before?"

"No."

"Are you nervous?"

"No."

My heart felt like the lump that was lodged in my throat as I put on my sunglasses. He got on the bike and fastened his helmet.

"You're going to have to hold on to me."

"O-Okay."

"C'mon, get on."

I cautiously climbed on behind him. Almost as if it were second nature I wrapped my arms around his waist. I already felt my heart beating strong and furious against his broad back. He turned to look at me, grinned for a moment before he kick started the motorcycle and it rumbled to life. He leaned back.

"Hold on."

"Okay."

When we'd retreated down a few blocks and were out in the thick of the summer sun he slowed to a crawl.

"I've got a full tank of petrol so where do you want to go Samarra?"

...Forsyth Park was grand this time of year. The fresh air and glorious gardens were wonderful and desperately needed sights. The fountain in the center of the square radiated refreshment on a hot day like today. Damon pointed to one of the footpaths. We walked along slowly, passed couples and kids and a few dogs. We wandered and sat at the fountain. When a vendor with a pushcart strolled by, Damon flagged him down and we shared a soft pretzel.

"When's the last time you sketched something?"

He licked the salt from his fingertips.

"Um, it's been a while."

I couldn't divulge how I'd spied on him, how he'd been my secret muse as I'd drawn bits and pieces of his features that night. I took off my sunglasses and put them in my bag.

"Do you show your work around anywhere?"

"Back home I'm part of this art collective at a place called The Rogues Gallery. A lot of different artists would display their canvasses and sculptures for a week out of every month. Andy Calhoun, the owner, just let me do whatever kind of paintings I wanted and he always gave me honest feedback."

"Have you always painted?"

"For ten or eleven years. I just started sculpting about a year ago. I can teach you if you want."

He finished his pretzel.

"Okay."

"It'll be fun!"

"Yeah, it will!"

We both laughed at the same time.

"How's your mum?"

I wiped my mouth with a napkin.

"I'm supposed to go see her Monday. She's going to be moved to another room by then."

"That's good."

"How's Nathan?"

"He's fine. He's over at Jeremy and Anna's."

"Can I ask you something?"

"Mmm Hmm."

He wiped his hands and looked back up at me.

"Why did you help me that first day we met?"

He turned away from me, his attention caught away by the ripples that were echoing from the falling water in the fountain.

"Do you think I can make a wish in here?"

"That's a well. This is a fountain."

"Same difference."

"You're not going to answer me, are you?"

He sighed, sort of laughed.

"I helped you because you looked like you needed a hand."

"So, do you think there was a reason we crossed paths?"

Damon took a quarter from his pocket and tossed it behind him where it plunked in and floated down.

"We'll see."

"What did you say?"

"Oh, nothing."

"I wish you'd stop being so passive aggressive!"

He looked at me and laughed.

"Hey?"

"Hmm?"

"Where's Nathan's mom, Damon?"

His smile slowly disappeared, and he took a deep breath.

"She's gone."

"Oh, you mean she died?"

"No. I mean she's gone. She doesn't see him."

"Oh."

"I don't want you to get the wrong idea about me, okay? I have to look out for Nathan and I wasn't about to let her use my son as a bargaining chip every time she wanted something. He matters more than anything to me and--"

"I know you're a good father. I can tell."

He extended his hand to me and when I accepted he kissed it (something I'd only seen happen on TV) and held it firmly in his own for a second. It made me see him as someone whose friendship might be both valuable and fruitful, even adequate. The contrast between his skin and my own brown sheathing was apparent, but lovely.

"Are you hungry?"

"Famished."

"Where to next?"

...When the bike stopped Damon took off his helmet and waited while I got myself in suitable order. He stepped up onto the curb and offered me his arm.

"Miss."

At the door of Applebee's, I passed my hand over my left wrist where the still faint scar had healed itself over. In time we were seated in a booth next to the window. We still hadn't talked about how I'd gotten bashed the other night and made a fool out of myself. I figured that he didn't make a big deal out of ridiculously petty incidents the way I sometimes did. Damon slouched down in his seat and I sat across from him. I set my bag down next to me. He put his shades on top of his head.

"When did you move to the States?"

"I came here when I was about eighteen. I had just graduated and I wanted to see if I could make a go at living here."

"It's a big jump, isn't it?"

"Yeah. Cape Town's a lot different from New York or L.A. in some ways."

"Or Savannah."

He smiled and nodded.

"'Ya know, my mum and dah would take Aaron and me through different townships when we were younger."

I leaned forward and rested my head on my hand and listened.

"Some of these places were so bad, little more than shacks, 'ya know? Whole families lived there. I never could've imagined that people could live that way, until I saw it for myself. It made me so grateful for what I have. It doesn't matter how many times you turn on the news and see it, until you're standing there looking at it face to face, it doesn't even begin to sink in, 'ya know?"

"That's some peoples' every day. No one should have to go without, though."

He nodded.

"It made me see a lot of things for the first time."

"Like what?"

"That I needed to get over myself and stop being so selfish."

Just then our server arrived at our table. After we'd both ordered our conversation continued.

"So, tell me some more about your family."

"What do you want to know?"

"What's your mother do?"

"She's a teacher. Fifth year math."

"What's her name?"

He paused and laughed to himself.

"Her name's Rachel."

"You're not used to all these questions, are you?"

"No, not at all."

Our server set our drinks down and scurried away again. He moved his glass of water closer, opened his straw wrapper with his teeth, sipped it down.

"What's you mum do?"

"She's a legal secretary."

"I could see her resemblance in you. She's quiet mostly, but friendly, your mum. Good neighbor."

"She talked to you?"

"Yeah, she held Roxy's leash one time when she wandered into your yard and she lent me some books."

"Oh."

"How'd you pick art as a career then?"

I sipped my tea.

"I didn't want to be a nurse or a lawyer or a debutante and I always liked to draw and paint. Art was the only thing I was ever really good at."

"That's cool."

"I just wish some other people knew it. My mom hates the idea."

"I think it's impossible to live up to our parents' expectations. If my folks would have had their way, I would have entered the seminary. I'm too every day for that."

"Your parents wanted you to be a priest?"

"Yeah. I used to be a bit of a hell raiser when I was younger. You don't even know! I used to drive my folks nuts!"

"Oh, I'll bet. So, what made you want to become a photographer?"

"Somebody at the paper gave my dah a camera and when I was younger I used to mess around with it. I liked it more than a lot, I guess."

"The makings of a legend."

"Yeah, right," he laughed to himself.

He polished off his water.

"What about your dah?"

I looked down into my glass and responded without looking up.

"I don't have one."

The server brought out the entrees, a new glass of water for him. After he'd thanked her, and she'd left, he turned back to me.

"M.I.A, huh?"

"Sort of."

"Mmm. 'Ya know, my parents have been married for so long, it's like they're joined at the hip or something."

We both laughed nervously. He unwrapped his silverware but stopped.

"We should bless the food."

Afterwards, I took out a small bottle of hand sanitizer and rubbed some into my hands. I gave Damon a squirt as well.

"Thanks. What did you get?"

"Something with chicken in it, I dunno. Do you want some?"

"Okay!"

We were trading part of each other's meal when another server walked by. She looked at us, frowned, her nose scrunching. Damon turned around and looked at her, did a double take.

"Can I help you?!"

She abruptly turned away, walked on. We looked at each other and laughed, talked between bites of food.

"You're gonna get us thrown out of here."

"Do you mean all of the Applebee's in the States or just this one?"

I laughed, my mind roaming over these last three weeks and how every word that fell from my lips secretly held some sort of contingency plan that wasn't based on anything other than my ability to escape, though I would not have wanted to be anywhere else now. He took his last bite, wiped his mouth on his napkin.

"Are you ready to go?"

"Okay."

We slid out of the booth. He reached into his back pocket and took out his wallet. After he'd tucked the money under one of the glasses he offered me his arm...

...He stopped the bike and helped me down. I stretched my legs, took off the helmet. Damon handed me my bag.

"Thanks for dinner, Damon."

"No problem."

I gasped, feigning shock.

"Was that your idea of a date?!"

"That depends."

We walked back across his driveway, past the hedges to my side where we stood on my front lawn.

"On what?"

"Whether you liked it or not."

I felt myself blush, fight the urge to bite my lip.

"Good night Samarra."

"Good night."

He gazed at me for just a moment before he turned to go home, a wide smile glued to his face as the amber porch light softened his features. When he'd gone, I walked to my car. There was a green Post-It note stuck on my windshield. I peeled it off.

{(828) 295-3016 If you ever need to talk. Damon}

"I did like it."

I found myself whispering, smiling uncontrollably...

TWO BLUE LINES

I sat on the bed and braided my hair. I couldn't help staring out into space, my fingers mechanically moving over and under. My mind went blank, stretched out into the vastness of time until it fell on some pale, but not too distant memory: Jason paced back and forth in front of me like a caged tiger while I waited for him to speak. I didn't ask if he'd heard me, I knew that he had. His stare felt so cold, so penetrating that I stood in place momentarily waiting to thaw. The rain dampened streets were slick and glossy at night like they'd been soaked through and I could see our breath as a fog when we spoke.

"Get rid of it!"

"If you're not sure about--"

"It's not up for discussion Samarra!"

I quickly averted my eyes to the pavement.

"Why weren't you more careful Sunny? You know I can't deal with this now! Why would you even tell me this?!"

"I thought that you'd be happy!"

The two blue lines on the stick came to mind.

I struggled not to scream out, tried to reach for his hand, but he pulled away.

"Do you know what it would look like to people if they knew I had a child without being married?! I can't do this!"

"Jason!"

"This is on you Samarra, you deal with it!"

"I'm sorry!"

Though I'd meant to say more, the two words had crept out as subtle as whispers, tiny bombs that killed the conversation dead before it had even begun. The same conversation that had started with only two little words, little words that had left massive fallout behind them. I couldn't make myself take in anything that had happened tonight, like the way he'd finally answered my call on the fifth try, come home in an agitated state and cursed under his breath when I'd asked to talk to him, grabbed my elbow and all but dragged me from the apartment until we walked up the street in near silence.

I saw it as raw and as plain as the day until the switch began being flipped on and off, back and forth, dark to light repeatedly. I cupped my hand over my mouth and suppressed the surge of delirium that followed. I couldn't trust myself not to cause a scene, even though we were alone, but I knew that what he was saying wasn't right. It couldn't be.

Hadn't this been what we'd both wanted? What I'd wanted with him? Did that mean that if I did what he said things would go back to normal between us? I watched as he turned around and walked back home. He never spoke of it to me again. My hands were shaking.

I showered, got dressed and got in my car just in time for my phone to ring.

"Hello?"

"Samarra? Samarra Wells?"

"Yes. This is she."

"Miss Wells, my name is Doctor Matthew Gleeson and I work in the oncology ward at Savannah Hospital. The reason for my call is that you're listed as next of kin for Angelia Wells, is that correct?"

"I guess so. Has something happened?"

...After not having seen her in almost three days I was finally becoming okay with not knowing what I'd say to her. Nothing practiced, nothing rehearsed. I drove to the hospital in a daze, rode the elevator up to the fourth floor and stood in the visitor's lounge looking around at all the other people there and wondering with a healthy dose of skepticism, if any of them would ever do what I was about to attempt.

As I walked down the corridor I prayed a Psalm of David, 27:1-2. "The Lord is my light and my salvation; Whom shall I fear? (Please let her be okay) The Lord is the strength of my life; Of whom shall I be afraid? (I don't want her to die) When the wicked, even mine enemies and my foes, came upon me to eat up my flesh, they stumbled and fell (I'm sorry for all the wrong things I said) Though an host should encamp against me, my heart shall not fear; though war should rise against me, in this will I be confident (Give me a chance to fix this please). Amen."

The door was ajar, and I didn't know if I should knock or just come in. I finally moved toward a nearby chair and sat down. There were monitors everywhere, an I.V. in her arm, tubes all over. I watched her chest rise and fall with restful ease and made up conversations in my head that might've happened between us. If only she weren't so distant, and I was not so lost. I wanted to crawl into her bed and lie beside her, to rest my head on her chest and listen to her beating heart, but I did not move until she slowly opened her eyes. She looked at me, eyes shifting from side to side, as if I had been someone that she'd known a long time ago but had now forgotten, some temporary friend or classmate that she knew would move away eventually and cease to be part of her life.

"Samarra?"

"Hmm?"

"Do you remember when your father and I went to your school play?"

I fought back tears.

"Yeah, of course."

"I never told you how proud I was of you!"

"Why can't you be proud of me now mama?"

It was so strange when she and I were alone and there were no more distractions to take away from this moment, just silence and time.

"I know your grandparents already told you how bad it is. I just want you to be secure, Samarra. I thought that you'd be married with a house and children and a degree you could actually use."

"But what if that's not what I want?"

She turned away from me and stared out the window at the gathering traffic. I could hear the steady beep of the heart monitor and the irksome drone from the ac unit on the floor above us, nothing else.

"Mama, why didn't you tell me you were sick?"

"I doubt that it would've mattered."

"Wow! If I didn't care I wouldn't have come here! You should've told me!"

Her facial expression didn't seem to have changed at all. Finally, her head rolled to the other side of the pillow and she closed her eyes, drew in a breath. Her profile was so different from what it had been even two days ago. There were dark circles beginning to form underneath her eyes, though there was a tiny draught of vitality still present in them and her skin had become ashen, her face gaunt and thin. I involuntarily sniffled.

"Do you know what your father said to me a month after we were married?"

"No."

"He told me he didn't want children!"

I couldn't keep my train of thought steady enough to process this scrap of verbiage and looked down at my shoes instead. Even now, she thought about my father. He'd never treated me harshly, had never been around enough, forced me to find him guilty of cruelty in absentia. When I didn't respond, she changed tactics.

"How's Jason doing?"

Hearing his name again was grating and it felt nearly impossible to move away from him in the space inside my head.

"I dunno. We don't talk anymore."

Her brows creased and I heard the repetitious clicking of a button. I looked down at her hand. She was self-administering pain medication, through her I.V.

"I'm really sorry, mama."

I held her hand for as long as I dared without feeling tense, tried to even out my breathing. She didn't readily make any movements.

"I don't want you to pity me! Please don't make it a habit of coming here."

Just then a nurse came in. Despite the austere expression on my face she proceeded toward the bed, tray in hand.

"It's okay. It doesn't matter. I still--"

"I'll talk to you later."

I got up and walked out of the room, down the hallway into the waiting room. When I got halfway to the exit doors I saw Grandma Camille coming in. I approached her, tried to keep it together.

"Samarra! I didn't expect to you to--"

"What's happening to her? Why does she have to be so cold all the time?"

My grandmother sighed.

"The doctor says that her brain cells are dying. It's like she's rapid firing random things. She doesn't mean any of it."

"Doesn't she? All I know is ever since I got here she hasn't had nearly one kind word for me--not one! Am I doing something wrong? What've I done to her, besides be born?"

I watched my grandmothers' eyes fill with tears and I grew afraid at the thought that my family may not ever mend. She looked up at me and finally spoke.

"When God speaks to you Samarra, all you can do is listen and obey..."

THE RISK

I could hear guitar playing coming from the inside as I walked to his door. I rang the doorbell and waited. The melodic drawl continued for a moment then the coda ended in a flourish of strings before the door opened. I straightened my dress.

"Hey!"

"Hi! C'mon in."

I stepped inside. Roxy wandered in and stood next to Damon. She leaned her massive frame against him and he scratched her soft head. He took the strap from around his shoulder and set the guitar down. I let my bag fall to the floor.

"You look nice."

"Thanks. Where's Nathan?"

"I put him to bed a little while ago."

He motioned for me to have a seat on the couch then sat beside me.

"I talked to your grandparents and um, I got you something."

He reached around and picked up something from the side table, a book. He glanced at it before he handed it to me. I read the cover: *100 Questions and Answers about Advanced and Metastic Breast Cancer* by Lillie D. Shockney and Gary R. Shapiro.

"I think it might help."

"Thank you. I appreciate this."

I opened it to the table of contents, stared at it, then closed it again. My mind was blank, like the canvasses that I started with each time I created something new and I quickly shut my eyes and looked away.

"I don't know why I came over here, I just--"

"It's okay. What is it?"

"My mom doesn't care about me anymore!"

"What makes you think that? What happened?"

Damon shifted around until we faced each other.

"It's okay, honey. What happened?"

"I went to see her and she, she just completely shut me out."

I broke down, though I hadn't wanted to. The freefall of tears made him move a little closer to me. He looked at me but didn't say anything, only cautiously reached and wiped my tears with the back of his hand.

"It's okay."

I shook my head.

"No! I can't go back there!"

"You don't have to think about it right now, okay?"

My whole body shook as I sobbed. He put his arm around me and drew me against his chest.

"Please, don't cry. It'll be alright."

My words came out in splintered fragments that needed connecting.

"How-do-you-know?"

"Because God will make a way. You'll see."

I sat up and rubbed my eyes. There were tears on his shirt.

"Oh, I'm sorry. I ruined your shirt."

"It's okay."

Damon smiled a little.

"Hey, do you want a cup of tea?"

I nodded.

"Yes, please."

"Okay, I'll be right back."

He disappeared around a corner and I heard him put the kettle on the stove. All sorts of ideas accosted my thoughts about the night I'd stayed here on his couch. I wondered (and worried) if he'd seen me in my skiives or if I'd been talking in my sleep or drooling on his pillow.

In another ten minutes he was back, cups in hand. As I looked him over there was a quiet uncertainty about him that made him seem timid at times while at other times there was a dark confidence, an arrogant attractiveness to him that made me want to listen to him, if only for nothing more than my own selfish gratification.

"Sorry for unloading all that on you."

"You really shouldn't be apologizing."

He drank from his cup and set it down on the table. I pushed the hair away from my face, tried not to smile, though it was impossible.

"What should I be doing then?"

"You should be happy, even if you still haven't figured out what that takes."

Of all the things I could describe myself as, happy had not been one of them, not for a long time.

"So, what are you going to do about it? You have to make up your mind."

I shrugged.

"I dunno yet."

"How about this--you've got the rest of the summer to figure it out, see what happens, is it a deal?"

I put the risk out of my mind.

"Okay."

"Good."

CHICKEN TERIYAKI

I didn't know if there was a clear definition for what Damon and I were or if a label even needed to be applied but spending time with someone without having to sever any strings that had been attached felt good and really easy. This Thursday evening found me sitting outside his bathroom door while he gave Nathan a bath. He'd laughed when I'd mentioned giving them some privacy. Nathan started singing and splashing in sync.

"Don't splash Nate! Hey Samarra, you said your dah wasn't around, so when's the last time you saw him?"

"Can I opt out of that question?"

"Alright, but I get to ask an extra question later."

"You can't make up the rules as you go!"

"I'm not, (he laughed) you're choosing which ones to answer."

He pulled the plug from the tub and was toweling off Nathan when the phone rang.

"Could you get that?"

"Your phone?"

"Yeah. Could you answer it, please?"

I knew that if I hesitated any longer he might think I was a weirdo, so I answered his phone.

"Marsden residence."

The caller on the other end paused.

"Hey, is Dame there?"

"Um, yeah hold on for a minute."

I walked back to the bathroom and handed off the phone and stood with Nathan. The little boy, wrapped in a towel, motioned for me to pick him up and I obliged willingly. His arms locked around my neck and he pressed his head to my chest. I pretended not to notice that his dad had taken off his wet shirt just a few feet away from me before he withdrew down the hallway, shirt in hand. While I got myself together and tried to focus his doorbell rang. I slowly put Nate down, opened the door and froze in my tracks when I saw my grandparents standing on the front porch and heard an audible breath seep out.

"Hey y'all!"

"Samarra, what're you doing here? We--"

Grandma Camille gasped just in time for Grandpa James to turn and see what I saw: Damon pulling his shirt over his head.

It felt like things were in slow motion, as my eyes stayed trained on him. Grandma Camille cleared her throat and waited for him to join us. He spoke first.

"Good evening."

"Hello."

My grandmother grabbed my arm and took me to the other side of the porch. Damon picked up Nathan.

"Samarra Lee Wells what's going on?!"

I raised an eyebrow.

"What?"

She leaned forward and whispered as her eyes narrowed.

"You're in that man's house and he's practically naked! What are you doing?"

"Nothing--he's just my friend!"

Grandpa Jamison walked over to where we were standing and quietly listened as I was being read the riot act. When there was a pause he interjected in his undemanding, understated way.

174

"I think what your grandmother is saying is that we're just trying to understand why you're here."

I knew that Damon was within earshot and I lowered my eyes, like we were having 'the talk' for the very first time.

My discomfort made them more resolute it seemed, and I could see that I wasn't going to win so I began to strategize.

"He was giving his son a bath and his shirt got wet so he changed it. That's all."

"Well, we have to go. Dinner's almost ready."

"'Ya know, this would be a great time for everyone to get to know each other. I mean, we haven't eaten, they haven't eaten, so we could all eat-together."

While they exchanged glances, I joined the neighbors. My face felt flushed.

"I'm sorry."

"It's okay. I'll see you later, right?"

"Um, would you and Nate like to come have dinner with us this evening?"

"Really?"

"Yeah! I'll draw you a map."

I sketched out directions, stole a glance at my grandparents. They looked a little stunned as they walked back to the car and got in.

"Make sure that you burn this once you get there."

We both laughed.

"See you around seven?"

"Yep."

I took a deep breath and whirled around to walk back to the car. Once we were on our way my grandmother spoke up.

"What's going on Samarra?"

"Nothing."

The car pulled up into the driveway and I unbuckled my seatbelt.

"I'm going to go finish making dinner."

...Damon rang the doorbell promptly at six fifty-nine and when I opened the door he and Nathan stood on the other side. The older Marsden was dressed in a blue polka dot shirt, heathery brown blazer, brown boots, and dark jeans.

"Hello!"

"Hey!"

Nathan was smiling, looking adorable in his shirt and tie. I stooped down and hugged him.

"Hey Nate!"

"Hi!"

I invited them into the dining room where we stood for a moment. Damon smoothed down his hair as he looked around the room, got acquainted with his surroundings.

"I wore this to a wedding once. Am I overdressed?"

"No. You look nice."

"Thank you."

My grandparents emerged from the kitchen, plates and silverware in hand. They were cordial.

"Good evening."

"Good evening."

Damon handed Grandpa James a bottle of red wine, much to his delight. He and Grandma read the label together and grinned.

"Thank you!"

"You're quite welcome."

"I'll get the glasses."

When they'd left the room, Damon turned to me.

"Are we going to talk about what happened the other night with your mum?"

I stared at him, but he was unmoved.

"Later?"

"Okay."

"We're having chicken teriyaki."

"Nice."

The clock chimed away.

"C'mon. I think it's ready."

The three of us walked into the dining room. There were pillar candles alight on the table and something about the softness, the melancholy in the atmosphere that made me aware of how precious and fleeting this night would be once we'd found some level of comfort among each other. We stood around the table, heads bowed, and all holding hands. Grandpa James cleared his throat and began:

"Dear Lord, we would like to thank you for being able to receive this food for the nourishment of our bodies and we thank you for our guests this evening. In Jesus' name we pray. Amen."

When Damon pulled out my chair for me I nibbled at my lip and quickly thanked him. I glanced over at my grandparents, who were intrigued by our guests. Damon checked on Nate, who was fumbling with his chopsticks. Father and son exchanged a few words among themselves and Damon took a fork from his pocket and handed it to the little one. We all laughed at the same time.

"With this one you always have to be prepared."

Grandpa Jamison seemed pleased to have another guy to discuss the finer points of Alabama football with or the socio-economic system in Africa or which bourbon was the best. The night seemed like it had barely begun when we were done eating and drinking. My grandparents cleared the dishes from the table. As a guest they had insisted Damon make himself comfortable when he offered to help with the cleanup.

"Thanks for inviting me Samarra."

"Thanks for coming."

"Your grandparents are awesome cooks!"

I chuckled.

"I know."

My phone rang, and I excused myself into the corner of the kitchen. It was Crystal. She wanted to know if I was sitting down and when I told her that I was she poured out a stream of information that she said had been burning a hole through her. In last week's edition of *The Carolina Times* section B, page fifteen there was a photo of Jason and his 'fiancée' Tiffany Roberson. They were to be wed at the First

Baptist church on September ninth, a month and some days from now. Pastor Acklin would be officiant. The bride's parents were to give her away in front of the two hundred seventy-five guests that would be attending. Crystal wanted to know if I was okay, if I already knew about any of this. The truth of it was as transparent as glass. This woman was the same one that had called me at some ungodly hour a few months back and tried to convince me that she and Jason were nothing more than friends, as if I were some fool. She was the same woman whose photos had turned up on Jason's phone, dozens of them from different 'incidental' meetings at various places. She'd tried to effortlessly slide into my place and take over my relationship, as if they'd been the originals and I was the outsider, but none of that really mattered now.

If I'd opened my eyes even as soon as last month I could've seen how many times he'd lied to me, how he'd been purposefully sabotaging our relationship. He could do all sorts of things to me, to us, when left to his own devices so this wasn't entirely odd, but it still stung just the same. Crystal and I talked for a few more minutes about work and Zara and what was happening back in Raleigh. Just before we hung up she stopped herself.

"Samarra, Dorian hasn't talked to Jason in a while. They got into an argument and they haven't talked since. What he did to you wasn't right."

"Thanks Crystal."

"Call us if you need us or if you need to talk or something!"

When I returned to our dinner guests they were in the living room looking at pictures of me in second grade and church choir and high school graduation. Damon held Nate in his arms, his back towards me. The sound of my high heels on the floor made him turn around.

"Sorry about that. I didn't mean to leave you guys stranded."

"We were checking out your pictures."

He stood close enough for me to see the tiny russet colored flecks in his green eyes. We walked back into the kitchen.

"My grandparents made you up some leftovers."

"Thank you."

Damon put Nathan down on the carpet, where he could play with his action figures. I handed him the storage container and glanced down at his left hand. It was free of its band, a light colored indentation around his ring finger.

"When my brother called earlier today he thought that you and I were an item."

"Really?"

"Yeah, it's been a while since there was a woman in our house."

He looked away, then down at his shoes. I smiled a little, reached out and grabbed his hand suddenly. He didn't flinch. Instead he rested his free hand on my back, moved closer and whispered in my ear:

"Makes the truth sweeter, doesn't it?"

"I don't know what you mean."

He motioned toward the other room with a nod. He'd heard my phone conversation.

"You're the one who has control now."

My grip around his hand tightened and then the tension that flowed through me seemed to ease up.

"I don't know if I want that."

"You said it yourself, everything happens like it's supposed to."

"I guess it had to eventually."

He smiled.

"I knew that you had enough sense to see when the ship was sinking."

Grandpa Jamison came in and stood next to the window before he cleared his throat.

LIGHT A FIRE

The next morning at breakfast my grandfather and I sat at the table. He drank his orange juice and read his paper.

"Are you excited about the reunion?"

"Yeah. I guess so. It's just been so long."

"Nervous, huh?"

I nodded and poured myself a glass of juice, took a few sips.

"Hey grandpa?"

"Mmm?"

"Do you think that Damon would like to go to the reunion?"

He set down his glass, folded his paper and gave me his rapt attention.

"Damon?"

"I haven't asked him yet or anything, but--"

"I'm sure he's nice Samarra, but he's, he wears earrings and he has long hair. He's so different."

"Could you define different? Do you mean different like Christian-Jewish different or like grape jelly and grape jam different?"

His gray eyebrows lifted on one side and I thought that he might say something else, but he was silent. I thought about Damon and tried not to smile, though I could see Grandpa James replaying the incident on his front porch when they'd thought something untoward had happened between us.

"What about how he's raising his son or how he goes to church or how he helped me?"

"How did he help you?"

"He replaced the carburetor in my car. He's been nothing but nice to me. I think he's sweet."

"Yeah, but we're not talking about a new bike here, kid. You really have to get to know someone first before you jump off the deep end."

"I know. He's only my friend."

"I saw the way he looked at you during dinner Samarra."

I was trying to laugh it off, but he sensed that I was coming away less than truthful. All that I could do was grin as I watched him sigh, smirk, and return to his paper. I reached for my phone with Damon in mind. At the risk of seeming desperate I closed it again, couldn't see how jumping the gun would make things easier between us or make him want to harbor a friendship with me, though I wasn't completely opposed to the idea that it might be fun getting there with him. The fire had been lit...

PRIDE OF PLACE

Grandma Camille looked radiant in her blue sheath dress and Grandpa Jamison, distinguished as always, was outfitted in a vest and tie. I hugged them.

"You look great!"

"You're not so bad yourself!"

"Hey, have you guys seen Damon yet?"

"Did you try the restroom?", he said.

"Mmm. Not yet."

While they talked I went off to find a drink of some sort and ended up at a table, standing in front of a man about my age with his hair in cornrows and deep dimples that showed whenever he smiled. He handed me a red plastic cup with ice in it.

"Hey, you don't remember me, do you?"

I tilted my head to the side, tried to recollect.

"Um, I'm not sure~"

"It's me--your cousin Sanchez!"

"Hey!"

Sanchez was one of my Uncle Michael's five children. He and I were closer in age and had more in common than most of the other kids and had always had a good time in each other's company. He hugged me from across the table and I almost instantly remembered the one or two summers he and I had spent together as kids, how we'd stay outside all day until it got dark, jumping on the trampoline, or catching fireflies or eating popsicles as they melted and left red and purple streaks down our arms.

"You're what, nineteen now?"

"Twenty."

"It's been a while."

"How's Uncle Mike doing?"

"Oh, he's good. He had to work."

"I can't believe how time's flown!"

"Yep. Where've you been?"

"Here and there, 'ya know. Busy with school and stuff."

Sanchez filled my glass with fruit punch then turned and conspiratorially looked over his shoulder.

"Do you want something else in that?"

I laughed.

"No, this is good. Thanks."

"Okay, suit yourself."

We were discussing school when the door swung open and Damon walked in. I watched him sifting through the faces in the room as he looked for me. I waited for a moment before getting his attention, trying to take him in and wondering to myself where the wellspring of confidence inside him came from. He was debonair in a button-down shirt and slacks. I walked over to him.

"Hey!"

He smiled and offered me his arm.

"Hi! I'm glad you made it!"

He greeted my grandfather with a fist bump and hugged my grandmother. We stood in a huddle discussing how many people were here and which ones we hadn't seen in ages. I looked over at Damon. It seemed like he was checking me out, so I leaned over and whispered:

"What are you looking at?"

He grinned, stared a moment longer.

"You. I mean, you look beautiful!"

"Thank you!"

"Mmm Hmm!"

I squeezed his arm.

"C'mon, let's get you a drink."

"Alright, but don't think you can ply me with alcohol then take advantage of me!"

"What?"

"Takes a lot to get me drunk, just saying."

We were both still giggling when we arrived at the refreshment table where Sanchez stood. He looked at Damon, his mouth twisting into a frown. I held Damon's arm as if he were escorting me to a dance. Sanchez refilled my cup. Damon extended his hand to my cousin.

"Hey, I'm Damon."

Sanchez didn't respond to him and soon he dropped his hand down at his side.

"I didn't know you liked saltines Samarra."

"What I like is none of your business Sanchez!"

He looked at one of us then the other and back again.

"I can't believe you brought him here! Seriously?"

Sanchez slammed the bottle down onto the table.

"Bar's closed!"

"C'mon Damon. Let's go."

"No. Hold on a second," he turned back toward Sanchez, "Is there something you want to say to me?"

"I don't even know you, man!"

"That's right--you don't!"

They were staring at each other ominously, dangerously aggressive on both sides. I leaned in and whispered in Damon's ear:

"Let's go, please!"

"You keep on running your mouth and I'll shut it for you! I can promise you that!"

Sanchez looked over at me as he was shaking his head.

"You Oreo!"

Before he could utter another word, I heard a barstool crash to the floor and saw Damon push Sanchez back against the counter.

"Damon!"

He didn't pay attention to me at first and it wasn't until I'd walked over to them and loosened his grip on Sanchez's shirt that he seemed to snap out of whatever had come over him.

"We just got off to a rough start, that's all. C'mon let's go get some air, alright?"

As we walked out of the ballroom, I reached out my hand and held his, unclenched his fist. We stood out in the lobby with our backs against the wall. Damon's grip tightened around my hand, but his gaze didn't change as he looked down at the floor. Neither of us spoke for a minute.

"Sorry. It's like a force of habit. When I don't like someone, I tend to go all out."

We laughed.

"Forget about it. None of it matters."

"Yeah."

"Do you think that if we go back inside you can behave yourself?"

"I think so."

The DJ started up and I was ready to dance and forget about the exchange that had happened. We walked to the dance floor and I set my hand on his shoulder. We moved in slow circles past my grandparents and a host of others. I was glad that the music slowed because it gave me time to think. I laughed to myself a little.

"What?"

"I was thinking about when I was six or seven and I got into my mom's makeup drawer and made myself up."

"Really?"

"Yeah. I had on this bright red, glossy lipstick and all this glittery eye shadow."

He spun me around.

"Glittery?"

"It was the eighties."

"Oh, that explains it then."

"She didn't even get mad at me. She just laughed and helped me clean up."

"Do you really think she doesn't care for you?"

"It's hard to say."

"Why?"

"She stopped returning my calls. She wouldn't talk to me. She still won't, really."

"Samarra, all you can do is keep loving her. Nobody can fault you for that, believe me."

Just as the song ended Grandpa Jamison dipped Grandma Camille and the room erupted in applause. I excused myself to go to the restroom.

...After I'd flushed and was about to open the stall door I heard someone walk in amid laughter and a conversation already in progress.

"Did you see who showed up?"

"Yeah! I can't believe it!"

"Her mother's in the hospital and she still came."

"I wonder where she's been all this time."

"I know right?"

I heard the door swing open and their voices began to die down as they walked back to the ballroom. I came out of the stall and stood at the sink, washed my hands. More people here had green eyes than I thought. When I came back into the room I found Damon dancing with a little girl. She giggled and squealed as he spun her around. After he'd been dumped by his junior dance partner he walked over to me.

"Our family doesn't do this kind of thing. It's fun! I like it!"

He smiled, but it soon vanished as our eyes met.

"Are you okay?"

"Is it wrong for me to be here when my mother's stuck in the hospital?"

"Don't let it get you down, alright? You've got nothing to be ashamed of."

We walked to the table where most of the other members of the Owens-Carson clan were beginning to gather. At the head of our table sat ninety-two-year-old Mrs. Beatrice Owens-Carson our oldest member and matriarch. She blessed our gathering, our families, our health, the food. The spread was massive: Fresh garden vegetables (two ways), salad, casseroles, chicken with sauce, beef skewers, rolls, pasta...

Damon pulled my chair out for me and we sat next to each other. A woman seated across from us looked over at her date and half whispered to him:

"You never do that for me!"

He fluffed his napkin and placed it in his lap. I found myself admiring his hair, the way it fell around his face and forehead, how much it had grown.

No sooner had we sat down, one of the attendees I recognized as a younger cousin, Naomi, began staring at Damon. She took a drink from her glass, looked over at her sister Olivia, who snickered.

"It's Damon, right?"

"That's right."

"Who's your favorite black artist?"

"I love Henry O. Tanner's work. There's so much depth in his paintings, 'ya know?"

"Yeah. I guess so."

I laughed to myself.

"Weren't you in the 'crazy hospital' Samarra?", she said.

I set down my fork. I couldn't see anything past her sitting across from me. We both knew that she'd been in the county lockup no less than four times and that her younger sister emulated her at every turn. She wasn't fit to pass sentence on anyone, least of all me. I turned to Olivia.

"You should really watch the company you keep, sweetie. Makes you look bad."

Olivia lowered her head and cut her eyes at her sister. Damon grinned without looking up from his dinner. The chatter at the table started up immediately, as if nothing had happened. After dinner there were cigars and drinks for the adults and dessert and treats for the kids.

Damon and I talked to my grandparents and Mrs. Owens-Carson for a while before we ended up alone on the balcony. We leaned against the railing, talking.

"Is what that girl said in there true?"

I closed my eyes.

"Yeah. Last year I didn't feel right, like I couldn't keep my mind still enough. My mother stopped talking to me and there was all this stuff going on with Jason. It was really hard to focus and I missed almost a week of classes."

I felt my eyes darting from side to side as I spoke. Damon reached for my hand, but I made a tight fist for a moment as I looked straight ahead.

"How long did you stay?"

"Almost nine days."

"Look at me."

I felt like I could barely lift my head.

"Samarra, look at me."

We stared at one another.

"Please don't! I can't--"

"I don't know anybody that hasn't been through something! We've all got baggage."

"Not like this."

"Having a garment bag and two carry ons doesn't make you a freak."

He smiled a little.

"Even if I voluntarily checked myself in?"

"Sure."

"Don't pretend like it's not a big deal Damon, 'cause it is!"

"It is if you want it to be! Quit trying to be perfect every second of the day, honey. It's only going to make you go off the rails for real!"

He moved closer to me.

"Do your grandparents know about what happened?"

"They know that it was stress induced, yeah. Do you trust me around Nathan still?"

"Still? Always."

"Don't tell him, alright?"

"What is there to tell?"

He hugged me.

"Better?"

I nodded, managed a weak smile. The DJ was playing his last song of the evening, 'Happy Feelings' by Maze featuring Frankie Beverly. I gasped.

"Oh! I love this song! C'mon!"

We ran back to the ballroom, back to the dance floor. It was crowded, but the milieu kept us all dancing, some of us singing. One of the younger kids, Langston, cut in on my dance with Damon. Mr. Marsden graciously stepped aside while suppressing his laughter. While we danced I saw Sanchez approach Damon. They seemed to talk in calmer, more measured tones then they shook hands. When Sanchez handed him a bottle of alcohol, Damon laughed.

We circulated around the room one more time. I looked around and felt a lot less like an outsider, a lot more like I belonged with them. I felt a pride of place. When the last song was done, Langston fist bumped me and went to hang out with the other kids in the ten and under set. Damon found me soon after.

"That kid's hilarious!"

"Yeah, he's great!"

"I'm ready to see Nate now."

I smiled at him. One of Jeremy and Anna's sons, Thomas, was having a sleepover and Nathan had been invited. He'd be returning tomorrow.

"It's great that he's got so many friends."

"Good way to keep him occupied."

"I'm sure."

The emcee carried two cardboard boxes out to the stage and began passing out t-shirts. Damon looked surprised that he'd been given one and he stood admiring it.

"Did Sanchez come to his senses?"

"Yeah. He apologized."

"Whoa!"

"Yep."

When it was time for us to take the photo, our thirty eight person party huddled together. The photographer counted us down, the buzzwords were practically yelled by most of us and the photographer snapped away. As I said 'Good night' to Mrs. Owens-Carson, the cousins, aunts, uncles, (others), and my grandparents, Damon went to go get the car. When I turned around Sanchez was standing beside me. I spoke first.

"Hey."

"Hey."

"Thanks for apologizing to Damon."

"I'm sorry about all that."

"Apology accepted."

"How do you know him?"

"He's my mechanic."

"He seems pretty cool, 'cous."

"Yeah, he's a real sweet guy."

Damon walked over to us.

"Are you ready to take me home?"

He raised an eyebrow and smirked.

...Back in the driveway of his house he took off his seatbelt and twisted around in his seat.

"I haven't had that much fun in a long time!"

"What was your favorite part?"

"That group photo!"

"Of course!"

As I looked into his eyes I knew I wouldn't get any sleep tonight. On the way inside, I checked my phone. Doctor Gleeson had left a message almost two hours ago.

LOOSE ENDS

Doctor Gleeson was waiting for me in the hallway outside my mothers' room as I approached. His face looked careworn by the tiny creases on his forehead, but a kind patience stayed in his eyes and did not leave.

"Miss Wells, may I speak with you privately for a moment?"

"Okay."

I was glad I'd come alone this morning as the doctor and I walked to the cafeteria. Whatever it was I was about to hear would be better consumed singly, quickly and without fear. The doctor offered me a seat and poured us both coffee. I wondered what everyone else was doing right now. Maybe Dorian and Crystal were changing Zara's diaper or perhaps Professor Sullivan was preparing for a lecture or Damon was taking Roxy to the vet. I looked at Doctor Gleeson and wondered how many times he'd told someone else exactly what he was about to tell me, how many peoples' lives had been changed irrevocably here in this very room.

As he fixed his coffee I could only stare down into my paper cup as if my future was looming dark and dangerously in its insulated walls. I sat back in the chair.

"Miss Wells, I'm going to level with you right now. There's a more immediate threat to your mother's life."

"What do you mean?"

"She's refusing to take her medication."

"What kind of medication?"

"It's a type of stabilizing medication. It will even out her liver function and help with the pain, for now," he looked at me, blinked a few times, "I need you to try and convince her that she has to take this medicine."

"How long have you practiced medicine, doctor?"

He drew in a breath sharply.

"Twenty five years."

"That's as long as I've been alive."

"Miss Wells?"

"In twenty-two years she's never acted like I was her daughter! I can count on one hand the number of times she's ever told me she loved me! That's why--"

"Don't you think I've heard it all before?"

"I can't do that, what you're asking."

"Do you understand what I'm saying to you? If your mother doesn't take this, her kidneys will shut down, her liver will fail, and her heart will stop and all you'll have left is your guilt and your regret. Please look at me."

My eyes flickered up to his where they caught. They were as blue as ocean water.

"All you can do is try!"

I looked down into my cup again.

"I don't usually ask a patients' family to do this kind of thing, out of respect for their privacy, but your mother doesn't have a DNR order in place, so I felt like I could ask you."

"What's a DNR?"

"It's a do not resuscitate order, should she become unresponsive or comatose and end up on a life support system."

"Oh."

Doctor Gleeson's eyes flitted back and forth over my face in confusion at what must seem so strange a thing. I slowly lifted the cup to my lips and drank even though I'd never liked the bitter taste of black coffee.

"Okay. I'll try."

I found myself regretting what I'd told the doctor with each step I took down the hallway. I'd made up my mind to get it over with as quickly as I could. When I came into her room she was awake and transfixed on the doorway.

"Hey, mama."

She stared at me as I sat down.

"Look, I'm here because Doctor Gleeson needs you to take your medicine."

"Do you want me to take it?"

"Of course, I want you to take it!"

She shrugged and looked out the window.

"If it'll make you feel better, why won't you take it?"

"I don't want you to come here anymore Samarra! I mean it!"

"Why are you acting like this?!"

"Because I can't just flip a switch and change the way I feel about you!"

"Do you want that to be the last thing you ever say to me?"

"No. I want it to be this: You never did anything to be worthy of your father and me!"

"I know you don't mean that!"

"I do! You're ungrateful and stubborn and your father and I would still be together if it weren't for you!"

My face felt flushed, but I was determined not to cry, never again in front of her. I'd already used up all my tears on an outcome that would end up the same way that it always had.

"I'm sorry you feel that way, but if anybody has a right to be disappointed it's me! 'Ya know, you never bonded with me, you never got to know me--you never wanted to! I can't pretend like none of that ever happened! Not anymore!"

She crossed her arms.

"Mama, you have to stop blaming me for whatever it is you think I did. Stop punishing me!"

"Then stop playing the victim!"

"You're clinging to his ghost like your life depends on it! Just stop, please!"

A nurse walked into the room.

"If you can't keep if down in here, I'm going to have to ask you to leave!"

When he was gone I looked back to my mother.

"You have to quit being so bitter. He's gone!"

"Do you think I don't know that? Ever since your father left, every day I've wanted to lay down and die! You'll never understand!"

I rubbed my hands over my face and sighed aloud.

"I don't have all these memories about him the way you do!"

"That doesn't mean that he wasn't a kind and decent person!"

"He still didn't see anything in us that was important enough for him to stay."

"It's never as black and white as you think Samarra! It's so easy for you to tie up loose ends because you've never had to sacrifice anything!"

The clock on the wall kept the minutes.

"'Ya know, I can't figure out if it's worse that he ignored us or that you just couldn't see it."

She stared at me. There was so much to say, but the crush of time pressed in on all sides of the small hospital room.

"Are you going to take the medication? I need to know what to tell Doctor Gleeson."

"I don't know!"

I picked up my bag and stood up.

"You just can't make this easy, can you?"

"What I said before still stands! Don't come back here Samarra!"

Her eyes narrowed, forever maintaining the steely facade that was all her own.

"Do you know what's so different between you and me mama?"

She shook her head.

"I have enough sense to see when the ship's sinking."

I walked out of the room and down the hallway past Doctor Gleeson, unable to keep the nihilism from spreading across my face...

PRECIOUS CARGO

I had hoped that I would wake up and find that the visit I'd made to the hospital to see my mother had all been a dream and that the argument, the drive back home, the coffee with Doctor Gleeson were all part of a sleep induced state, but it wasn't to be. It was just beginning to grow dark when I pulled into the drive. I only wanted to kick off my shoes and rest for a little while. I had taken the keys out of the ignition and gotten out of the car when I heard the screen door slam open next door at Damon's house. The frantic pace of hurried small footsteps approached and I turned to see Nathan standing in front of me, his eyes wide, his face marred by tears.

"Nate?"

"S'maruh! C'mon hurry! You have to come!"

He tugged at my hand and pulled me toward their house.

"C'mon!"

We ran at full speed up the steps and into the house. Aside from the television being on there was a supernatural quiet in the house as I closed the front door. There was an overturned chair in the living room, a rug crumpled up nearby. The phone was lying on the floor, the error message repeating.

"Nate, where's your dad?!"

I walked a little further into the kitchen and saw his bare feet there, unmoving. I instantly clapped a hand to my mouth. Nathan retreated to a corner, bawling his eyes out as I knelt beside his dad. There was broken glass scattered across the floor. I turned back to Nathan.

"It's okay sweetheart. It's gonna to be alright."

I touched Damon's face, tried to feel for a pulse in his neck. His heartbeat was faint and so broken that I thought I might be watching this man's last moments. I threw off my jacket. His body began making involuntary back and forth movements, jerking that was painful to watch as he gasped for air, his hands postured in a rigid stance. I rolled him onto his side.

"Damon!"

I ran to the living room and grabbed a pillow from the couch and slid it underneath his head. I tried again for a pulse, felt a slight throbbing. His eyes were half open, staring out into space, but seeing nothing as I moved him onto his back again. A thick stream of blood gushed from his nose. I wiped it away with my hand and smeared it across my t-shirt then tilted back his head to check his airway, listened to his labored breathing with a mounting uneasiness. Nathan started to whimper. Damon's nose was still bleeding. I snatched a dishtowel off his drainer and ran cold water over it in the sink, wrung it out. By the time I reached him his shirt was drenched in sweat and his skin was clammy.

I dabbed his face and neck with the dishtowel, wiped his nose, then when I could trust myself enough I tilted back his head again and breathed into his mouth, even as sorrow began to slight my hopes and I knew that I could not let it. I started doing chest compressions and rescue breathing over and over. Suddenly, as if I'd been directed by The Almighty Himself, I thought about his diabetes. Damon had told me that he had to take insulin shots. I ran to his fridge and tossed its contents aside, checked the door and pull out drawers.

At the very back, nestled in each egg tray slot were at least ten tiny vials of insulin. I grabbed the insulin and his test kit from the counter, knocked over something that I didn't stop to watch hit the floor as I yanked at the pouch's zipper and sent hundreds of test strips and his meter flying across the kitchen. At the bottom there was a bundle of his syringes. I pulled up his shirt, pulled it over his head. He was still seizing as I pulled off the tiny orange cap on one of the syringes, filled it from the glass bottle and pushed the needle into his arm, jammed down the plunger with my thumb.

Ten or fifteen seconds passed by before the convulsions slowed. Nathan came over to me and stood close, tearfully watching Damon. Finally, he gasped for a breath and drew it in wildly. He focused in on me and the weight of the moment came down on all of us. His eyes shifted feebly from side to side as he pulled himself up.

"Nathan!"

He ran to his father and hugged him.

"Dah!"

Damon kissed Nate's head and hugged him for a long time, stroking his hair and softly reassuring him. He looked over at me through eyes that were lachrymose.

"What happened to me?"

He slid back against the cabinets and rubbed his hands over his face. I sat up on my knees and pretended not to see the trembling in his hands.

"You had a seizure."

"What? Wait, how'd you get here?"

"Nate came over and got me. What's the last thing you remember?"

"I went to get a glass of water and..."

His voice trailed off and we were mutually silent for a moment.

"Samarra?"

"I'm here. As long as you need me I'm here."

"Okay."

I hadn't thought about whether I'd just made him an empty promise that was void in the space of my heart where I kept the most precious cargo. Damon winced. There was a shard of glass lodged in his right hand, glass lying near him. I took his hand, palm side up, and gently pulled until it came out. I wrapped his hand with the dishtowel and helped him to his feet. He braced himself against me and we stood in the doorway looking at the aftermath in the kitchen. In my peripheral vision I could see him staring at me.

We walked to the couch where Nate sat down and rested his head on his dad's arm.

"Where's your first aid?"

"Hall closet. Third shelf down..."

..."Samarra?"

"Hmm?", I didn't immediately look up from my work as I bandaged his hand.

"Thank you."

His eyes moved in on mine in a way that they hadn't before and an odd sort of trepidation forced me to stand up and straighten my clothes.

"You're welcome."

I walked over to the ottoman and searched through my bag to keep myself from his face. I handed him and Nate each a granola bar, the last of Grandma Camille's care package.

"Thanks."

"Mmm Hmm. I'll help you clean this up."

I quickly excused myself to the kitchen where I hung up the phone and swept up the mess on the floor, then picked up, straightened, and put away until everything was set to rights. When I came back into the living room Damon had put Nathan to bed and changed his clothes. I thought back to the first time I'd ever laid eyes on him, not knowing who he was or what his life contained. He joined me on the couch.

"Are you alright?"

He nodded, spoke slowly.

"You don't know what you've done for me tonight Samarra. I thank God for letting you be here. I just~"

Damon was clenching his jaw, a tenseness spreading through him. I thought about how quickly life could change and go crazy and turn into something so unexpected. I didn't want there to be this awkwardness between us and when he continued I could see that he was struggling. He pressed the heels of his hands against his eyes and wiped away tears as he breathed slowly. I put my hand on his arm. He looked at me for a long while.

"I was thinking that was the last time I was ever gonna see my son Samarra."

I couldn't think of a single thing to say to him, but I felt so much for him, of him at that moment that I forced myself to look away so that I didn't have to see him hurt or feel what he felt, so that I didn't have to try and resurrect such feelings in my heart for anyone else ever again. I got up to leave, was walking toward the door when he grabbed my hand.

"Where are you going?"

I looked at him then back to the door but didn't answer.

"Just stay with me a little longer. Please."

He still held my hand and as he ambled back to the couch I was being towed along. We both sat down.

"You really are good at caring for people."

He smiled, used his bandaged hand to move my hair to one side, away from my face. I nodded.

"It's not so hard."

We were moving closer together, as if a gravitational pull was inching us inward. I stopped short and looked into his eyes. He folded me into his arms where we sat hugging. His voice was faint now.

"Thank you, Samarra."

"It's okay."

I didn't want him to see me cry and tell him how safe and honest it felt to have his arms around me, so I broke free from his embrace and bolted for the door, still thinking about what it was I was running away from.

"I'll see you tomorrow."

"Okay."

I opened the door and stepped out onto the porch. The stars were on display tonight just like they'd been on that evening when we'd first met. Was it a sign from God? Was I supposed to tap my brain and figure out if I'd missed the times He'd told me this would happen?

I walked back across the driveway to my house. Back in the foyer I felt safe enough to sit down, although my heart was doing somersaults in my chest. The exhilaration was leading me into a breathless distraction. I couldn't explain, not even to myself, what I felt must've been happening to me at that moment. Had I almost...?

I rummaged through my bag and felt for my phone. The green Post-It note with Damon's number scrawled across it lay at the bottom of my bag. I picked it up and began dialing...

THE DEEP

...My mind had abandoned the grocery list in my hand in favor of my sudden departure from Damon's house the night before and the weighty unease that was sunk deep in his eyes, his arrested breaths as he came to, as he shook off the fear that had tied the stone to his heart and threatened to drown all that he was in a sea of uncertainty. I thought about the hours long phone conversation that ensued and the ways it had been awash in words that were so personal that they bordered on the sacred to me. When I asked him if he was okay he seemed to be thinking.

"I'm better now."

"That's good. How's Nate?"

"He's okay. He's sleeping like a rock."

We both laughed.

"Are you alright Samarra? You left in such a hurry."

"Yeah, I'm okay."

"I'm glad."

I was thinking of how he must have been smiling as we'd talked, and I almost didn't hear someone calling me as I stood in the produce aisle, basket in hand, unsure of her at first until she approached me.

I tried to match her face with her name then realized where I'd seen her before: The cookout at Damon's house, Natalie. She wore her hair in a sleek chignon and a cute blue trench coat cinched at her waist. She pushed her glasses up on her face.

"Hey, how're you?"

"I'm good. How have you been?"

We chatted about small things (organic blueberry muffin recipes) and important things (public schools versus private ones and which their kids would be attending) until the conversation turned to Damon and his son.

"Damon went through a rough patch about a year ago. After his divorce he just fell into such a deep depression. He stopped taking care of himself. He was so down. Mic and I started going over and sitting with him. We took turns helping out with Nathan until he felt better."

"He was that bad off?"

She nodded.

"You do know that his divorce was just finalized this past January, right?"

"No, I had no idea."

"Now you'd never know he was the same person," she nodded as she spoke, "You should see the way he gets when Nate talks about you! There's this look on his face, like he's stuck deep down in something and he doesn't want to get out of it."

I felt an immediate discomfort at the direction this conversation was taking and when her phone rang I was sort of glad. We exchanged 'Goodbyes' before moving off in different directions. As I gathered the rest of tonight's dinner ingredients I could only focus on getting home to clear the space in my head and recover what I'd buried there.

VERITAS

When I opened Nate's door and peered in I couldn't help but stand there, motionless, dazzled by the mass of plastic stars and planets affixed to the ceiling as they phosphoresced in the near darkness. I was about to turn and leave when he stirred in his sleep and sat up in bed.

"S'maruh?"

"Hmm?"

I walked toward him and sat down on the edge of his bed.

"Are you gonna stay here now?"

"I don't know sweetheart."

"I wish you didn't have to go."

"I know."

He rubbed the back of his hands across his eyes, defending himself against sleep.

"How 'bout you get some rest and I'll see you tomorrow? Sound good?"

"Okay."

I pulled the covers over his shoulders and tucked him in.

"Get some sleep now. Good night."

"Good night."

He closed his eyes. I rubbed his back for a moment and thought of the lullaby my mother used to sing to me some nights before I'd fall asleep, 'P'tit fleur fanee' as the French Creole dialect mixed with her gentle voice. As I looked up at the artificial galaxy above us I sang to him as best I could remember:

"P'tit fleur fanee, p'tit fleur aimee, Di a moin toujours, kouk c'est l'amar. Vi machais dans la foret Y faisait bon y faisait frais. Dann z'herbe l'avait la rose'e. Dans le ciel z'oiseaux y chantaient." / "Little wilted flower, little beloved flower, Tell me always what love is. We were walking in the forest. It was nice, it was cool. In the grass there was dew. In the sky, the birds were singing."

I didn't leave until I saw the rise and fall in his breathing. When I stepped out into the hallway Damon was standing there. As we walked along he looked over at me.

"'Ya know, Nathan's getting attached to you."

"Yeah. I kind of guessed that."

We migrated to the living room and the wall where his record collection was stacked. He sat down on the floor cross legged and delicately let his fingers slip over each record cover and fall against the previous one as if they were important files. When he had found the one that he wanted he pulled the vinyl record from its jacket.

"Why don't you own a cd player?"

Damon laughed and shook his head as he put the empty cover at the front of the stack and got to his feet.

"I searched around a lot of record shops in Savannah 'til I found this. It took me a long time."

I flitted a smile, thought that he was giving me a clue about himself in that he was patient, determined, persistent. He placed the record on the Crosley turntable and dropped the needle. In a matter of seconds, the whole room was engulfed in music. He sat on the couch.

"Do you remember what you said to me in the kitchen the other night?"

"I remember, yeah."

"Does the offer still stand?"

I could scarcely feel my feet moving, but somehow, I made it to the ottoman.

"I thought you would've forgotten about that."

"Why would I?"

"Damon, I have my own life!"

"You've been over here so much that Nate gets anxious when you leave now."

I sighed.

"Why are you trying to--?"

"I'm trying to get you to see that not everybody has a hidden agenda! Not everything's about the take Samarra!"

I walked over to the mantle, looked at the pictures.

"Until a few weeks ago, you didn't even know me, though."

"So, what?! Everything has to have a starting point."

I shook my head, looked away.

"You just don't want to take a chance, do you?"

"It's got nothing to do with that!"

"It's got everything to do with that and you know it!"

"I'm not going into this blind and end up getting my feelings hurt, or worse--hurting Nathan! You have NO idea what it's like to have to carry around this weight on your back, so things don't fall apart Damon!"

He got up and walked over to me.

"You're joking, right?! I've had my heart ripped out Samarra, but I'm not shutting you out because of it! I'm, I'm standing here, and I'm trying to be your friend!"

Our voices had elevated to the point where we were yelling at each other like contestants in a shouting match. He pushed back his hair and I turned away from him.

"At least tell me being here doesn't feel like a mistake to you! Tell me that at least."

I didn't verbally respond, and he stood staring at me.

"Quit looking at me like that!"

He looked away.

"I don't know why I expect you to be honest with me if you can't even tell yourself the truth!"

"I don't owe you anything!"

I walked to the door, flung it open, long past infuriated at his audacity to think that he was just going to tell me how things in my life were going to be while I simply rolled over. He came over to me and all but cornered me up in the doorway, refused to let me pass. It was the first time I'd seen him so angry. He grabbed the doorknob and slammed the door shut.

"Stop running like a scared rabbit! Just talk to me, please!"

We stared at each other and were quiet for a long while. I sat down on the ottoman again. Damon was still standing at the door. I thought of what Natalie had said about the way he was a different person after his divorce, how his heart must have been kept in a suspended state, contained in a jar that was already filled to the brim with sadness. He slowly turned around.

"Samarra-"

"Damon, what happened with you and Nate's mom?"

He closed his eyes and his breathing slowed, as if he was trying to forget. I could see even now, an enduring darkness engulfing him, drawing him back into some painful remembrances that no amount of equivocation could mute as he spoke softly, his eyes glazing over, his head sinking. He sat down across from me.

"About a month before we separated I came home and found Nate by himself. She didn't even care that something might have happened to him. She told me that she'd only been gone for a few hours, like that was supposed to make it okay."

Damon was staring down at the patterned rug on the floor as he spoke.

"I couldn't trust her. No matter what she said I couldn't look at her and not feel~"

"Empty?"

"Empty."

In such close quarters I felt my face growing warmer, wondered if he noticed. Suddenly, he looked up at me and I couldn't look away.

"I wish you were the first man I'd ever met."

He shook his head.

"Not me."

"Why not?"

"I like you just the way you are."

I felt a bit confused, as if I weren't equipped to accept what he'd said.

"You know what pain feels like?"

I nodded.

"Then that makes you who you are. I don't think you should forget it, but I don't ever want you to have to feel it again. If your boyfriend can't appreciate you, then he should step aside and let someone else."

"I don't have one, a boyfriend."

"Oh. How long were you with him?"

"Almost five years. He wasn't good for me and now I feel like I'm one of those people that's only in love with the idea of being in love."

"We like the fire, but we hate the burn."

After a time, he stood up.

"Would you like a cup of tea?"

"I would. Very much..."

...There were two cups set out on the counter, tea tags dangling from them, diffidence mixing with the sugar and the creamer. He picked up his tea bag and steeped it before adding sugar substitute.

"Are you taking care of yourself?"

He looked up from his task.

"I didn't know you cared."

I bit my lip, watched him grin as I sipped my tea and looked elsewhere.

"I've been taking care of myself, I haven't had any more problems."

"That's good."

We both laughed at the same time. He took a drink then set aside his cup. He was looking at my wrists, at the stars. I turned my arm over and he leaned in.

"How many tattoos do you have?"

"About four apart from the sleeve."

"Which one did you get first?"

"The one on my ankle, the feather."

Damon picked up his cup again.

"What's it mean?"

"It reminds me of resilience. No matter how many times the wind batters a feather, it still manages to rise back up again. And it reminds me not to become a stranger in my own life."

"Mmm."

"What?"

"I don't see how you could think something like that could happen to you."

I laughed to myself.

"There's a lot you don't know about me."

"I could say the same thing."

"Is that right?"

"Absolutely!"

I finished my tea.

"If I answer one of your questions you have to answer one of mine. Tit for tat, okay?"

"Okay."

"Ladies first."

He stood smirking at me across the counter.

"What's the last thing you prayed about?"

"I asked God to watch over my family and friends, Nate, of course, your mum and your grandparents, you. And world peace and all that."

"Really?"

"Yep. You sound surprised."

I shook my head.

"Your turn."

He scratched his beard, seemed to be thinking of a question to pose to me. I sat back in my seat.

"Have you ever been in a relationship where you were the one who cheated?"

"No."

"Yeah, me either."

"What makes you happy?"

I clasped my hands together, tried to think.

"I dunno."

"Really?"

"Yeah. Your turn."

Our exchange, our confession session, kept us relying on each other to release the truth and hold back nothing. He drained the tea from his cup.

"Have you ever been arrested?"

"Yes!"

"So have I!"

"Why're we excited about that?!"

"I dunno."

"How many relationships have you been in?"

"Do you want to ask me that or do you just want to know how many women I've been with Samarra?"

"Sure."

"Three, including my ex-wife."

"Quality versus quantity?"

"Nah. Style over substance."

He continued.

"What scares you?"

"Dying alone."

"I thought about that when..."

He stopped, looked away.

"Damon?"

"Hmm?"

"It's okay."

From where we stood I reached over and ran my hand through his hair. It was soft and full like down feathers and I was satisfied that it was as glorious as I'd imagined it would be. He didn't stop focusing on my face and I found my heartbeat quickening, my breath escaping me even as I stood before him struggling to master my own fragility, the vulnerability I felt at that moment, trying to take hold of myself before it was too late.

"I know, I know. Keep going."

"Alright. What's your idea of success?"

"Knowing God wakes me up every day. Having a son that's healthy and happy. Getting to do what I love for work. Good friends. Making memories with new ones. What's yours?"

"Getting the chance to be better than I was the day before."

"Mmm. That's good."

"Can I see your wallet?"

"What? Are you serious?"

I nodded.

"I'll show you mine."

He paused, but still couldn't keep a smile off his face. "Okay."

Damon reached around into his back pocket, disconnected the chain from his belt loop and produced his wallet. I handed him mine as well and we each opened the others at the same time. I felt like I was opening a gift. I unsnapped the two closures and unfolded his wallet. I looked at his driver's license first. He took a very fine picture.

"You were born in nineteen eighty-two. You're three years older than me!"

He was shuffling the cards that I kept in the zippered slot on the side. When he got to my license he stopped. He grinned.

"I like your picture."

"Thanks."

I opened his bill keeper and snuck a peek while he was still looking at my library card. Inside there was an unusual red tinted paper currency with a lion on the front.

"What's this?"

"It's a fifty rand note. One dollar in the States is the same thing as eleven and ninety four rand in South Africa."

"Oh. That's interesting."

"You think so?"

He was staring at me.

"Yeah."

"It's a little bit of home."

I looked through his cards. There was an ATM card, a picture of Nathan, a medical card with information about his diabetes, a photographers' union card along with some other business cards, and a few slips of paper with handwritten notes on them. He'd taken an interest in a month-old receipt of mine from Walgreens. I'd bought a bottle of green tea, lip balm, and a birthday card. I handed him back his wallet and he gave me back mine.

"That was fun."

He nodded.

"Yeah."

"Can I ask you something else?"

"Anything."

"Do you think that Nathan notices I'm different?"

His brow furrowed.

"How do you mean, 'different'?"

"I mean, I'm not vanilla."

"I prefer chocolate. Dark chocolate."

I smiled as I shook my head. His expression, his grin, held steady.

"I think that he knows that you're not the same, but I've taught him to look at the content of a person's character and not the color of their skin."

"Well, does it bother you?"

"No, why would it?"

"Just wondering."

"I don't know, I just think that you're the first woman that ever made me want to use my imagination."

"What do you imagine?"

"That you could be~"

My phone rang. I looked back toward the living room where it lay in my bag atop the ottoman.

"I'll be right back."

"Okay."

I walked into the other room and picked up my phone. I scrolled down through the missed calls. There were several, all from Jason, along with one new text message dated today, an hour ago:

SUNNY, IDK WHAT HAPPENED. IM SO SORRY. CALL ME PLZ. LUV U. J

I deleted the message with one button, swiftly erased the sorrow that I might feel if I had back pedaled. I lifted my head. Damon was standing at the kitchen window drinking a glass of water. I threw the phone back in my bag and as I walked into the kitchen he turned and approached me.

"Are you alright?"

"I will be."

"Good."

"When are you going back to work?"

"Probably around the first of September."

He was absentmindedly staring off into space and I tapped him on the shoulder. He instantly came around.

"Hmm?"

"What's on your mind?"

"I can't tell you."

"Why not?"

Damon looked down at his feet, like a kid with a bad grade on his report card.

"It's too indecent to repeat."

I put a hand over my mouth.

"Oh!"

His head snapped up.

"Nah, I'm just messing with you!"

"That's not funny Damon!"

"Sorry, (he stopped laughing) I was thinking about which lenses I need to take to work. And that you look beautiful tonight."

"See, why do you say stuff like that to me?"

"Stuff like what?"

236

I rolled my eyes at him.

"Friends don't make friends feel awkward Damon."

"Okay."

"Okay!"

He kept looking at me until my scowl-like frown melted away and I found it impossible not to laugh.

"You can't stay angry for long, can you?"

"It just seems like a waste of time to be mad when nobody really cares to begin with."

"I still meant what I said before, you do look beautiful."

"Thank you."

"You're very welcome."

I only smiled back at him...

...The hours were winding down and it was late when I got up to leave. He walked me to the door.

"How's your mum?"

"I'm going to go see her tomorrow."

"We're all praying for her, us and Mic and Jeremy. She's on our prayer circle list."

"Thanks."

He nodded, tugged at his ear lobe.

"Thanks for the tea. It was perfect."

"Anytime."

"How's your hand?"

He held it up for me to examine. On his palm there was a small incision-like scar a few inches across that was still a little red.

"Better, thanks to you."

Damon hugged me and just as he let me go I felt him slip something into my sweater pocket, something lightweight, barely there. I pretended not to notice until he had gone and I was back across my own driveway. I put my hand in my pocket and felt around for some evidence of my suspicion, palmed the piece of paper at the bottom...

...Back in my room I unfolded the note. It was the size of an index card. Handwritten in marker was the remainder of our conversation that had been interrupted by the ringing phone:

I imagine that with you, I leave no dare undone.

-Damon.

I read it only once, folded it up and put it away in my Bible in the book of Ecclesiastes...

FAMILY

The elevator door opened and as I walked down the hospital corridor I could hear my heart beating like a snare drum until the repetition became my mother's words echoing in my head:

'Don't come back here Samarra!'

On the ride up to the fifth floor of Savannah Hospital-Memorial Health University I'd wondered if Doctor Gleeson had had any luck convincing my mother to take the medication. It seemed like time was catching up to us all. Another week had passed and September was quickly approaching. My thoughts today were like a rubber band ball. The looser outer elastics were like school and sleep and Jason, the furthest from me. The tighter, more rigid bands were my grandparents, and my mother and Crystal and Dorian and Zara and they were closest to my heart.

I couldn't make up justifications for being away from my friends anymore or to stay in a place where I was transparently not welcomed. I'd decided this morning while I was brushing my teeth that I'd tell her that I was going home tonight. I knew at some point during this week that I'd stopped fighting, that the last bell rang, and I'd returned to an empty corner for the last time, hung up my gloves and iced my hands. I thought about my family and the way the inner workings between my mother and her parents had always seemed so foreign to me.

I couldn't mesh her life into theirs, to her childhood growing up in Louisiana with grandpa and grandma or any shred of comfort or happiness now when she didn't possess any of it for herself. The slow fuse in my heart began burning as I stepped inside her room and approached her bed. Her eyes were closed, but the rapid movement behind them seized my imaginings and I began wondering what she dreamed of, how far the roots of her tree of life ventured down. The plaid gown she was wearing all but swallowed her up and the information bracelet reminded me of a paper shackle the way it lay flatly against her wrist. She looked over at me from the corner of her eye, never turning toward me fully or lifting her head. Her hair had grown a lot since I'd last seen her.

"What do you want?"

"I just came to tell you that I'm going back to Raleigh tonight."

Her eyes narrowed and zeroed in with a missile-like precision as the friendly fire dispersed. It seemed like she wasn't even breathing, just frozen. I lowered my eyes, contemplated trading places with her, wishing it were so already. It was difficult knowing that she was disappointed, but not how to fix it.

"Good. If you promise never to come here to see me again I'll tell you the last thing your father said about you. I'll tell you how he died, just promise me you won't come here anymore. Promise me."

"What?"

"Promise me!"

I couldn't make my feet move, but even if they did where would I go? My mouth had gone dry. It wasn't so hard to pick up the truth when it was laying at my feet, so readily offered and easy to take up.

"I can't."

"I told you he died in a car accident, but that's not what happened! Give me your word!"

"You're lying! Grandma would've told me."

"Samarra, she can't tell you about what she doesn't know."

I stared at her.

"Do you want to know or not?"

"Why are you telling me this now?"

"I have to see this through without you clinging to me!"

"I can't believe you!"

"You already do! Promise me and I'll tell you. Just say it and you'll know the truth."

She sat up in bed and leaned forward stiffly with what strength remained as her eyes blazed with the heat of contempt, even as I slowly nodded and mumbled:

"Yeah, I promise."

My mother beckoned for me to sit next to her as she sank back down on the pillow.

"Your father and I met when I was seventeen. He was nineteen. He was the reason my heart beat Samarra, the reason I breathed. He was so intelligent and sophisticated. He had the most beautiful eyes. I loved him so much."

There was a faraway look in her own eyes as if he were standing in a corner of the room with us.

"When we got married your grandparents didn't know. I forged my birth certificate. At first, I told them that the reason I wasn't coming home was because I'd extended my study abroad trip, but by the time I got back, I was showing. I couldn't hide it anymore."

"Why'd you lie? You were married, so what were you afraid of? They would have understood, right?"

"I didn't know what they'd say. It was complicated. I threw your father's whole life into chaos. He didn't mean to really end up..."

She slowly looked off, out the window.

"He didn't mean to end up how?"

"With a child that he, (she looked at me) didn't want or a wife that he never cared for."

"You knew he wasn't going to be monogamous before you got married and you still went along with it? You thought just because you got pregnant with me you could make him stay?"

"Yes."

What could I say when I'd done the same things, when I'd made the same mistakes as her? I swallowed hard, sat back in my chair.

"He was the one that named you. He said it meant 'reward' in Arabic. You were a reward after what I'd said and done to him."

"So what happened between you?"

"I forced him to stay. I all but held him hostage. He told me that I was never his first choice and that he didn't want to be responsible for someone else, but I wouldn't let him go!"

"Maybe things would've been better if you had, mama."

Her lips parted, but she was temporarily silent. Tears ran down her cheek. A nurse walked by with a stack of charts in her hands, but I couldn't be pulled away not even for a split second. I hadn't known which questions to ask next, in which sequence. I'd never guessed that we'd even be here at this moment, having to catch and release the truth of our lives in quite this way.

"I sent you to live with my parents so that we could work on the problems in our marriage. I thought he'd get help. He just kept on drinking and it went downhill from there, and finally he left in the middle of the night."

She wiped her eyes.

"So, what happened to him?"

"He moved out to California, started a life there."

I sat up in my chair.

"That was the first time I tried to end it, after he moved out."

I looked up at her, but felt flat and oddly unaffected, perhaps numb in the knowledge that the thought of me wouldn't have been enough to stop her.

"What did he say about me?"

"He called you his baby hummingbird. He didn't want you to know that he felt like a failure his whole life because he never wanted to be a father to you, that he couldn't be."

"How did he die?"

"He went on a two-day binge. He died of acute alcohol poisoning. It just didn't make any sense. There was so much in his system, I--"

"He did it on purpose?"

She nodded.

"Oh."

I hadn't meant for it to come out in such a tiny whisper, but since I'd come this far I had to know more, to go a little further. She pressed her fingertips to her temples and moved them in little circular patterns as she closed her eyes.

"Why couldn't you feel differently about me mama?"

"You were my baby. You were such a good child."

"Why do you keep talking about me like I'm gone when I'm right here in front of you?"

I moved to the other side of her bed, into her direct line of sight.

"Did you love him more than you love me?"

If she was surprised by my question, it didn't wash over her face.

"Yes."

Suddenly she wasn't looking at me anymore, only past me, over my shoulder at my grandparents standing in the doorway. The specter of consciousness loomed, and we were momentarily silent as they walked in and stood beside me, hovering protectively like my guardian bees. I could see them gauging my reaction to what had just been said in the way that they greeted us, warily eyeing my mother. My first solo visit here to see her came to mind and the conversation I'd had in the downstairs lobby with my grandmother that had undammed an avalanche of old resentments.

Perhaps they had never seen her so venomous or been exposed to her in quite this way before. I took in the faces in the room. My grandfather's gray beard, kind eyes and tortoise framed glasses. My grandmother's sweet smile, beautifully coiffed hair and soft set eyes. Patient, wise demeanors that only time could raise. Then I looked at my mother. Her meticulously arched brows hung over eyes that were tired, but brilliantly colored and her chest rising and falling slowly with anticipated rest as her broad lips parted into a smile.

"Bye, mama."

"Goodbye."

I collected my bag and left her room. On the elevator ride back down, I cried.

WITNESS

I was almost done folding the laundry when there was a knock on the door. I opened it to find Damon standing on the porch with Roxy. He leashed her to the bannister and turned to me again.

"Can I come in?"

"If you want to."

He stepped inside and stood quietly next to the sofa. I started putting the clothes back into the laundry basket, didn't acknowledge him really.

"So, where've you been?"

I folded and stacked a few shirts.

"I've been around."

I knew that my prolonged silence was probably making him uncomfortable, but I couldn't tell him that in the four days since I'd last seen him, he'd been like the quickening, repetitive beating of my heart or the sweet dizzying motion in my head or that I secretly couldn't wait until I saw Nathan or him again. He cautiously took a step forward.

"I just wanted to see you."

"What do you mean?"

"I thought~"

I threw the last pair of socks into the basket, but still didn't meet his gaze.

"Look at me. What's wrong?"

"I'm tired of talking about it!"

I'd folded my arms across my chest in silent protest. I sensed he was growing frustrated by my sudden swing in mood and that he wouldn't stay much longer.

"Are you worried about your mum?"

Even when I knew that I had to start letting go and that perhaps the man standing before me was the most beautiful path of least resistance to happiness I still could not talk myself off the ledge of guilt that I presently dangled from. I was losing my nerve, it seemed. I nodded.

"I think I'm going to go home soon."

"What about our deal?"

I sighed.

"What about it?"

He turned away from me and put a hand over his mouth. I put the laundry basket on the floor and flopped down on the sofa. He spoke without turning to face me.

"'Ya know, I don't get you! It's like you enjoy being a sad version of yourself, or something."

"You don't get to be a critic in my life! YOU don't get a say Damon!"

He turned around.

"What's waiting for you in Raleigh, Samarra?"

"Nothing now."

"So why are you going back then?"

"I dunno. I just have to."

Damon sat down next to me on the sofa. I looked down at his hands.

"What's that?"

He picked up my hand, smiled a little.

"Nate made this for me in vacation Bible school. Do you like it?"

"Yeah, it's great."

The bracelet on his left wrist was a red band, tightly woven, made of parachute cord, perhaps. I could tell by the frayed edges and tattered condition it was in that he kept it on always--showering in it, sleeping with it on. When I looked back at him, he was looking at me.

"Damon?"

"Hmm?"

"Can I tell you something?"

His back arched then straightened and he pushed himself up and faced me.

"Alright..."

...An hour later found us sitting on the sofa still. My legs were folded underneath me. He rested his face in his hands, not seeming like he was allowing everything I'd said to sink in suddenly or completely. I'd hoped that he wouldn't see me any differently or condemn me as I continued:

"He didn't know that I was pregnant because we barely saw each other. He had his work and I couldn't--"

"I'm just trying to understand why you would--"

"What? Why I would still stay with him after that?"

He nodded.

"Maybe it was easier! Is that what you want to hear? Maybe I couldn't hurt him that way! I loved him enough not to complicate his life."

He stood up slowly and walked toward the door and I could see him clenching his jaw. It was hard to know how to not feel ashamed.

"You couldn't hurt him?! Do you even hear yourself? How could you defend him? You were carrying his child and he treated you like a common--"

"Damon, stop it!"

I got up and walked over to him. He shut his eyes tightly, shook his head then his brow furrowed, as if he'd thought of something dark and ghastly in the very threads of its inception. I'd never wanted to make anyone else a witness to my indiscretion, though I felt sure that we'd all stood at the precipice of change at one time or another or made a decision so final that it could not be revoked. Still, letting him in felt like some epic sized self-betrayal.

"Anyway, I lost the baby about a month after that. I hadn't even made an appointment, but I was going to that week. It just happened. I never told anybody."

"Oh, Samarra. I'm so sorry."

I couldn't speak. He moved a little closer to me and pressed his face into my hair. I felt utterly bottomless, breathless. I thought that I might collapse beneath the crushing weight of my own shame and self-disgust until I heard his voice in my ear.

"Shhh, it's alright now Samarra. You're alright."

THE MONOLITH

I'd packed up the last of my things and set my bag on the landing. Across the hallway my mother's door was shut and in the length of her absence I'd thought of her constantly. I walked into the room where I stood at her dresser and took in some of her possessions. Her things were neatly laid out there: Her hairbrush, her car keys and lipstick. There were pictures of Grandma and Grandpa, a blue glass bowl full of bobby pins. The desk and floor held a dull shine and the sharp redolence of furniture polish stayed, but my eyes never left from what didn't fit:

In the almost clinical space of her room, at the bottom drawer of her bureau the corner of a piece of paper stuck out near the pull, a manila envelope. I pried it from the drawer and turned it over in my hands. It felt sort of heavy. I searched for a return address, but there wasn't one. I sat down on her bed and couldn't stop thinking of what her reaction would be when she discovered that it was missing, of how many times she'd opened the envelope and studied its contents or laid it all out or held it in her hands. I tore off the seal and let the papers slide out into my hands. Amid the darkness of the background, grey flecks surrounded a small orb that floated in an invisible jelly. Six weeks of life and I'd only been a tiny blip on a very large screen. There was a letter addressed to my mother. Its three pages were neatly folded, handwritten on stationary paper with the navy blue letterhead from the architectural firm of Wells and Klein embossed at the top.

The script was clear and tidy, my father's handwriting, his voice long absent. I read:

{My darling Angelia, I know that something very real existed between us, if only for a short while. I am sorry that I could build everything for you with my own two hands except for the thing that could most make you happy. I know that you thought this would turn out differently, but you put us both here knowing that I never wanted this, not with you.}

Fade

Words like responsibility, guilt and love battered at my brains.

{There was a time when I couldn't wait for the hour that we could be together again, to look into your eyes without this distance that separates us now. I can recognize that you haven't been the same. I can recognize that I'm to blame for allowing you to believe that we had a chance after you lied to me about the pregnancy.}

The last page was the hardest to read:

{When you became pregnant with our Samarra, I knew that we were done, because you chose to jeopardize everything. It was enough that I stayed with you. You should know Angelia that some sentences can never be commuted and that the locks of some lies have no keys. ~Anderson}

I slid the letter back into the envelope and placed the three ultrasounds toward the front. I took a closer look at the postmark on the envelope--six months to the day that he'd filed for dissolution of marriage. I tried to collect my thoughts, but there was an indefinite, red, raw pain in my head that forced my eyes shut, My mother and father were the orchestrator and architect of this monolith that had caused our family to disintegrate. I still needed some answers...

...The drive to see Grandma Camille felt torturous. I pulled into the driveway and sat still, the letter resting in my pocket, waiting to be opened and re-read, to be mulled over and thought about or simply be forgotten again at the bottom of some bureau drawer forever, but not tonight. In the soft glow of the porch light her face wore concern like an old shirt. Jazz music was playing softly in the kitchen.

"Where's grandpa?"

"It's bridge night. What's wrong? Did something happen?"

"I found this, and I don't know what to do."

She took the letter from my hands and read it. For a long time, she didn't say anything.

"Where did you get this?"

"I took it from her room."

"Samarra--"

"You always said that family was the most important thing."

"'Ya know, Samarra your parents were young, and your father was working all the time. I think they felt like they couldn't care for you."

"Or they didn't want to?"

She looked at me with raised eyebrows that seemed to speak of tandem thought. She nodded.

"What if you and grandpa weren't here?"

"Nothing that happened between them is your fault, okay?"

I nodded.

"I think that I should go back tomorrow..."

TURNING POINTS

Grandpa Jamison and Grandma Camille taught me to pray when I was younger. They'd said that when times get hard I should find the Lord and 'go to work'. This time wasn't as difficult as it had been on the first day back in my old room or forcing myself to lay through another sleepless night when things had become unbearable between Jason and me or trying to explain to my mother what it felt like to be locked up in a place like Haven Harbor. It was late when I got home. The feeling was just beginning to come back into my hands, as if I'd been holding on to the steering wheel so dearly that everything was dependent on my not letting go.

I closed my eyes and breathed for what felt like the first time in my life. I wasn't completely surprised that my mother had chosen to follow my father into the hereafter. I opened my mouth and let a stream of unconscious words flow freely as I lost track of time, sitting in my car in the dark, praying. I got out and went inside the house. Everything was quiet and most of the lights were off, aside from a tiny green orb on the coffee pot, the digital numbers on the microwave, the nightlight in the upstairs hallway.

I looked around my room, hoping that I could remember the way that I'd left things. I made it to the bottom of the steps just in time for the clock to begin its chime. I closed the front door and was halfway to my car when I turned to see Damon standing on the other side of the long row of hedges that separated his house from ours.

"Hey Samarra. What's going on?"

He beckoned me over with a wave of his hand as he drank from a brown glass bottle and after he'd taken a few sips he offered it to me. The suds of the cream soda slid down the inside as I tipped it up and drank. In the back of my mind I'd filed away this summer and how it had been the most memorable one of my life so far. To be leaving now was bittersweet. I was too much of a coward to tell him that this was my last night in Savannah. I thought that he deserved better than having to listen to my piss poor excuses. He stared at me for a moment, tuning in perhaps. Ever since I'd left the hospital almost everything seemed as slow as stop motion, like we were all being painstakingly moved frame by frame. It was cool this evening and I could just make out the arborvitae being rustled by the breeze.

"Mmm. I got you something."

He handed me the bottle and I watched and waited as he pulled a small envelope from his pocket and handed it to me. I gave him back his bottle and opened the envelope, took out a black and white photo of us standing next to each other at the BBQ. While I was smiling into the camera he was smiling at me. I thought about my grandfathers' dinner recollections and tried not to nibble at my lip.

"Oh, thanks."

He took another sip from the bottle.

"Mmm Hmm. It's a nice picture."

"Yeah."

"C'mon."

Damon grabbed my hand and we walked to a corner of the yard where there was a low wall made from roughly hewn tumbled stones. We sat down, neither of us speaking into the night. No apologies, no pretenses between us.

"Nate's turning four next month."

"Really?"

"Mmm Hmm. His mum wants to come up and see him."

My lips parted, but I was speechless.

"I haven't talked to her in", he exhaled sharply, "I don't know when. I can't let her back in. Not now."

"What do you mean?"

"Are you serious?! Just because she gave birth to him that doesn't mean nothing! What is she to him? NOTHING!"

"She's his mother Damon!"

He shrugged.

"So, what?"

"What would you do if the tables were turned and she wouldn't let you see him?"

"That would never happen."

"Never say never."

"Whatever Samarra! You don't have a kid! What would you know about it?"

"That's not fair!"

"Doesn't make it any less true though, does it?"

He got up and walked back toward the house. I followed behind him, feeling the anger rising off me like steam.

"Damon!"

He didn't answer me and wouldn't turn around, so I walked in front of him.

"Who the hell do you think you are?! You're no better than me! Do you hear me! I-"

"I never said that I was!"

"No, you just act like it! You're SO perfect! This is the reason I don't talk about this! I should've just kept it to myself! Just forget I ever said anything."

"No, I'm not going to forget it! I told you that you can talk to me Samarra. You--"

"I changed my mind."

He rubbed his hands over his face and sighed aloud.

"Is this a game to you? 'Cause if it is, I'm not playing!"

"I didn't tell you about me and Jason so that you could judge me!"

"I'm not judging you, honey!"

"That was the hardest thing I've ever had to live with Damon and I think about it every day! Every day!"

I leaned against the breeze that was blowing, tried to regroup.

"The only place that feels safe anymore to me is in my heart."

"I can understand that."

We stood staring at each other and soon afterward I felt the warmth of his embrace. His beard was coarse beneath my hands. He held on a little longer than usual before he released me.

"I'm sorry about what I said before. I shouldn't have taken it out on you."

I nodded.

"I'm glad that you trusted me enough to tell me, okay?"

"Okay."

"Are you leaving because of your mum?"

"Yeah."

"Nate's going to miss you."

"What about you?"

"Every day."

"Some summer it's been."

"Best one yet."

Whether I knew it then I can't say, but what flowed next from his lips would be the turning point of our quasi-relationship. He pushed back his hair.

"Do you think that I could--?"

"What?"

"Do you think that I could be enough for you?"

264

"Damon, I--"

"You don't have to answer right now. I know how crazy it sounds. I hadn't really planned on asking you, it's--"

"It's not crazy."

I wished that he hadn't caused certain sentiments to flourish and not set loose those emotions in me that kept me feeling completely unworthy of him. I was certain that I would never be able to forget the way his eyes would twinkle when he smiled like the gossamer threads in a spider's web when the sun hits it at the perfect angle and dew drops dance on its invisible strands...

BUYING TIME

As soon as I opened the door of the apartment I knew beyond any doubt that I was alone now. The bed hadn't been slept in, laundry was in heaps on the floor obviously sorted through and the mail was strewn across the coffee table. Jason's clothes were gone. The empty hangers dangled in their places inside the closets. He'd taken his laptop, books and his papers. The couch was gone, but the microwave remained. He'd taken his toiletry bag and empty shoe boxes littered our bedroom floor. Everything was gone along with the man whose life had been wrapped up in mine for the past four years, but none of that mattered now because I knew that the residual feelings that had caused me to doubt even my very existence at one point had evaporated. The things that remained of him were easier to forget now that he'd become someone that was of no consequence to me. I set down the pile of boxes that I'd brought with me and began gathering up my things and thinking about how I'd buy myself time...

THE IMMORTALITY OF INK AND PAPER

The leaves on the trees were finally beginning their slow descent into fall, morphing from green to crimson and bronze and gold as the air grew chilly. On Tuesday I called Crystal and we ended up meeting for coffee at Poole's Diner. I'd just moved my possessions (two suitcases and a few boxes worth) into my hotel room the day before. Even when Crystal and Dorian had insisted that I come stay with them I couldn't have possibly burdened them down with my issues. I had never meant to leave the landlord in a lurch, but my half of the rent was tucked into his mailbox, same as always. I'd signed the lease termination agreement and cleaned up and now that it was all over. I couldn't help feeling lighter, easier. While Dorian was at work and Zara was with her grandparents Crystal and I chatted over tea. Since we'd seen one another her hair had grown down to her shoulders and the sun had darkened my skin to a beautiful shade of deep sienna. I thought of the Hensons as I felt a growing pull of self-satisfaction and a brand-new craving for wedding cake. When the conversation turned to what I'd done in Savannah I had to fight off the urge to blurt out everything in no particular order and when I talked about my mother she listened attentively.

"It's weird, having to watch someone you love turn into a total stranger."

"Maybe she's not supposed to remember what she's done, 'ya know?"

"Yeah. I wouldn't want to remember."

When I talked about how much I missed Raleigh food we both raised our cups and toasted to that. When we talked about Zara there was a glow on Crystal's face from the joy of her baby and I thought of the way that I had all but given up the right to expect the warmth and love of a child ever again. Perhaps just to assuage my own guilt I'd taken on the role of godmother and my first official duty had been to paint Zara a picture (bunnies were her favorite) that I'd taken first thing this morning to have professionally framed. I'd held her for nearly an hour upon our first meeting. After the initial excitement had died down and she had called to check on Zara I pulled the black and white photo from my bag and slid it across the table. We both shrieked at the same time and drew in stares from the other patrons.

"Cute white boy!"

"I know, right?!"

"Details!"

"His name's Damon. He lives next door to my mom. He's a photographer and he plays guitar--"

"Where'd you meet him?"

"It's a long story, but he helped me fix my car and we just started to talk."

She held up the picture and looked at him again.

"Girl, if I were you, I'd be all up in his business!"

Her sincerity made us both laugh and after the racket had stopped I told her about our walk through Forsyth Park, the BBQ, the things he'd said to me and the way he'd looked at me at times. I took a sip from my cup.

"Samarra!"

"What?!"

"You don't get it, do you? He likes you!"

"I really don't know him like that, though."

"Sounds like you're in some serious denial."

"No, I'm not!"

"Do you know how you can tell if he likes you?"

Her energy and enthusiasm regarding my love life were a bit unnerving, but I knew it was coming from a good place, considering what I'd been through.

"How?"

"If he fights for you."

"What do you mean?"

"If he tries to defend you against something somebody else says or does, then that's how you know."

I drank my tea and listened to her advice because, after all, she was married.

"Crystal I might not ever see him again. I dunno."

"Do you want to see him again?"

She put down her cup. In truth, the landscape of my heart had changed from being callous and coarse to velvety soft and pliable in such a short time with him that it scared me.

"Maybe."

"What would you say to him if he walked in here right now?"

"I don't know."

"C'mon! Think about it! He really likes you, so he already knows what he would say to you!"

After some goading I had a thought.

"Okay. How about: 'Hey, how are you?'"

She rolled her eyes at me.

"You can do better than that," she held up the photograph again, "Look at him!"

I looked at it, at us, and thought about how we'd been immortalized forever on ink and paper in that moment. I thought of how our paths had crossed and the way that we had so easily warmed to one another. It didn't matter if we never spoke again, on that day (and many others) I'd felt more welcome among (then) strangers than in my own mother's house, more accepted on that night than I could ever be rejected by anyone else.

"I just don't want to make a big deal about it."

Crystal sat back in her seat. My phone rang just then as if it were on some sort of timer.

"Hello?"

"Samarra, it's Damon. I was just calling to see if you made it home alright."

I looked at her and silently mouthed the words, 'It's him!' as her eyes grew wide and she moved over to where I was sitting.

"Yeah, I made it back okay. Thanks! How's Nate?"

"He's doing fine. Still learning to read."

"That's great!"

"How's your family?"

"Everybody's doing okay. Mmm, almost everybody."

When I called my grandparents, they weren't home so I left a short message promising to try back later. I had talked to my mother a few times since I'd seen her last. There was a slight pause in my conversation with him, though he soon continued.

"I'm going to L.A. to see Aaron. I'm leaving Nate with Natalie for a bit. He loves playing with their three girls. It's sort of hard, too 'cause I've never been apart from him longer than a day. (He exhaled) It's a bit nerve wrecking."

"How long are you gonna be gone?"

"About a week."

"Oh."

I really hadn't bothered to mask the sadness in my voice with cool nonchalance. I suspected that he knew.

"Don't worry. I'm bringing my camera, so I'll take some pictures for you."

"That would be great!"

"So can I see you when I get back? Maybe we could get together and see a movie or something?"

"Sure."

"Okay."

There was noise in the background and I could hear Nathan talking. Damon muffled the phone while they talked for a second or two. I found myself smiling uncontrollably.

"Nate says 'Hi!' Samarra."

I laughed.

"Hey Nathan!"

"It's kind of funny, 'ya know, he's never warmed up to anyone as quickly as you before."

"That's sweet."

"Well, I have to finish packing. We just wanted to see how you were doing. Talk to you later, okay?"

"Okay. Bye."

"Bye."

I hung up but felt like I couldn't crawl out on a limb altogether just yet. Crystal stared at me, a mischievous smile surfaced on her face.

"Did he ask you out?!"

I put my phone back in my bag.

"Yeah, I guess he did."

"Does he have an accent?"

I nodded.

"He's from South Africa."

I looked at her and laughed as she all but jumped out of her seat.

"Samarra!"

"What?"

"I can't believe you! You met a guy that obviously likes you and has all these great qualities and here you sit, stalling!"

"I can't help it. Jason just moved out his stuff. It's still a little weird."

It would've been moot to drudge up his name in conversation were it not for what was going to take place in a mere seventy two hours.

The volume at the table dropped and the mood turned somber and I recognized the look of sheer unconcealed disappointment on my best friends' face.

"I'm sorry Samarra."

"I guess it's better that it happened this way. It'll be okay. Besides, we don't want it to seem like I've been holding on to sour grapes, do we?"

I downed the rest of my tea.

"I should go wish them luck."

"You're going to crash their wedding, aren't you?"

"Crash is such a strong word."

Fade

This time nothing could contain the laughter that ensued...

2 DRESSES

"Room two eighty, please."

The hospital operator patched the call through. As I waited on the front steps of the small boutique the chilly air made the back of my neck cold. I'd never had my hair shorter than the few inches of a trim, but it's amazing what you'll let a hairdresser talk you into at least once. It had turned out nice, I thought: A much shorter, chin length bob and bangs that moved whenever I turned my head. Not having hair in my eyes all the time felt glorious. The phone was ringing. I thought of the promise that I'd reluctantly made her three weeks ago and how every day since then I'd found it a little easier to stay away. Finally--

"Hello, mama?"

She hesitated.

"Samarra?"

"Yeah, it's me. How're you?"

"I'm not getting any better, if that's what you mean."

"No that's not really--"

"Thank you for respecting my decision to do this alone."

"I don't really respect it, but you're welcome."

She acted as if she hadn't heard me.

"Your grandparents came by yesterday."

"Really?"

"Mmm Hmm. How're things going down there?"

This time I was the one that hesitated. The civility of the conversation was frightening, but I continued.

"I'm trying to get some things in order."

"Oh."

"Have you eaten something today?"

"I tried to eat some soup, but I can't keep anything down right now."

"Mmm Hmm."

My eyes were shut tightly, and I held the phone away from myself to keep her from hearing me break down. My voice was still shaky when I came back to the phone.

"Hey mama, do you remember how I wanted to be an acrobat and join the circus when I was little?"

I wiped my face and for the first time since I could remember I heard her laughing. It sounded light and untroubled, almost melodic to me.

I knew that something in her memory had triggered a thought of me and that I wasn't lost to her entirely.

"Of course. You know that was after you wanted to be an astronaut and a ballerina and a concert pianist."

"I remember."

I could imagine her looking out the window, enjoying the sunshine as it blanketed the room, the brightness of her eyes. I chimed in.

"I'll be coming home soon."

"Why?"

"I should be there just in case. I don't think it's safe for you to be alone anymore."

"Samarra, I'm not coming home."

"What do you mean?!"

"The doctor says that I have to start having more aggressive chemo treatments. I'll be too weak to do much moving around."

I was never a rebellious child. In fact, it seemed that my eagerness to comply had followed me into adulthood, incessantly tagging along as my near constant companion, but I shelved it for a short while.

"No! You can--"

"The nurse is here now. I have to go."

"Mama, I love you."

I heard her shallow breaths and expected her to respond in kind.

"I'll talk to you later."

I held the phone close to my ear.

"Goodbye Samarra."

The line went dead, and I snapped the phone closed. I hadn't had a chance to tell her about last week and my hope of seeing her again was fleeting. I walked into the boutique. A tall, slender woman, presumably the owner approached me.

"May I help you?"

She wore a huge, sincere smile.

"I'm looking for two dresses. One's for a wedding and the other's for..."

My voice trailed off and I looked away.

"The other's for something else."

She took a step forward.

"A baby shower, bar mitzvah, an awards ceremony?"

"No, a funeral."

Emelia, according to her nametag, let her hands drop by her side, her eyes widening. At last her surprise gave way to sympathy.

"Oh, I'm sorry."

I didn't say anything else as she turned to a rack of dresses. She wouldn't look me directly in the eye after that and promptly cleared her throat.

"If you need help I'll be back in the shoe stockroom."

"Alright, thanks."

I began skimming the rack but felt rather indecent for thinking of my mother's resolve to live as non-existent. While I was in the fitting room all the things I was going to have to let go of played in my mind, like my need to be the good daughter that warred in the emotional trenches everyday or my refusal to recognize that something was wrong with my mother or that the role that I played in helping her be better might require me to never learn certain things about her, knowing that a chance at reconciliation may not be possible. I stood in front of the mirror.

The first dress had been a lot easier to choose. A deep purple knee length dress with a sweetheart neckline caught my eye and never left my hand. The second, a simple black

A-line dress with pin tuck detailing and a fuller skirt and Peter Pan collar seemed to make sense. The impulse buys were next to the cash register and I picked up some tights in black, a pretty hair barrette, some Skittles and a really cool knit hat with ear flaps for Nate. I walked up to the counter with my things just as Emelia came up to the register. She looked at me carefully as I stood there.

"Did you find everything okay?"

"Yes, thanks."

After she'd processed my transaction I handed her the platinum American Express card that had Jason A. Henson's name emblazoned across the front, one last hoorah for old times' sake.

"Thank you."

I went to take out my wallet when the picture of Damon and I fell out of my bag. I stooped down to pick up the photo and suddenly Crystal's words flooded my mind. She had been right. Had Damon come close to saying 'the sacred three' as we jokingly referred to them? The way that people on television said 'the sacred three' one would think that it was perfectly normal to tell almost anyone that you loved them. We preferred to save them for special occasions or only when we meant it. I actually giggled aloud. Emelia stopped and looked at me.

"Sorry. I just thought about something."

I could see that she wasn't going to understand what she had no idea about in the first place. She neatly folded the dresses, wrapped them in tissue paper and boxed each one.

"Never mind."

I thought of all the people that I loved and the different ways that I loved them and the duration of my love: I loved my grandparents with a permanence and a concentration that would outlast us all. I loved Andy, art gallery owner extraordinaire, who'd displayed my first piece with a gratitude that still persisted.

I loved Tucker, the boy who had a crush on me all the way back in second grade (and who had kissed my cheek on the playground then run away), with a simplistic kind of love that was loose and naive. I loved Crystal, Zara and Dorian with a love that was bonded as tightly as a family's --tried and ever true. The love that I felt for my mother caused my very core to ache as it reverberated from sadness, a deep sorrow, still an ever growing loyalty that had not yet reached its zenith.

And I adored Nathan and Damon in a different way completely. The 'love' that I felt for my new friends, this man and his child, was fragile and transoceanic and exigent. The tiny pangs in my head were like the truth, a warning, a blessing, or something else. I thought about the last question he'd asked me on that evening back in Savannah. The dots did not have to be connected and it was all so plain, so obvious. I knew what I had to do the minute I got home...

THE BEST REVENGE

Sometimes the plans we make don't work out because we unwittingly sabotage ourselves. Sometimes the people you love turn on you or forget that they ever loved you at all. Sometimes no matter how much you may want something to work it may have never been God's plan for you to begin with and sometimes the best revenge can be to live well. I had fully intended on leaving every resentment and hurt and regret there at the wedding ceremony. As I sipped my lemonade I stood wondering, mostly about myself and halfway in denial about where I'd found this new, astonishingly high threshold for pain that would bring me here.

I prayed for a strength that only God could grant me. I hadn't worn high heels in a while, but the leopard print stilettos were irresistible, and I acclimated quickly enough. I took in my surroundings: The spacious dining hall was immaculate. Crystal chandeliers hung from the center of the room, sparkling and catching the light as they cast brilliant reflections onto the tables. The finest china, glassware and linens were set before their guests on freshly starched and pressed white tablecloths. Centerpieces complete with clear cylindrical vases adorned with turquoise blue ribbons and Phalaenopsis orchids sat atop each table. The atmosphere was rife with a lightness, the unmistakable banter of conversation filled with excitement and joy of expectation. I saw people I knew, but most I did not.

His parents, replete in their priggishness, regaled their guests and I couldn't help but feel cold at the sight of them. It didn't take me long to find Jason. His frat brothers were gathered around him. I lingered in the background until they dispersed. The sound of my heels on the floor made him turn around and when he looked up at me he almost gasped.

"Samarra, what are you doing here?"

I stood there for a moment and stared at him, a swell of finality seeping in. He smiled at me but grabbed my arm and squeezed it tightly. We both spoke in hushed tones.

"You didn't mean anything! Don't you get it?"

He laughed to himself and let go of my arm, leaned forward, and whispered.

"She's nothing like you!"

"It's not who you lie with Jason, it's who you lie to."

"I'm not lying to her."

"It won't be long before you're lying with someone else, though. It's only a matter of time. You're a whore and you can't help it."

We both looked over at his brand new wife all bright and shiny, her hair in spiral curls, with the train of her mermaid style gown fluttering along as she walked.

"Why didn't you stop it?"

"Why would I stop someone else if they got you out of my life? I'm not mad at her."

"You're just jealous! You'll never be half the woman Tiffany is!"

I laughed out loud. It must have looked like we were getting on well. In a split second I'd scanned the room and not seen either of his parents nearby.

"You're right. I could never dumb myself down just so some man can pretend he loves me."

"The only one pretending is you Samarra!"

"No. You'll pretend with her, but you'll never love anyone more than you love yourself."

"You're crazy!"

"Keep telling yourself that!"

I smirked, sipped my drink.

"Did you really think I'd marry you? I've been with whores that were better than you just because I could!"

"Was she one of them?"

I strongly suspected that the truth was rolling around somewhere in his silence, in his angry stare and furrowed brow.

"You can't accept that it's over. I can't blame you."

"I loved you with all my heart! More than our baby's life once, Jason. Now the only one you'll ever matter to is her. I feel sorry for you."

"I don't need anything from YOU!"

She was talking to his parents, a glass of white wine in her hand and as they laughed and carried on every word they'd ever said about me resonated like a bell ringing. I thought of ways to cause a disturbance or break up the party, but quickly brushed them out of my mind. His voice brought me back to the reality in front of us. He was trying (and failing) to keep himself calm.

"You were so weak that you did whatever I said!"

"That doesn't matter now. I forgive you, for everything."

"Why did you come here?"

"I didn't have anything else to do on a Saturday night."

I sipped my drink slowly as he stood eyeing me, as if his stare could permeate me and make me vanish.

"When she asks you about me I know you'll tell her everything."

"Why would I do that?"

"When you get angry, your ego won't let you keep your mouth shut."

He quickly moved toward me.

"I can back up EVERYTHING I say, sweetheart!"

"Haven't you always?"

I looked down at his hands. His fists were clenched so tightly that they shook. This time, this moment had eclipsed every argument we'd ever had, but it had made the beautifully euphoric ones between us seem that much less important, too.

"See? It doesn't matter how you--"

"You just couldn't let it go, could you?"

He looked away, then back at me as if we'd gotten off to a false start and he wanted to say more or reach out for me. He swallowed hard.

"I'll bet you hate me, don't you?"

"No, I don't hate you. I hardly think of you at all now."

I knew that the road that had led us here had been a bumpy one paved with disappointment, but love in its purest form and a genuine compatibility. I'd traveled it so long that it had left me feeling kind of fatalistic, perhaps because now I was secure in the knowledge this saga was over. I drained my glass.

"Goodbye Jason. Congratulations."

I smiled then turned and walked away from him, knowing that he'd be watching every one of my steps...

EXPECTANCY

It was a crisp still afternoon that found me back in Savannah. I honestly couldn't drive fast enough to get here and I felt like saying my peace at the wedding had stripped away the weakness and doubt in me. One month had gone by more like a week and as I walked up my grandparents' driveway I felt a flood of joy as I laid eyes on Grandma Camille sitting on the front porch. She hugged me like we had never been apart.

"How have you been?"

"Good!"

She planted her hands on my shoulders and leaned back to look at me. I could see her checking out my hairdo.

"Do you like it?"

"Of course! It really becomes you."

"Thanks."

"How's mama doing?"

"She's stabilizing."

"What about the chemo?"

She shook her head as she spoke.

"It's a fifty-fifty chance. Doctor Gleeson thinks that she should try a more aggressive type of medicine."

I nodded.

"What does she think?"

"I don't know. She's trying to see how she feels without all the drugs in her system, I guess."

We stepped inside the house and walked into the kitchen. Grandpa Jamison came in a moment later.

"Samarra!"

"Hey!"

We hugged each other. This felt like when I was eighteen, back for my first visit from college, still very homesick and very green. My grandfather interrupted my nostalgia.

"That boy you like called looking for you-- twice."

My grandmother chuckled.

"What?"

He walked over to the desk, opened the drawer, and began rummaging around for something. He looked over his shoulder at me for a moment.

"He left you a message."

I hadn't asked him who he was referring to, though we all knew. Finally, he handed me an expired pizza coupon.

"What's this?"

"It's on the back."

He turned it over in my hand. I looked up at him and grinned as he shrugged.

"I couldn't find any paper."

There was the date and time and a brief message about some photos, not having to work on Wednesday and his number. I could only guess that my grandfather had wanted to ask Damon twenty questions but had held back.

"He said that if I saw you to ask if you'd call him."

"I can't believe he called here!"

"Don't act like you're shocked."

The thing about them was that I knew they'd never lie to me. She grounded me back into reality again.

"Do you think it's too soon to be in a relationship after Jason?"

I grew serious, having asked myself that very question over and over when I wasn't even sure if I was in a relationship with Damon to begin with.

"I don't know," I turned toward the window, stared out. "He's just so different. He doesn't try to be someone he's not and he's so sweet and smart and kind."

In the reflection of the window pane I saw my grandmother nudge my grandfather. They looked at each other, smiled. I turned back toward them again.

"Did he say anything else?"

Grandpa Jamison sat down at the table and unfolded his newspaper.

"No, but today's Wednesday."

...After breakfast I drove to McCarthy Avenue and parked at the curb outside of Damon's house. The way we'd parted company was fresh in my mind. I thought of what his words meant to me and I wondered if I would be able to express these things verbally to him or if he even cared by now. I put my hand on the car door handle but stopped short as his front door opened. He held it open for a woman and they stepped out onto the porch amid their laughter. They seemed to know each other and were friendly. There was something hovering in the back of my mind: She seemed to have a nervous energy that looked like something more, a crush perhaps.

I felt hot and anxious almost immediately at the way she stood there next to him, the way her hand would fortuitously fall next to his on the bannister, the way she tucked her hair behind her ear.

Knowing that I didn't have the right to fight for someone who wasn't really mine made me scared, though in some corner of the universe I was being courageous for all the right reasons. I slid down in my seat when she walked past my car, got in her SUV and soon disappeared around a corner.

I waited for a moment to cool off, play it back and analyze what I thought I'd just seen, what I was going to say, whether I was making a mistake. I got out slowly and walked to his door. I rang the doorbell and waited, listened to my heart beating in my ears. Damon stood wide eyed then smiled at me.

"Samarra! I thought you weren't coming back."

He took a step toward me and I backed away until I was up against the bannister.

"Damon, who was that woman? Don't lie to me!"

"Damn, it's really good to see you too, Samarra."

"Who is she?!"

"Her name is Vivian."

I felt an unadulterated anger for him for the first time, shoved him.

"Who is she?"

"Samarra! Vivian's my DCFS case worker, alright? Calm down!"

"What?"

"She stops in every few months and checks on Nate 'cause he's a minor. She has to make sure that I'm taking care of him properly. She checks on all the single parents in this county."

I lowered my eyes, my legs feeling rubbery.

"Oh."

"So, do you want to come inside or what?"

He held the door open for me.

"C'mon."

We walked inside and stood in his foyer.

"Damon, I am so sorry! I understand if you want me to go."

"No harm done."

"I can't believe I--"

"You were jealous 'cause you thought I was seeing somebody?" he crossed his arms across his chest and smirked, "Does that mean that you like me, then?"

I laughed but looked away.

"Maybe."

"Yeah, I know."

He grabbed my hand and we walked through his house.

"I called you a few times. I wanted to show you my photos. I've got a ton. I almost used up all of the memory on my camera."

We stopped in front of a door that was covered in all kinds of stickers from dozens of bands, car parts, and instrument makers. They ran the gamut.

"This is my darkroom. At first the lights might hurt your eyes, so be careful."

"Okay."

He held open the door for me and walked in after me. The light from the red bulbs hanging overhead wasn't as bad as I'd imagined. Damon flicked a series of switches that produced a soft ambient light. There was a long table on one side of the wall with four large shallow bins on it and a soft flokati rug on the floor. There was a drafting table with a slide sorter on it and a chair parked beneath it and dozens of photographic slides in plastic boxes (meticulously labeled) and a basket in the corner with long rolls of paper in it.

"Are you okay?"

I nodded as he walked over to the drafting table and pulled out the chair for me.

"Miss."

I sat down and watched as he walked over to a corner of the room and retrieved a long cylindrical tube.

"I've been working on these since L.A."

He opened the tube and unfurled a stack of prints. He laid them out across the desk and stood beside me explaining each one and what kinds of things had inspired him through the lens. When he got to one picture near the bottom of a skyline and sunset, its staggering simplistic beauty made me gasp.

He looked over at me.

"Yeah, I really like that one a lot, too. It reminds me of creation."

"You're really good."

"Thank you."

"What do you do with these?"

"I sell them to magazines and archives and people who collect and stuff."

"Oh."

"I like your haircut. It looks good on you."

I ran my hands through my hair.

"Thanks."

"Mmm Hmm."

I stood up and faced him, but neither of us split the silence. He came closer to me, his eyes never wandering away from mine. What I felt after being gone for so long was anything but ephemeral as the back of his hand swept across my cheek and we stood only inches away from each other.

We both slowly leaned in until I felt like my heart would cave in beneath the weight of expectancy. We were both startled when his phone rang and I jumped. He lowered his head, almost as if in defeat, laughed to himself and held the door open for me...

BEYOND THE SEA

We waited on the front lawn. Damon paced back and forth, started with each car that drove past. It seemed that nothing would make his anxiousness recede except the sight of his son. He and I had already blown up the balloons, wrapped the presents and set out the cake. The sodas and popcorn balls were ready and the stickers, party favors and decorations inside the multicolored tent were truly fit for a kid turning four. The very idea of Nathan being happy to see me made me happy, too.

He couldn't wait to show me all the stuff he'd made in vacation Bible school when he returned a few days ago. There was his Jacob's ladder made from pasta, his coloring book pages and drawings, his collection of things that represented what he was most thankful for stored inside an old-fashioned canning jar. When I asked him what the paper butterfly was for he looked up at me.

"That's you S'maruh!"

Each time that I saw him he seemed to be minutely getting a bit taller, growing steadily into the man he would one day become, though to me now he was perfect: A boy that was vibrant and energetic and loved his dad and his dog and his friends, whose favorite food was mac and cheese and who liked to paint and read and listen to music. He was steady on his feet and was a budding soccer player.

He'd really loved the hat that I'd bought him and had worn it to his day camp and vacation Bible school and to the store. When I looked up again, Damon was staring into the distance toward the direction of the sinking sun.

"I think that's him!"

The seriousness subsided and he dashed to the edge of the asphalt, eyes wide as a minivan pulled into the driveway. I stood watching as he scooped up his child and hugged him then hoisted him up onto his shoulders.

"Airplane!"

Nate held out his arms and Damon ran around, turning and twisting, making a myriad of noises as they laughed. After a moment Damon stood still and Nate climbed down. A flock of kids filed out of the van and approached. I saw Natalie and her three girls: Charlotte, Sia and Brionna with a few new faces mixed in. Anna and Jeremy, whom I hadn't seen in a while arrived with their kids Jackson and Thomas. They didn't have trouble finding a game to play and a quick round of tag or something like it began as the adults congregated on the lawn. Anna turned to me.

"I hear you've been busy!"

"What do you mean?"

I looked at Damon. He was scanning the street again, oblivious to the conversation. I refocused on the partygoers and tried not to let him see me watching him.

"The party. I'll bet you spent weeks getting everything ready."

I smiled.

"Something like that."

He'd thought that the specter from his past would suddenly reappear and pervade this night. I wasn't naive enough to think that things always ended completely or that feelings settled in the dust just because two people weren't together anymore, but I couldn't help feeling a little on edge, just the same.

"Damon?"

He glanced down the street a second more before looking at me. There was a smile superimposed across his face.

"Hmm?"

"What're you thinking?"

He didn't answer right away but stared wistfully at me.

"A lot of things, mostly 'bout Nate."

His hand interlocked with mine and we walked to the backyard. I couldn't help smiling as the guests 'ooohed' and 'aaahed' at the decor. Damon had set up a projector that shined on the back of the tent and we all sat for a screening of the Charlie Chaplin film, 'The Circus'. In the dark I leaned over to Damon and whispered:

"Is this the movie you had in mind?"

He laughed. Both kids and adults hooted and hollered during the entire movie, one moment funnier than the next. When I looked back at Nate he was giggling, lost in what I hoped would be his best birthday ever. After the movie we sat for cake and sweets, music and presents (a watch, a color changing flashlight, a new soccer ball, some books and an RC car) and a firework show that bagged it. Jeremy and Anna and company were the last to leave and after we'd escorted them to their car and they'd gone, Damon looked at me.

"You're incredible!"

"Thanks. I know."

He laughed. Nate emerged from inside wearing his hat and stood with us in the driveway. Damon picked him up.

"Happy birthday kid! I love you!"

"I love you, too, dah!"

Nathan hugged his neck then turned to me.

"I love you S'maruh!"

If Damon or I had blinked, we would have missed the subtle glances we'd given one another. I couldn't keep him waiting or tell him I needed a second to get it together because I wasn't sure or that I couldn't be someone's mother after I'd fouled it up the first time, even though he hadn't asked me to be.

"I love you too, Nathan."

He stretched out his arms and I held him tightly. Damon stuffed his hands into his pockets and looked at me with a sideways grin as if we'd reached some important milestone. What kind of family would we make, I wondered? Damon scratched his beard and as we stood in surrounding silence I thought of a quick subject change.

"What else did you do in California?"

"Hmm. I went swimming in the Pacific Ocean and I had the most amazing fish tacos and ceviche and Aaron and I went to see some bands play."

We walked back toward the party area. There were paper plates, cups, trash scattered. As he picked up the yard with me we talked.

"How's your brother doing?"

"He's been hinting around that he'd like to meet you. He won't shut up about it."

"What's wrong with that?"

"Samarra you don't understand, alright?"

"What am I not getting?"

"He's scrutinized and picked apart every relationship I've ever been in."

"Uh huh, so this is a relationship, then?"

"I certainly hope so, or people will start talking."

We stared at each other until neither of us could suppress our laughter. Damon noticed that Nathan was quiet.

"Is he asleep?"

I looked down at him. His eyes were closed, his breathing undisturbed, his body limp under the throes of heavy sleep. Damon put down the trash bag and walked over to us.

"Here, I'll take him."

He lifted his son into his arms and turned back to me.

"Will you stay for a bit?"

"Okay."

"I'll be right back."

He walked back inside cradling Nathan's head with one hand, turning on the lights as he walked through the house and when he returned he held what looked like a primitive walkie talkie. He saw me checking it out.

"It's Nate's old baby monitor. I use this sometimes when we can't be in the same room at the same time, so I can hear if he needs me."

After the yard was clean we walked past the tent, a little further to the corner with the Bradford pear tree.

"Have you ever camped out before?"

"No."

"There's a hammock over there. Do you want to give it a try?"

I wasn't entirely sure at first, but once he sat down on it and helped me in I felt safer, almost like being in a cocoon. We lay there for a moment before he spoke.

"Thanks Samarra. It was great! You know he loved it!"

"I had fun, too."

"I know it seemed like I wasn't paying attention, but I thought that Kirsten was going to show up."

"What if she had?"

"I would have told you where I keep the emergency bail money."

We both laughed. I squirmed around to face him.

"No, seriously though, she would've had to go."

"I can understand that."

"Samarra?"

"Hmm?"

"Do you know what a handira is?"

"No."

"It's a ceremonial marriage blanket that brides and their families make in North Africa. They're beautiful, so ornate. They make it out of sheep's wool and they sew on thousands of these tiny sequins by hand. It's meant to bring good luck and protection to her marriage."

"It sounds like a special thing, huh?"

He nodded.

"I used to see them hanging up in some of the houses that I photographed in. The colors were so intense and powerful."

"I'd like to see that one day."

"It could be on your bucket list."

"Yeah. We should go."

He pulled a blanket over my shoulders and around my back. I traced his strong, masculine jawline with my eyes, though I wanted to reach for him.

"Samarra?"

"Hmm?"

His eyes closed slowly for a moment just before he looked over my face.

"I'm glad you're here."

"So am I."

We talked until either one or both of us fell asleep. The last thing that I remembered was our conversation about the deep sapphire blue waters, out beyond the sea, in the Gulf and how much he missed and dreamed about them before I drifted off, unaware of my surroundings aside from the rhythmic pace of his breathing and his hands steadying me in the hammock beneath the stars...

DEALBREAKERS

Dinner was on the table, as always promptly at seven o'clock. This evening as Grandpa Jamison passed around the bowl of homemade Caesar salad we talked. Our seating arrangement was a little different with Damon and I sitting across from each other. For the first time since he'd started coming over for dinner he'd been late. He was unusually quiet. I noticed that he only took small bites or watched as Nathan ate. When he finally did look up at me I smiled a bit then mouthed the words, 'Are you okay?' He nodded, but there was a solitude in his eyes.

I sat back in my chair, dared my mind not to turn in on itself with a thousand questions. I sifted through everything that I knew about him and thought I'd figured out just enough to know that perhaps things were about to change between us. While my grandparents talked about the family reunion I gingerly picked over my fish and waited. I didn't want him to be mired in emotional debt because of me, because of something I'd done. I called out his name just loud enough for him to hear.

"What's wrong?"

He sighed, took his napkin from his lap, and put it on his plate. He put his elbows on the table, clasped his hands together.

"I feel like I ought to tell you that I went and saw your mum today."

"What did you say?!"

The sudden elevation in my voice made my grandparents' prattle instantly stop and they looked at the two of us. Damon was clenching his jaw.

"I don't appreciate you going behind my back!"

"I don't need your permission Samarra!"

"Yes--you do! She's my mother!"

"I have never met anyone as stubborn as you in my entire life!"

"I don't care what you think!"

"I know that it's not what you expected to hear, but just let me explain. I--"

"Damon, you don't even know her!"

It was a kneejerk reaction that would have made me tear up, but instead of letting him see that I threw my fork onto my plate, moved back my chair, excused myself and walked into the great room. I caught a glimpse of my grandmother, her hand to her mouth, her eyes wide in disbelief. I stood in front of a picture of my great-grandparents with my back toward the door. I couldn't see myself in the reflection, couldn't accommodate this wild eyed, untamed woman with the way I saw myself.

It took a minute or two before I could bring myself to look at Damon, even though he'd entered the room just after me and was standing close. He was the first to speak after he'd thrown back his head and sighed. I turned toward him fully.

"Samarra, honey, I wasn't trying to go behind your back."

"Then when were you going to let me in on your little parent teacher conference, hmm? After she was dead?"

His eyes narrowed.

"Why would you say a thing like that?!"

"Did she know you were coming to see her?"

"Yes, she did!"

"I don't believe you!"

311

"I don't care if you do or not!"

He took a deep breath and looked back toward the dining room where it had grown a lot quieter.

"I'll talk to you later."

"What did she tell you?"

"I don't want to talk about it right now Samarra! I'll call you later."

"Don't bother!"

"Don't you start something that you can't finish!"

My grandfather came into the room and stood next to us, looked at us both.

"I believe that's enough for one night."

He never had to raise his voice to hold his point and at once we both were quiet.

"Now if you can't settle this before he leaves then maybe you should sleep on it, but don't go your separate ways being angry, understand?"

"Yes."

"Yes, sir."

When my grandfather left the room, Damon looked back at me.

"I'll call you, okay?"

"Okay."

I watched him go back into the dining room and collect Nate, apologize to and thank my grandparents then walk out the door. I went up to my room and waited...

...The phone rang only twice before I picked it up. It felt so peculiar hearing his voice without being able to see his face, so handsomely august. It seemed that knowing so much more about a person opened you up to their habits and idiosyncrasies, which kinds of offenses constituted deal breakers for them or what made them cry tears of joy or left them glowing hot and frenzied from anger like a coal taken straight from the fire. His voice was heavy and raspy. It was late, on the brink of morning, but I was certain that my grandfathers' words had saved us both from lingering mistakes.

"Is Nathan alright?"

"Yeah, he's fine."

"I'm sorry about the way I acted."

"No, it's my fault. That wasn't the appropriate place."

"Damon--"

"I pulled your mum's name from the visitation hat, at church. We draw names and visit the person whose name we pull. There were a lot of people's names, but I drew hers. (He laughed to himself) I know everything happens according to God's plan. That's how I ended up going to see her. Mic went with me, too. You can ask him if you want. We prayed with her. She told me that your father was studying architecture in Corsica. She said that they talked about the Madame Butterfly opera and that he had wanted to know why she was so far away from home by herself. That was all she said."

The freefall of information had left me badly wanting more, though I was sure I'd reached my emotional limits for the day.

"Could you play a song for me?"

"Alright."

I could hear him place a record onto the turntable of his Crosley. A John Coltrane piece began to play. I slid down onto the bed and lay there listening to the music.

"Damon, tell me some more about where you've traveled."

"My last big overseas job was in Singapore. Then I went to Mali and Makassar then back home, but that was before Nate was born."

"I've never been out of the States, but I'd love to go to Africa."

"To me, it's the most beautiful place on earth. You have to see it to believe it."

"Yeah. Where do you think you'll be in ten years?"

"I don't know. Living off of retirement."

"In ten years?!"

We both laughed together.

"I just want to be able to see enough to draw and paint, maybe sculpt a little."

"And as long as my thumb and index finger are in okay condition and I can snap a picture, I'm good!"

His sense of humor was just what I needed to quiet my mind. I could envision him as a silver fox, camera in hand, retired and en route to some far-off destination to capture something no one else had ever laid eyes on.

"Good night Damon."

"'Night Samarra."

I closed the phone and turned back the covers...

OATHS AND OVERDRAWS

Damon stood beside me and rested his hand on the small of my back as I steadied myself enough to sign the last of the papers. The tiny room just off the lobby of the courthouse reminded me of a bookstore. I wondered if anyone had ever read all the books on the shelves from cover to cover. Time was of no consequence to either of us and if Damon was nervous he never showed it. My black and white polka dot dress made me feel inappropriately clad, though no one else seemed to mind. Damon, in a white button-down shirt and khaki pants was the poster guy for genteel dapperness.

The look in his eyes was serene and I felt like all the hopes and second chances of my life were tightly woven up in that moment, in him and in Nathan and I knew that I loved him beyond any earthly measure. I knew that he was my all. He reached down and held my hand. His thumb ran across my wrist. The witnesses, a court clerk and a probate lawyer from down the hall were solemn and thoughtful as they stood at the back of the room. I felt my heart tumble over itself and took a deep breath. My bouquet was simple, greenery tucked between white peonies. Both of our hands were joined together by an elderly man of the Baptist church, a Mr. Thomas Bryant.

A few very important words were exchanged, a band (silver this time) was placed on his hand, a diamond studded band on mine and in another five minutes or so it was official, an electrifying newness declaring itself in us.

Damon shook Mr. Bryant's hand and then he turned to me again, resting his lips against mine. I could scarcely see him through my tear dimmed haze and just before he touched my face I opened my eyes. I sat up in bed, startled by my reaction to what had been so gloriously real until I looked down at my hand and studied it carefully. It was bare as always, with the same tiny scar on my thumb left from a paring knife accident over a year ago, the same long, delicate fingers as my mothers'. I had begun to see myself in her a little more each day and I didn't mind it. I climbed out of bed, picked up my phone and walked to the bathroom, my bare feet plodding along the cold floor. After I'd switched on the light I waited to look into the mirror but wasn't surprised by what I saw: There were puffy creases beneath my eyelids and signs from my bloodshot eyes that I'd been crying.

I turned on the water and splashed some on my face. I dabbed at my eyes with a towel and sat on the edge of the tub. All I could think of was how no oath I'd ever made to myself or no overdraw I could have produced would ever free me from the way I felt. I picked up my phone from the sink and called Crystal.

"Samarra, hey! How are things? How's Damon?"

I peeked out of the window. His SUV was gone from his driveway.

"That's why I was calling, actually."

"Okay. What happened?"

I set the phone back down and pressed the speaker button.

"This morning..."

THE REWARD

In an hour Damon had Nate tucked in for the night and we stood in the dining room making small talk after dinner. I started to clear the dishes from the table when he approached me. He took the plate from my hand and began stacking everything together.

"Let me."

We walked into the kitchen and stood at the sink.

"That was wonderful! I never knew that I liked asparagus. Thank you."

"You're very welcome."

Damon dropped the dishes into some hot, sudsy water and dried his hands on a dishtowel. Then he reached out and took my hand, pulled me into the living room as he walked a little way in front.

"C'mon."

We stood in front of the fireplace where he suddenly knelt in front of me.

"Damon~"

His hands grazed my legs as he lifted one of my feet and then the other and slowly slipped off my shoes. I steadied myself against him.

He got back to his feet and pushed the ottoman and chair against a wall and walked over to the record player, untucking his shirt as he went along. He switched on the music then turned back to me.

"Dance with me."

He spun me around and pulled me toward him. The music (old blues) was low and I could feel my body automatically begin to stiffen and grow tight. He leaned in.

"It's okay."

I nodded as the space between us grew thinner. I twirled around and ended where we had begun. He took up my hand and we traversed the room until we came together again.

"Where'd you learn to dance Damon?"

"I'm pretty good, huh?"

"No, you're horrible!"

I threw back my head and laughed and he couldn't suppress it either. When we were both level headed again he continued.

"You seem like you know what you're doing."

"I don't dance much anymore."

"Okay, so when was the last time you danced like nobody was watching?"

Before I could answer the music started up again. Damon shook his head, never stopped laughing as I danced--really danced on his living room rug. He snapped his fingers and kept time with the music from where he stood watching my solo effort. When I was almost tired out I grabbed onto his hand and we slow danced in tiny circles. He rested his head in the space between my neck and shoulder.

"Damon?"

"Hmm?"

"What's your favorite picture?"

"Mmm, it's one that someone else took a long time ago of a girl."

I stared at the flames in the fireplace.

"Oh."

Damon spun me around again.

"Before I forget, I'm making dinner for everybody before the kids go back to school. I'd really like it if you came."

"Okay."

"I'm the live entertainment for the evening."

"Yeah, I'm sure you are!"

His waning smile concerned me, and I grew a little fearful.

"Hey, what's wrong?"

His hands encircled my waist and he pulled me closer as the warm embers from the fireplace cast shadows on our faces that flared then disappeared on the walls behind us.

"Nothing. Absolutely nothing."

"Damon, I've been thinking, and I don't want you to feel like I'm just hanging out with you because I'm getting over Jason or because I'm trying to deal with my mom being sick."

"'Ya know, you don't have to compartmentalize us. You can just let this be what it is."

I laughed to myself, looked down at my bare feet in tights.

"What is it?"

"What is it to you?"

I thought that it was strong and uncharted and wondrous and tangible and that it reminded me of a beautiful inky blue color. I only wanted to silence the final remnants of fear that plagued me. Without another seconds' hesitation, I grabbed his collar, pulled him forward and kissed his lips. When he finally released me, an edge to edge smile had formed across Damon's face. He whispered in my ear:

"You can't possibly imagine what you're doing to me right now."

He placed my hand on his chest over his heart. It was beating fiercely.

"See?"

Damon closed his eyes as if he'd found the thing he'd long been searching for and exhaled slowly.

"Why, what do you see in me?"

"Everything. You could be the reward at the end of it all."

I watched his warm, familiar smile arrive in time to distract me and make me blush.

THE GAME CHANGER

I looked at Damon, dressed in his finest and thought about how he'd juggled apples to make Nate laugh and our conversation in the kitchen just a few hours ago:

"So, how often do you have these dinners?"

"Once a year. This is the sixth one."

"Why's it black tie?"

"Somebody wore a suit one time and it just stuck."

"Oh."

"I appreciate you helping me with the setup."

I shrugged and smiled.

"You're welcome."

"I have to go back to work day after tomorrow."

I pretended to be crying.

"Your sympathy is touching, really."

We both laughed.

"I should probably go get ready."

324

"Okay."

...I set down my bundle of accessories on the tub and hung my dress up on the hook on the back of the door before I took stock of the contents in my toiletry bag: One bar of Olay soap, an eyelash curler, a small tube of Vaseline, mascara, deodorant and a container of body butter. As I took off my shirt and folded it neatly the sink was just about half full. I took a towel from the shelf and was lathering up the soap when I heard footsteps approaching the bathroom door.

"Samarra are you in there?"

By the time Damon opened the door I'd just managed to turn my bare back toward him. I couldn't be sure what he'd seen as I gasped and pulled my shirt up next to me.

"No, I'm not ready yet!"

"Sorry!"

He backed out of the room and shut the door. It took a moment for the embarrassment to subside as I hurriedly finished bathing, getting dressed, brushed my teeth and combed my hair until it was perfect. I didn't expect to see him standing there, but when I stepped out into the hallway in the purple party dress, he wheeled around and faced me, his eyes wide.

"Samarra, you," he took a step toward me, "You look stunning!"

"Thank you."

I'd noticed that he'd shaved for the occasion and the absence of his beard or stubble pleasantly surprised me. His jacket played off his broad shoulders and his tie complemented his white shirt. I was momentarily at a loss for words, too.

"I'm sorry about walking in on you like that!"

"Why are you sorry? Did I disappoint you?"

"No. You couldn't disappoint me even if you tried."

One of the guests called for him from downstairs. He responded then turned back to me.

"See you downstairs?"

I nodded, watched his eyes linger on me before he turned and walked downstairs. There were candles lit everywhere. The dim glow made the mood effervescent, mirthful as I mixed with everyone. Damon was standing in the kitchen talking with some of his guests when I walked in. He handed me a bottle, a ginger ale with a clean, light taste.

"Thanks."

He nodded without looking away from my face.

"I'm just glad you came."

"Me too."

Damon and I walked around, and he introduced me to some of his friends that I'd never met before, some from work or around the neighborhood, others like Anna and Jeremy I knew. He motioned toward the guitar in the corner.

"Do you have any requests tonight?"

"You should surprise me."

He smiled as I sat next to the other guests. Nathan and one of his playmates, Felix, were rolling around toy trucks behind the sofa. Damon took a seat and tuned his guitar. The guests clapped and cheered, some even whistled as he played a slower more stripped-down version of a Van Morrison song, 'Brown Eyed Girl'. Four songs later (including a perennial favorite, 'Over the Rainbow' and an encore of the second song that we all sang along to) it was time for dinner. My place card was next to Damon on the right side of the table next to Chris, Damon's other neighbor. There were hurricanes with pillar candles alight on the table. I watched Damon take in each face before moving on to the next. Then we bowed our heads as he said grace:

"Father, we don't know what tomorrow will bring, but we trust in your wisdom. We come to you Lord in the knowledge that we are weak and that we stumble, but where there is great need of you, Father, we ask you to abide in us. I thank you for everyone here tonight and I ask that you watch over us all and bless us. This we ask in Jesus' name. Amen."

For whatever reasons we each had, we remained standing a little longer before we took our seats. Each of us passed around the salad, cornbread, soup, roasted chicken and okra and tomatoes.

I was helping Nathan cut his chicken when I looked up to see Damon, elbow on the table, gazing right at us. Before long, everyone was laughing and talking. The man sitting next to Nathan and another woman turned to Damon and they conversed. I learned that his name was Marcus and that he was a biology teacher. His beautiful chestnut skin was exquisite. He'd come with his wife Kiva and their son Felix, one of Nathan's best friends. They'd both be starting school together next year.

"Where'd you find these tomatoes? They're really good."

He put down his glass.

"At the farmer's market on Third and Bailey."

"Oh yeah", Marcus nodded. "I know where that is."

Damon stirred his soup and took in a spoonful as Marcus turned to me.

"Where'd you two meet?"

I wiped my mouth on a napkin.

"He helped me with my car and we just got to talking."

Damon was staring at me, for so long actually that Marcus jokingly snapped his fingers to bring him out of his daze. He smiled a bit, picked up his glass. Marcus continued.

"I met my wife at a bookstore about six years ago."

He turned to the woman sitting next to him and picked up her hand.

"Kiva's the one that helped me get sober."

"That's, that's wonderful! How many people actually find a bond that strong with another person?"

Marcus looked at Damon then back at me again.

"Yeah. It's extraordinary."

As he returned to his plate I believed that I saw him smirk from the corner of my eye. As the dinner wound down and we all remained seated and at rest Jeremy looked at Damon after a pause in conversation.

"So, what's the question?"

Damon sat back in his chair. I leaned over to Marcus, my brows wrinkling with curiosity.

"What's he mean?"

"It's a tradition. At the end of every dinner, Damon asks a question and we each have to answer honestly. Every year it gets tougher."

"Oh."

The potential for something radical seized me as I waited and the chatter at the table lessened until it was quiet. I looked around at everyone. Finally, he put down his glass and rubbed his hands together. There was a calculating tone to his voice that brought me up short, though I couldn't keep myself from eyeing him.

"The question is this: If you'd never felt it before in your life and no one had ever told you, how would you know that you were in love with someone?"

The query settled on the table the way a light blanket of frost rests on the ground at the start of winter and the man to the left of Damon, Chris, answered first.

"For me, there's a nervousness in the pit of my stomach at first, a feeling that I get."

Someone else spoke up.

"Are you sure that's not heartburn Chris?"

Everyone at the table laughed. Jeremy was next.

"I think that you know it when you can't stand to be without that person."

His wife Anna chimed in.

"When you trust them with your life."

There was mutual agreement from all the adults. Felix and Nathan were playing underneath the table, laughing, and giggling. The guest to the left of her was one of Damon's co-workers. Travis, a bright eyed, clean shaven man with a shy smile and an affable disposition was next to speak.

"I think that the essence of love is putting the other person before yourself, that if you love someone you'll do for them first."

Kiva, Marcus' other half, looked at him before she began. The spark that had ignited them was evident in the way that they saw one another, at times seeming unaware of anyone else.

"Being willing to keep a relationship going when you can't be with that person every single day."

The spray of freckles across her fair skin, her sandy hair and pale lips put her and her husband at completely separate ends of the spectrum, but I found the contrast in them hypnotically refined. Marcus moved around in his chair.

"You know that you love somebody when you'll sit through an eight-hour marathon about fashion because she wants to see it."

Everyone laughed. When it was my turn I felt aware that all eyes were on me and that having had time to think of an answer hadn't made me any more prepared. I folded and unfolded my napkin. The only thought that flashed in my head before I began was when Damon and I stood in his darkroom and talked, the stalwart feelings I got when I saw him again, how they had not changed.

"Well, I think that you know you're in love with someone when you'd sacrifice everything for that person without thinking about the cost."

The others nodded and there were tiny cues from a few people in the form of 'Mmms'. Then it was Damon's turn. He looked up from his glass, directly at me as he answered.

"I think that you know if you're in love someone when your heart tells you that you're home when you look into their eyes."

I bit my lip, smiled. Travis raised his glass and we all followed suit.

"To love and recognizing her when she comes to call!"

After our celebratory toast we took pictures together and exchanged numbers. Around twelve thirty the party broke up, each of the guests stopping at the door to wish him well and thank him before taking their leave. Damon joined me in the dining room where I was standing next to the table waiting for him. He loosened his tie and upturned his collar.

"How'd you decide on the question?"

"It just felt like the right one to ask."

"It was a good one."

For me it was the game changer as I considered telling him about the dream I'd had about us two days ago. He followed me into the living room. Nathan was half asleep on the sofa and it was quiet with just the three of us here until my phone rang.

"Hello?"

It was my grandmother. I opened my mouth to ask how she was doing, but she stopped me. Damon must have heard what she said to me next because his eyes grew wide. He reached for me and held me up, walked me over to the armchair and set me down before he took the phone out of my hand.

"Hello?"

I could hear his volume dropping as he spoke.

"Yes ma'am. She's here with us. Okay. I'll take care of her. Yes. Alright. I will. Tomorrow's fine. No, it's no problem. I understand. Alright. Goodnight."

Damon hung up and set my phone down on the arm of the chair. He sat across from me on top of the coffee table.

"Samarra?"

Without moving my head, I looked up at him. My back was straight, flush with the chair and I could all but feel the guilt seeping from my pores. I closed my eyes as the warmth of his hand engulfed my cheek.

"C'mon, let's go upstairs. I've got you."

He helped me to my feet and we slowly ascended the stairs one at a time. Damon let me rest myself against him, patiently waited when I wavered in some places before we reached the landing. He smelled like aftershave. His door was open and he sat me down on his bed. I watched as he walked over to his chest of drawers and retrieved a small stack of clothing and set it next to me, one of his t-shirts and a brand new pair of his boxer shorts.

"I'm sure you want to change."

"Yeah."

"Do you need some help?"

I grinned for a second.

"No. No, thank you."

"Alright."

He turned to leave.

"Damon?"

"Hmm?"

"Thank you."

He smiled a little just before he closed the door behind him...

...It was late when he came back into the room and sat down at the foot of the bed. He'd put Nathan to sleep an hour ago, but I couldn't rest. There weren't words for what I felt and as he looked at me I knew that he might understand, really understand, somehow.

"What if she doesn't wake up?"

"We don't know that now Samarra."

"What if she doesn't, though?"

I felt cold at the idea that I'd messed up too many times, that if I'd just said I was sorry we could have been free. He leaned forward.

"Hey?"

"Hmm?"

"I can take you to see her. We could go--"

"I can't!"

I knew that the tears would come and when they did I couldn't stop them. Damon moved closer still, held my hand.

"I wish so badly that I could keep you from this."

The second hand of the old-fashioned clock on his dresser was like a metronome. We were both listening to the pacing lilt when suddenly, without warning, my heart sank. It felt like the pause at the top of a steep roller coaster ride just before the drop.

"Damon, I don't want her to die!"

He released me from his cradle, wiped away the tears from my face.

"Do you want to pray?"

I nodded, bowed my head.

"Okay."

Before he began, the fear that I sensed was strong enough to make me want to get up and run out of the room. Just as I closed my eyes he took my hands in his and it felt easier to breathe, to settle down.

"Father, as we sit here Lord we know that you know all. We know that all power is yours, so we come to you,

Father asking you to move in us, to ease our pain, to give us your peace that passes all understanding, to wash us and make us clean again, Lord. We ask you to restore health to Ms. Wells because we know that you, our God, is able. We ask you to do a work in her, Father. We give you all the glory and honor, Lord. In Jesus name we pray, Amen."

"Amen."

When I looked up at Damon his eyes were shut. I thought of the way my once mustard seed sized faith had grown and how open my heart felt. I thought of how I had never prayed with Jason a single day during our relationship, but Damon had been ready from the start of our friendship. He opened his eyes.

"Damon?"

"Hmm?"

"When did you become a Christian?"

"I didn't fully commit myself to Christ until I was nineteen or twenty. I've done a lot of bad things in my life. Things that I'm sorry for."

He abruptly looked up at me, measuring my reaction. I stared at him, still.

"I have to just ask God's forgiveness and know that He will forgive me if my spirit is right. That's all I can hope for, 'ya know?"

"Yeah."

Damon hadn't let go of my hand the entire time.

"I spent months in jail on a gun charge. I couldn't go home. I disappointed everybody. I hadn't done right by what God had given me and I wanted to make it right so bad. Every day I just remember what I have to lose and I rely on God to save me."

"And He did?"

"He does. I never picked up a gun again. I gave it all up."

He nodded, smiled at me.

"What about you? You grew up in the church, right?"

"I did."

"It's a bit different when you become an adult."

I looked down at my hands.

"I've taken so many wrong turns just to wind up at all these dead ends. After all that, I know there's nothing that Jesus can't fix. I know that no matter how bad it gets, I can call on Him."

"'Ya know, that's why John 8:36 is one of my favorite verses. We don't have to depend on ourselves for salvation. We don't have to be perfect to come to Him."

I instantly recognized the verse.

"Yeah. I like that one, too!"

"I couldn't keep living like that. It was worth it. Every time I look at my son I know it. Every time I look at you, I know it."

I smiled and rested my head on his shoulder.

ANTIGRAVITY

As we sat at the table I watched the multi colored fruit flavored rings float around in the bowl of milk. Nathan was distracted this morning by almost everything: The background noise of the TV, Roxy, his disinterest in breakfast altogether. I looked at him from across the table.

"So, what do you wanna do today?"

"Can we paint?"

"Sure! What do you want to paint?"

He considered the question for a moment as his eyes roamed around and he grinned.

"A tree!"

"Okay. Good idea!"

While we were discussing what type of tree we would paint Damon wandered into the kitchen. His messenger bag was slung over his shoulder.

"Good morning!"

He kissed Nate's forehead.

"Morning!"

"Hey!"

Not even twenty-four hours ago I'd been dispensed a medicine so bitter that it had seemed impossible to absorb. Damon had been there all night until I fell asleep cradling my head against his arm. I could tell by the way he stood close to me that he was trying to feel me out, to see what was next.

"Are you alright?"

"Mmm Hmm. Better."

"Good."

Nate climbed down from his chair and ran into the living room to watch television.

"Thanks for keeping him for me. I won't be gone long."

"It's okay. I don't mind."

"So, you're painting, huh?"

I nodded.

"Trees."

I thought that he'd ask me more questions about my plans for the day, but he only looked at me. Then he leaned forward.

"Do you wanna talk about last night?"

I shook my head.

"Everybody needs saving from something."

I glanced down at his hands and thought of the songs he'd played at the dinner, what else his hands were capable of.

"Like you saved me?"

I nodded.

"Maybe."

Nathan was laughing at the TV.

"I'll be back in a little while."

"Okay."

We walked into the living room.

"Bye Nate."

"Bye dah."

"See 'ya Samarra."

"Bye. Have a good day at work."

"Okay."

I stood in the doorway and watched Damon back out of the driveway and drive up the street and out of sight. I turned to Nathan again. He matched my smile with one of his own...

...The brushes sat in old jelly jars full of cloudy water. Nathan stood over his handiwork and ran his tiny fingers along the paper like a seasoned artist christening his best masterpiece. We'd listened to a few songs on repeat as we painted. His tree sprawled across the page, a giant elm against an orange backdrop. His skill level impressed me. We sat on the bench outside while we waited for our paintings to dry and drank our apple juice out of paper cartons and talked.

"Are you ready for school?"

He nodded between sips.

"Your dah says that your reading is getting better. I'm so proud of you Nate, really!"

"S'maruh?"

"Hmm?"

"Are you going with me to the bus?"

"Would you like me to?"

"Okay!"

"I'd be happy to walk you to the bus, Nate!"

He grinned eagerly. The sun cast a reddish-auburn tint on him and the next breeze disheveled his hair. He rubbed his hand over the tattoos on my arm, as if he thought they, too, were painted on and could be wiped away. I smiled.

"Are you hungry?"

"Sort of."

We packed up his watercolors and my acrylics, our brushes and paper towels and carefully set out our art on the kitchen counter. We rolled up our newspapers and put away our smocks. Then at the table (again) I set out a snack: grapes, and cheese sticks, and went upstairs to put away the supplies. With the box in my hands I pushed open the door to Damon's room and went to his closet. I stood on my toes and reached my hand back into the shelf at the top. I had barely brushed my hand there, but I'd felt something rigid, textured and I arched up to grab at it and rake it forward. A book fell and hit the floor. I set the cigar box down, bypassed the book that lay there in favor of what was lying beside it: A 3x5 photo.

On the back there was an inscription in red ink: Samarra L. Wells, 16, c. 2001.

I turned it over and felt as if nothing could ever fasten me down to the earth again. I canvassed the photo as I held it in my hands: My hair was windswept, an avid glint shone in my eyes, a smile flared out on my face. I was my mother's daughter, after all. I stooped down and picked up the book and tucked the picture back inside then went back downstairs to Nate...

...A little less than three hours later his front door opened and Damon stepped inside as he took his key out of the lock. He picked up Nate and counted him down before tossing him into the air, only to catch him again. He set him back on his feet and flopped down next to me.

"How was your day?"

"It was good. I got a lot done. Did you and Nate have a good time?"

"We did. It was fun."

His eyes fell to the book on my lap and he stared at it. I thought he'd be angry by my nosing into his things, his life. The sum of him and me had blended into more than it had been even just hours ago. He sat up and looked at the wall farthest away from us and I glanced away to give him some time.

"Damon?"

"Your mum lent me the book and she must've forgotten that uh, that your picture was in there."

I moved closer to him. Damon took the book from me and leafed through its pages until he came to the picture. He turned it over in his hand and we looked at it together.

"I used to look at it almost every day, like you were a sable haired siren calling out to me. I used to study your face, your eyes."

"Why didn't you tell me you had this?"

"I didn't know what to say to you."

"You didn't have to be so secretive. It's only a picture."

"Not to me."

We stared at one another, but suddenly he averted his eyes and settled into a quiet reservation as if he'd spoken out of place.

"Damon--"

"I always thought about you, how you were or what you were doing."

"Do you remember when I asked you about your favorite picture?"

He nodded.

"This is the one. This is it."

I thought of my mother and the obsessive love she'd had for my father, the strength, and indissolubly intense feelings, even now. It ran through my mind more than once as we sat there that perhaps the way we loved was somehow passed on from parent to child. The silence told me that Damon was thinking, too. I spoke up.

"What about letting this be what it is?"

He glanced at his son then exhaled sharply.

"Just say whatever you have to."

He looked at me for a long time before he ran his hand over his face, tried to regroup.

"Samarra, I…"

"Uh huh?"

"Samarra, I smaak you stukkend."

He'd said this as if it were an axiom and I shook my head a bit and smiled as he pulled a blue Sharpie marker from his pocket and reached for my hand. I obligingly rolled up my sleeve.

He flattened out my hand, palm side up, and held it in his own. He carefully drew a perfect heart in the middle of my hand. He continued, added an "I" to the left of the heart and a "U" to the right. In a minute my smile ceased to exist.

"Whatever it is, I want it with you Samarra. All of it."

I was still staring at the heart in my hand.

"Hey?"

I looked at him, all the while fighting the antigravity as a deep concentration set in his eyes.

"When you showed up here in Savannah, I took it as a sign that God intended this. I figured that--"

"How long have you had that picture?"

"Truthfully, almost a year."

"Don't you think that's kind of one sided?"

"No! I didn't know if you had someone or if you'd even care!"

"You don't want to know me Damon!"

"Why can't I be the one who gets to decide that, huh?!"

"Damon, you just--"

"I'm not asking you to move the world for me. Just give me a chance, honey."

I looked away. He lowered his voice as he continued.

"I can't just turn it off, 'ya know? Besides, if you didn't feel anything between us, then you wouldn't have kissed me the other night!"

When I turned around he leaned in.

"I'm not gonna lie to you, I enjoyed it! Your lips are really soft."

His frankness made me blush and I had a sense that he'd accomplished his mission when he smiled.

"Just say the word. Ball's in your court."

Nathan was watching a show with singing robots and dancing kangaroos. He was smiling, unconcerned about anything outside of this moment. The light from the TV screen suffused our faces. I felt his fingers clench my wrist and his beryl colored eyes leave me bereft of loneliness.

"I need to go take my shot."

He got up and helped me to my feet. I looked over at Nate, still enthralled by the action on the screen.

"Be right back Nate."

"'Kay."

I followed him up the stairs into the bathroom where I sat on the edge of the tub while he gathered his supplies together. He produced something similar in size and shape to a pen and pressed it against his index finger. A tiny drop of blood appeared and he held his glucose meter with a ready test strip up to it.

After a second there was an audible beep. While he washed his hands at the sink we talked.

"Nathan asked me to go to the bus stop with him."

"Really?"

"Yeah. I said I would."

He dried his hands.

"He's so excited!"

"I know. He's been trying to get me to talk you into staying over all week."

"I meant he's excited about school."

"Oh, right."

We laughed at the same time.

"For a long time after his mum left he would cry. He used to keep asking for her. It's the most impossible feeling, 'ya know, not being able to comfort him. I told him that it was okay to be angry."

"Good advice. I think he's going to be really self-aware. He's going to know which mistakes not to make."

He nodded.

"I wouldn't trade him for the world, but if someone would have told me that I'd be divorced with a kid by the time I was twenty-four, I'd have called them a liar."

"I never wanted to be back in Savannah either, but I still ended up right here."

"You were meant to be in his life. I've never seen Nate so happy. No one's ever treated him like he was important the way you do. I appreciate that."

"He's a really special little guy."

"That he is! He gets all that bossness from his dah!"

We both laughed. He gave me a kiss on the cheek while I was still giggling.

"Um, I wanted to ask you something."

"Mmm Hmm?"

"Nate's going over to Marcus and Kiva's to hang out with Felix tomorrow night. It's kind of an overnight thing. I'm going to be alone and I was wondering if you had any plans?"

"Oh..."

PROOF

We all but waltzed into the bar. It was packed tonight and the music was blaring from unseen corners as clouds of conversation and cigarette smoke filled the air. Pendant lights hung from the ceiling and the bar was so vast that it covered an entire wall. Damon waded into the crowd, relentless in his search for a table with me in tow. I could tell by the way that he navigated through the room that he'd been here before.

"C'mon."

He and I settled at a tiny corner set. He took off his coat and slung it across the back of the chair.

"Do you want a drink?"

I shook my head.

"No."

"What do you want then?"

He got up from his seat, looked toward the bar at the infinite selection.

"I'm gonna get a tequila shot or a dop of--"

"Damon?"

"Hmm?"

"My dad was an alcoholic. I don't want to end up like him. I don't."

He sat back down rather abruptly and looked at me.

"Why do you think you'll end up like him?"

I shook my head, never answered.

"What do you mean by 'he was'? I thought your parents split up?"

"They did. He died when I was eleven."

"What happened to him?"

"He pretty much drank himself to death, probably on purpose."

Damon sank down in his seat. He let his shoulders slump, looked crestfallen as if he had known Anderson Wells himself. After a moment he looked over my face. The intensity in his eyes was maddening.

"Samarra, I'm so sorry. I didn't know. Do you wanna leave then?"

"No, it's alright."

He moved his chair beside mine.

"What was your dah like?"

"From what I remember he was tall and he--"

"No, I mean how was he, as a person?"

I leaned in, thought for a second, moved around the anchor pendant at the end of the chain around my neck.

"Mmm. He was quiet. He didn't talk much. He was a brilliant man, but I think he spent most of his life lost in his own head, 'ya know? Nobody could get to him."

People milled about, talking and laughing and drinking. A few couples danced together while others gathered around the stage listening to the live band play. Damon slid the empty ashtray around on the table. He smiled and rose from his seat and jogged over to the stage. The house band acted completely normal as he turned to them, whispered something, and adjusted the microphone. In no time the music started up again and I felt the pulsating of my own heart as it seemed to keep time with the music.

Damon seemed comfortable as he slung an electric guitar over his shoulder. I'd managed to get close enough to see him and he stared at me headlong, faintly smiled as if he'd been expecting me. The bass guitar started and the makings of a song soon coalesced into a catchy, fun tune.

His voice was good and clear and even though his song wasn't familiar enough for me to sing along to, I was startled by how frequently I heard my name being repeated in song. After we'd taken our seats again he was still being cheered on from all sides by raucous applause.

"I can't believe you just did that!"

He scratched his eyebrow and grinned.

"Did it cheer you up?"

"Yeah."

"Yeah? Good."

"What else don't I know about you?"

"My middle name's Emory."

Our attention was diverted to a woman that had taken the stage and was singing a rather loud and boozed up rendition of some overrated pop song. Damon snickered to himself. Just as suddenly as it had started a fight broke out between two men and quickly escalated to the point that we both stood up. Damon put on his coat, clenched his keys and grabbed my hand with his free one.

"C'mon, let's go."

He walked ahead of me, sorting through the throngs to get to the front door, but when I didn't feel him holding on to my hand anymore panic set in. When I called his name,

I got no response above the noise and chaos. The crowd was like a sea rolling back and forth. I had almost made it to the door myself when I was knocked off my feet and looked up to see a man nearly three times my size standing over me.

He held a beer bottle in one hand and as he dragged his sleeve across his mouth, a savage look flared in his eyes. I got to my feet and shoved him, though he barely moved. In a quick moment Damon had reached me.

"Are you alright?"

"Yeah, I'm fine."

"Are you hurt?"

"No. I'm, I'm okay."

He held my face in his hands as I tried to convince him that I'd not been harmed. Damon pivoted around and confronted the man.

"Don't put your hands on her!"

The aggressor kept spouting threats and pointing in my direction. Everything was happening so fast. Damon turned to me.

"Go home Samarra!"

He tossed me his keys, but I felt so completely immobilized by fear that I didn't move immediately. I'd wanted to cry so badly that I could feel a tingling in my throat. My voice was shrill.

"Damon, don't!"

"Just go! I'll meet you at home!"

I'd just made it to the door when I heard glass breaking and felt nauseated. The noise was clamorous, and I turned around in time to see Damon land a blow to the side of the man's face that fell him. He crashed to the floor with such force that I thought he may never get up again, although soon enough he was stumbling back onto his feet.

The crowd that had gathered roared with a sick enthusiasm that went unmatched by the raw terror, the still stranger adulation I felt for him as I ran back to the car. It was all the proof I needed. . .

...When I flung open his front door Damon was standing on the porch soaked through with rain. The taxi he'd taken pulled away from the curb. He was grimacing in pain and I couldn't help feeling sorry for him. In the light I could see a fresh bruise on the right side of his cheek just beneath his eye.

"Can I talk to you?"

"Yeah, of course."

He quietly stepped inside and waited.

"I'll go get you a towel."

I slowly walked down the hallway to the bathroom, fighting the urge all the way to turn and look back at him. I grabbed the biggest towel I could find and the first aid kit. There were other bruises and scrapes, no doubt. I quickly returned to him and took a step closer, reached out and pressed the towel to his face, held it there.

"Why did you do that?"

He didn't respond, only stared at me. Then he placed his hand over mine.

"What were you thinking?"

"I was thinking about you."

Damon winced as I helped him out of his coat. He peeled off his t-shirt and threw it on the floor, closed his eyes again.

"Let me see."

His ribcage was badly bruised. My eyes welled with tears. I pressed my hand to his side, but he didn't flinch. I picked up some gauze and tape and bandaged him up as he looked on.

"Are you going to stay here tonight?"

I packed away the contents of the kit but didn't make eye contact with him yet.

"I don't know."

Damon held my hand.

"Hey?"

"Hmm?"

"I don't want either of us to have to live with any regrets Samarra. I love you."

I set down the first aid box.

"I've only told one man that I loved him my entire life Damon. Look where that got me."

"Well, start over", he nodded, "If you mean it, say it to me now."

I did not hesitate.

"I love you Damon. I do."

He suddenly moved toward me and we came together like magnets, forcefully. He handled me so carefully, his hands pressed against me, as if I might break beneath his grip. I closed my eyes halfway listening to the rain as it broke against the roof. I saw Damon's face in my mind: The way that his bottom lip was fuller than his top one, the slight upward curve at the tip of his nose, the light in his eyes that was always present, mischievous and youthful. I heard his voice as a whisper in my ear and I felt myself begin to let go. A million varying degrees of joy and exhilaration pass over us in the gathering depths as I was left liberated and delirious by our closeness.

I had never embraced anyone so tightly or felt as weak or as overwhelmed, so willing to be overtaken by someone else or to be bound to him in such a way. In this singular moment there was no pause, no lull between the eager thudding of our own hearts and the fleeting moments that passed into the gradual darkness of another night, between the staggering weight of our words and the things that had yet to be said.

HALCYON

I could hear Damon softly humming a song to himself from the inside of the bathroom. The alarm clocks' bright blue display radiated five thirty- two a.m. and I turned away. We'd stayed up talking, traversing the beautiful fitfully unknown questions together, transcending the answers. The bathroom door opened and he stepped out a moment later. I pretended to be waking up from some dream laden torpidity when he sat down in the chair opposite me where he'd slept. He put his hand on my shoulder and I opened my eyes, smiled.

"Hi."

"How are you feeling?"

"I'm okay."

In the four and a half weeks since circumstances had grafted us together and love had claimed us for its own, I'd stopped thinking about myself. I could hear him breathing softly and I nestled my hand into his, moved closer to him until only inches separated us. In the dim light I could barely make out his features, though I felt him plaintively staring at my face. When the silence had become too great I spoke up.

"Damon?"

"Hmm?"

"She never told me that she was sick."

"One day you won't even remember any of that. It won't matter how many times you argued or who said what. You'll remember the way she wore her hair or her laugh. Not this."

I looked down at my pillow, determined to smile my way past the hurt. His grip tightened around my hand.

"I know this is really hard for you. It's not even something that I could imagine having to deal with."

"I'm, I'm okay. Don't worry, I--"

"I heard you crying last night."

I looked away, half whispering the words to him.

"I thought you were sleeping."

He shook his head as he smoothed down my hair. His voice was deeply inviting when he spoke again.

"Do you wanna talk about it?"

I shook my head.

"No! Haven't you ever made someone a promise before?"

"Not one I know I couldn't keep."

I sat up in bed, flung my legs over the side. The view of him from over my shoulder steadied me.

"She's dying! If you were in my position, what would you do?"

Before he answered, I felt my heart telling me that this was the halcyon that would come before an approaching storm of bitter disappointment.

"I would find a way to make sure that I saw her again. I'd go to her and ask for forgiveness. I'd be brutally honest if I had to be. I'd say all the things I needed to say."

"I'm scared that I won't be able, I won't be strong enough to see her."

"You don't have to be strong. Not when it comes to this, okay?"

"Okay."

"I need you and Nate needs you."

Sun rays trickled through the blinds and danced over the floor, the bed. He stood up and faced me.

"What do you need from me?"

I slowly got up and moved over to where he was. He leaned forward and pressed his hands against my back, pulled me closer. I threw my arms around him and whispered in his ear:

"Will you come with me?"

SURRENDER

Damon was standing in the dining room in front of my painting. When I approached he didn't look away but tilted his head to one side. He took his time, letting his gaze stay in one place and then another like he was in a gallery with time immeasurable on his side. I looked from the painting to him as he stared straight forward at the canvas, immovable.

"What's it called? You never told me."

"Umm, it's called 'Soliloquy.'"

"You just made that up, huh?"

"Maybe."

We both laughed.

"I see something new every time I look at it. It's bakgat!"

"Hmm?"

"It's awesome!"

"Thank you."

"Mmm Hmm."

I looked at the painting and thought about the way I felt when it was finished, the way I still felt. He was smiling. Perhaps we were both reliving the moment.

"C'mon, we should probably get going. We don't want to be late."

"Okay..."

Afternoon had worn down into evening and the streetlights flickered on as we walked to my car.

"Do you wanna drive?"

"Okay."

I handed him my keys and opened the passenger side door but stood looking up into the sky at the stars. He was about to get into the driver's seat, but paused and looked in my direction, then upward, seeking.

"What is it?"

I laughed to myself.

"I remember the way she used to recite poetry. Dylan Thomas was her all-time favorite. 'And you, my father, there on the sad height. Curse, bless me now with your fierce tears, I pray. Do not go gentle into that good night. Rage, rage against the dying of the light.'"

...Damon was quiet as he drove on. It was hard to know what to say in the moment. Perhaps the truth was there, laid at our doorstep and fawning to get in.

All of my adult life I'd felt like my mother's words were the pendulum of my own weaknesses, razor sharp, that she'd held against me, ready ammunition. Outside of myself and this moment I was just as angry as I'd ever been, but my mind wasn't made up about what I'd say to her, the mercurial laying waste to this night. I felt for the anchor pendant around my neck. I was about to break my promise to her, felt like I couldn't face myself again after this.

...Doctor Gleeson walked with us to the cafeteria, my ground zero, sat across from Damon and me. He began by offering us his apologies, then he looked at me directly.

"Miss Wells, your mother's I.V. was taken out this morning. Her respirator is still connected for now. You should expect..."

He continued, but it was abnormal how nothing beyond this moment was important enough to register: Not the numbness in my heart, not the chill that ransacked my spine, not the tightness I felt around my eyes or the sickness that rose up in my throat. I hadn't realized that the sounds of my own labored breaths were what filled my ears until

Damon reached over and grabbed my hand underneath the table. I looked up, looked at him as his conversation with Doctor Gleeson never plateaued and they talked on.

The clock on the wall behind the doctor read seven fifteen and I thought about my last visit as we rose from our seats and began the walk to room two eighty. Damon offered me his arm and I stayed close to him as we moved along. The room was dimly lit. There were flowers from my grandparents on the nightstand, a water pitcher and cup, a framed photo of us.

Two chairs had been placed next to the window opposite her bed and we quickly took our seats. The doctor closed the door behind us, sealed us off from the outside world for whatever time remained. I turned back to Damon and felt my breathing cinch in after I set my eyes on my mother. All of her long, beautiful hair was gone, stripped away by the chemotherapy treatments, shaved down to a close cropped nothing. Her eyes were closed as if she'd fallen into the deepest sleep of her forty- six years. It was hard to think of all the wasted hours between us and not feel the stain of sadness seeping through. The ambient glow from her lamp at the head of the bed gave her an almost saint-like appearance as she rested on the soft pillows.

Her respirator took and gave air in a rhythmic stream and I soon forgot why we were here, sitting in near darkness, waiting and watching and wondering if she was between plains yet; hearing, but not responding; being touched, but not feeling. I knew that tonight was all I was going to have with her and that I couldn't waste it on my career or how much we'd been slighted by each other or our differences. I glanced at the wall clock. It was eight twenty -three when she first began to stir in her sleep. She spoke slowly without opening her eyes and I leaned forward, listening to her susurrated speech.

"Samarra?"

"Yeah, I'm here."

"I knew you'd come back."

I wondered in her lifetime how many words she'd spoken.

"How do you feel mama?"

"It doesn't hurt anymore."

"That's good."

I reached over and held her hand. This time she squeezed mine tightly. Suddenly the phone was ringing and Damon excused himself out into the hallway to take the call. I turned my attention back to my mother.

"You bought someone along, I see."

"Yeah, that's Damon."

"Is that the boy from next door?"

I nodded and watched her blink slowly, smile a little.

"You seem different with him."

I hadn't expected her to broach the subject.

"Do you love him?"

The question left me on the cusp of a renewed kind of wonder and I smiled in spite of myself.

"How can you tell?"

"I know you Samarra. I can tell."

I nodded.

"Yeah, I do."

"Make sure that he knows it."

"Alright, I will."

Damon came back into the room a second later. He sat back down in his chair. Another hour had ended, and we'd sat and talked, listened to Damon read, eaten and looked at pictures together. In the sixth hour Damon and I watched her sleep and talked quietly.

"It was your grandparents on the phone earlier."

"What did they say?"

"They're on their way here. It won't be too much longer."

He held my hand.

"You okay?"

"I dunno."

He looked at me for a while.

"She seems so happy."

"That's not what you were expecting, is it?"

"No."

Her face was relaxed, soft. The sullen dullness that had once tempered her expression was gone and it was as if at any moment her lips could have eased into a smile. I moved my chair closer to her bed and pulled my bag up onto my lap.

I found a clean sheet of paper in my sketchbook and a ballpoint pen and I began sketching her face. My grandparents and Uncle Mike came into the room just as I was finishing. They hugged me and Damon and rallied around my mother's bedside in different positions, sentinels, one on either side and the other at the foot. At first everyone was quietly thoughtful, perhaps each well versed in goodbyes in his or her own way. My grandfather was the first to engage her.

"Angelia? Angie?"

She opened her eyes and took in the latest arrivals.

"Hey mama, hey daddy! How're you? Hey Mike!"

They greeted her fondly, though like me, their hearts must have been disintegrating where they stood.

"I was just thinking about you."

It was enough to know that God heard her thoughts, every one of them originated in anger or love or uncertainty. Just maybe we all collected hearts the way some people saved buttons or magazines or stamps, placing them in airtight jars on shelves. My grandmother smiled at my mother.

"I know you're not afraid."

She shook her head.

"Not anymore."

It was two in the morning when she beckoned me over. As I stood next to her she breathed deeper and looked directly at me. All of my angst and fear and sadness melted away.

"You are a good daughter Samarra. Your father may have named you, but you were MY reward! I thank God for you. I love you."

I turned away and shed bitter tears. She hadn't had to say that she was sorry or that she'd wanted me to stay away when she was hurting or that she wasn't really angry with me, just the circumstances. My grandparents held her hand, stroked her hair. We told her that we loved her as Grandpa Jamison put his hand on her shoulder, seemingly ushering her away to a more peaceful place. Grandma Camille dabbed at her eyes with her handkerchief. Uncle Mike stood at the foot of her bed, head bowed, voice firm, controlled.

"I will sing praises to my God even with my dying breath. Psalm one forty one, two."

A momentary flash of pain froze on her face then there was surrender, erasing all the fine lines from breath to vapor as she drew in her last and fading, left us...

...Damon opened the car door for me, fastened my seatbelt for me when I couldn't. We were home when he looked over at me, loosened his tie.

"I am SO sorry Samarra. You're not alone in this, okay?"

"Mmm Hmm."

"Samarra?"

"Hmm?"

"I mean it."

"I know."

I turned away from him and stared out the window, not leaning on any one thing for too long. The moonlight poured in through the windshield, the passenger and driver's side windows, crashed against the dashboard, drenched every surface then our faces. It felt like being at a drive-in movie, waiting for the curtain to pull apart.

"What did I do? I wasted so much time instead of trying to help her, now she's gone! What did I do?"

"What could you have done?"

"I dunno."

"Hey. It's not your fault."

"She didn't get to see any of this."

"No, but do you know what she did get to see?"

"No."

"She got to see you; her family, the people she loved, the--"

"Then why's it over for her?"

He shook his head.

"I don't know."

We were both staring at each other now.

"I think I need to be alone for a while. Just for a little while--"

"Samarra, look, either you can trust that we'll get through this together or you can't, 'cause if not, then where do we go?"

"Damon, I--"

"You can't go!"

"Why?"

"Because I promised your mum I'd look after you, alright?"

I shook my head.

"What're you talking about?"

"When Mic and I went to see your mum, she had taken some medication. She was drowsy and I thought she was just talking out of her head, but she asked me to take care of you."

"What are you saying?"

He sighed and looked out the window. I took off my seatbelt, sat back in my seat, covered my face with my hands.

"Damon, that doesn't make sense! Why would she talk to you and not my grandparents?"

He shrugged and sighed.

"Sometimes the craziest things just make the most sense."

The dream I'd had of us circled around. I wished for a spare heart, that I could break the glass around it and use it in this emergency.

"I knew that she wasn't joking. It was like she was in a trance. You weren't there!"

I hesitated, but broke free of the hold.

"She told me once that the women in my family had dreams, premonitions that came true. My grandmother had them, my mother had them, now~"

He nodded.

"So do you."

"Yeah."

"She knew I'd find your picture, I think. She wanted me to find you."

He held my hand.

"It's gonna be alright. I know it is."

I nodded, believed every word he'd said to me.

THE NIGHT WATCH

Roxy's tags gently clinked together as she walked, her stride seemingly endless. For a while after Damon and I had left the house and began walking up the street I was quiet. Damon moved inward, seemed to hold me up as we moved along.

"Are you okay?"

I nodded, the previous nights' conversation gilding my face as I thought of what we'd said to each other, what I could never recapture with my mother.

"We've had Rox since she was a few months old. She grew up with Nate."

The black and light grey specks in her coat gave it a marbled appearance. I scratched her fleecy head just behind her ear.

"She's sweet."

"I think her size intimidates some people, but she's harmless."

The birds were singing in the trees overhead and I felt, if only for a moment, like I was a fresher, more modern rendering of myself. We stopped in front of a house where a gorgeous saffron colored hibiscus bush grew near the curb. He handed me Roxy's leash as he warily glanced over his shoulder and plucked a fully opened bloom from the shrub.

We took up our unhurried stroll while he stripped the foliage from the plant and tucked the velvety soft flower behind my ear. It matched my belted dress.

"It's perfect. Thank you."

He smiled.

"It really doesn't take a lot to make you happy, huh?"

"Nope."

Roxy pressed her nose to the sidewalk, sniffed at a leaf before moving on.

"Did you have a pet as a kid?"

"I had a goldfish once."

"Just once?"

"Yeah. Burial at sea by way of toilet."

He looked at me and we both laughed. Damon took a deep breath.

"I was thinking about going back home with Nate at some point, just getting back to square one."

"Oh. To Cape Town?"

"Yeah. It was just a thought, though. I'm not going anywhere."

Nepenthe spread along with the beauty in his eyes as he held my hand, squeezed it for a moment.

"Do you think you'll go back to Raleigh to stay?"

"I don't want to anymore."

"I don't want you to either."

Roxy was growing restless waiting to move. I hadn't realized how close to home we were until he took out his house key...

...I sat down on the couch while Damon let Roxy out into the backyard. He sat down beside me and loosened the laces on his boots.

"I can't believe it's almost another weekend."

"I'm trying not to think that far ahead."

"Once I go back to work, I won't have a lost weekend for a while."

"What would we do if we had a lost weekend?"

"Listen to music, watch movies, take some pictures, eat, have a dance off, I dunno, other stuff."

I tried to choose my next words unwantonly, though none would come. I tried not to chew my lip, but it was hopeless.

"Oh, Samarra, I'm not talking about--"

His expression grew thoughtful as his eyes searched my face and I tried not to second guess myself in the moment, to understand what he meant.

I had never thought of myself outside the lines of Jason in any other way and the sudden push and pull of shyness stopped me.

"I don't know what you're used to, but I'm not going to be the one to mess this up for you again. I really want to be with you, but once we cross that line we can never go back. I just have to do this the right way. Do you understand what I'm saying?"

I nodded.

"Mmm Hmm."

His phone rang and he winked at me before leaving the room to take his call. I exhaled, took appraisal of myself. While he paced back and forth in the kitchen I read each title on the bookshelf. Damon walked back into the living room a short while later.

"I have to go get a haircut. Do you wanna come?"

"Okay."

...After he'd let Roxy back in, retrieved his keys and wallet from upstairs and changed his shoes we were off. In the car he looked over at me.

"How're your friends, the ones with the new baby?"

"They're great. Zara's really growing! I'll tell them you said 'Hello'."

He turned the steering wheel as we took a steep corner.

"There's nothing like the smell of a newborn baby."

"Yeah, 'til it wears off."

We both laughed and when he rested his hand against mine I felt my breathing change. Damon stopped the car, put it in reverse and backed into the parking spot. Outside of the red brick building with the green door that was the barbershop he turned to me as he shut off the engine.

"Not a lot of women come in here."

"Mmm Hmm."

"Some of the guys are kind of rough around the edges, so could you just try and overlook them?"

I nodded.

"Okay."

The shop took on the appearance of a members' only social club. Cigar smoke emanated from the front room as we walked in. There was dark wood paneling, lots of light, a spacious waiting area, framed portraits on the walls and a refreshment station. There were large leather armchairs in the seating area and the sounds of electric clippers and conversations in progress. Damon put his arm around me and walked with me to the lounge.

"Hey everybody this is my lady Samarra."

"Hello!"

There were cordial 'Hellos' and a whistle as I sat down next to a man wearing a bow tie and reading a *GQ* magazine. Damon walked to the chairs at the back of the shop and sat down to wait for his haircut. The man reading the magazine quickly dropped his reading material and turned to me, extended his hand.

"I'm John."

"Samarra."

"Nice to meet you. How long have you known Damon?"

"A good while."

It was completely clear that John was not in need of a shave or a haircut and that his visit was purely a social one.

Someone else, a guy getting a hot shave, peppered in commentary from the chair where he sat.

"You're a whole lot prettier than his first wife."

I found that I couldn't form an answer and I grinned nervously. '*GQ* John' laughed.

"He never brings a woman around here unless it's serious. You must be something mighty special."

They were all looking at me, waiting for an answer, gauging me to see if I was prim or loose or bossy. I read each of them before speaking.

"Damon thinks so. He's a good man and that's all I care about."

"Spoken like a true girlfriend!"

They all laughed and I felt a little less on trial. Another patron approached and sat down in an unoccupied chair. He was the most reserved it seemed.

"Where'd you get your ink done?"

"At a place back home called 'Anvil'."

He lifted his sleeve to reveal an octopus tattooed on his left bicep. It was packed full of color and extremely realistic.

"It's beautiful."

"Thanks. So are yours."

"What do you do Samarra?"

"I'm an artist."

'*GQ* John' interrupted:

"Oh, like a performance artist?"

I laughed.

"No. I'm studying art at UNC."

"I always thought that artists had a better understanding of the world, like their souls are more in tune."

"Thanks. That's a kind thing to say."

He nodded. I poached a glance at Damon. He was just sitting down in the barber's chair for his haircut.

I turned back to the group at the offering of another question.

"Where are you from Samarra?"

"I'm from Raleigh."

'Hot shave guy' turned from the subject.

"You know, you can tell a lot about a guy by the women he's dated."

"I don't buy that!"

He sat up in his chair.

"It's simple. Look, when you're in a relationship, you're defined by the person that you're with, good or bad. Take Damon for instance."

"Okay."

"When he was with the leech, he started out alright, then she started sucking the life right out of him. It changed him! He hardly ever laughed. And between her and you, he was just going through the motions with everybody else."

I thought about how high the stakes must've been for him.

"Now he acts like he used to. He's back to normal."

"Normal?"

"Yeah. He's healthier, he smiles more. You don't think you had something to do with that?"

I shrugged.

"I guess so."

"Trust me, you didn't see him before. You would definitely know the difference."

They all agreed on some level and I tried not to blush at the laudatory comments. Damon was paying his barber when I looked up at him again. He emerged from the back with a grin that matched his haircut.

"You look so handsome!"

He gave my cheek a peck while the others jeered and whistled. He laughed and rolled his eyes, but otherwise ignored them.

"Are you ready to go?"

I nodded, stood up.

"It was nice to meet you all."

'GQ John' shook my hand.

"Likewise."

As he held the door open for me someone shouted:

"You better marry that one Damon!"

AND

"She's a keeper!"

We sat in the car for a few minutes before he started the engine.

"That was interesting. They're like the sounding board."

"That's one way to put it."

"Is it like that all the time?"

"No. Just on special occasions."

"Oh. I see."

He put the car in drive and pulled away from the parking spot.

"I knew you would."

I was thinking about how he'd introduced me to the barbershop quartet, the words he'd used and the potency that had been contained in them.

"Samarra?"

We stopped for a red light.

"Mmm Hmm?"

"How would you feel if I asked you to stay with me and Nate?"

The traffic light changed and we accelerated.

"Permanently?"

"Yeah."

I looked down at my hands as he leaned back against the headrest, scratched his eyebrow.

My heart skipped a little and I wished that I could have said more in this paramount moment.

"Look, I know that the timing's bad, but I figured this way you won't have to worry about things for a while."

"That's really thoughtful, but I don't know Damon."

He looked out the window. I felt a strange dichotomy between what I should do and what I desperately wanted to do.

"I'm sorry."

"Don't be."

We pulled into a parking spot, unfastened our seatbelts.

"Ready?"

"Mmm Hmm."

Nathan was due out of his day camp at any moment. There were other parents waiting outside as we began to walk to Nate's classroom. He moved closer as we walked along and held my hand. I looked at him, his wry smile.

"I heart you."

"I heart you, too."

When we rounded the corner and got to classroom number nine, Nathan and his classmates were lined up and waiting to be dismissed.

His eyes brightened and he flashed a toothy grin at the sight of us. The other kids filed out and met up with their parents, but Nate ran at full speed and jumped into Damon's arms.

"Hey dah!"

"Hey!"

"Hey S'maruh!"

"Hi!"

"Did you have a good day?"

"It was okay, but at lunch they ran out of cookies and Tabitha didn't get one, so I gave her mine."

"Who's Tabitha?"

"She sits next to me in class."

"That was a nice thing you did Nate. We're so proud of you!"

Nathan swelled with pride as he held his head a little higher. Damon helped him into his seat. Only when we were all strapped in did we go. I looked at Nate in the backseat. He was reading a book quietly to himself. I glanced over at Damon. His elbow was propped up against the window. He had on his sunglasses and was the epitome of cool. I was trying not to be stare, but he already noticed.

"What?"

"Nothing."

We pulled into his driveway. Damon helped Nathan out of the car then he turned to me.

"What are you going to do with your flower?"

"Maybe I'll press it in a book."

"Really?"

"Yeah. Why not?"

He shook his head and laughed, picked up Nate's backpack.

"That's so old fashioned!"

"I know. I have my moments."

Damon looked over at Nate.

"How about some chocolate milk kid?"

"Yeah!"

"Yeah, c'mon!"

Damon took Nate inside and got him situated. My phone rang. It was Grandma Camille.

"Samarra, how're you?"

"I'm okay. How are you and grandpa holding up?"

"We're taking it one hour at a time, literally."

"I know. I just can't believe she's gone!"

Damon walked outside and stood on the front lawn next to me.

"Tomorrow? Okay. I love you, too. Okay. Bye."

I hung up the phone.

"Damon."

I grabbed his arm, half whispered his name again. Everything was becoming way too real suddenly and I felt myself turning inside out.

"What's happening tomorrow?"

"They're planning her memorial service and they can't find a pastor."

He exhaled deeply. I turned around and walked down the sidewalk. Damon ran after me and stood in the way.

"Wait! Where are you going?"

"Please, I just--"

The look on Damon's face was mnemonic to me. I thought of that night at the bar, how angry he'd been, the kind of action he'd taken to protect me. His demeanor slowly changed back to what it had been.

"Don't go, alright? I've got you. C'mon inside..."

...Damon coaxed me into the kitchen to help with dinner. Before I could finish one task, he had another one set before me. He'd made it clear to me that this was busy work and that we would talk later after Nate was asleep. I appreciated his candor. We were standing at the sink. I turned to Damon.

"What are we making again?"

He shook his head and laughed.

"Pepper steak with portabella mushrooms and green beans."

"Oh. Sounds good."

"I always thought that I'd cook my way around the world."

"That's really ambitious."

"Yeah."

"What's the strangest thing you've ever eaten?"

"I ate a scorpion once."

"Eww!"

He laughed.

"It tasted like chicken!"

"So gross!"

"That's considered a protein. It's a staple in some countries."

"I'll stick to pepper steak..."

...We all sat around the table after dinner. Knowing what I knew about my mother made it nearly impossible for me to wear the brave face, but I kept in step fairly well. Damon got up from the table and began clearing away the dishes. After he'd stacked them together he turned to Nate.

"Ready for your bath?"

He finished his milk.

"Mmm Hmm."

"Go ahead and get ready then."

Nathan hugged my neck then excused himself to go gather his bath necessities.

"I'll see you later, okay?"

"Okay."

"I'll be right up Nate."

"Okay, dah."

Damon finished scraping the dishes and he spoke without looking up at me.

"Thanks for not running out on me."

"Thanks for coming after me."

"We're gonna get through this, alright?"

"Alright."

Damon pulled me into a hug, gave me a quick peck then turned and went upstairs. I slowly got up from my seat and ran a sink full of warm soapy water for the dishes...

...Our evening was slated to end where it had many times before, in front of the fireplace. The dinner dishes were done, Nathan was freshly washed and asleep in bed, the recycling was waiting at the curb for tomorrow's pickup and Roxy was peaceful and at rest. Damon hunkered down in his chair. I'd already retreated inside my head and was thinking about how long I could stay there when his voice evaporated any designs I'd had for evasion tonight.

"Samarra?"

"Hmm?"

"I haven't had time to talk to Nate about what's happening, but when I can do you want to be there?"

"Okay."

I'd thought about tomorrow all during dinner: The way my mother would look, who else would be there, afterwards. The night watch was rigorous. Perhaps it had begun the day I'd set foot on her doorstep. It had forced me closer to Damon, closer to anyone else outside of my grandparents than I'd ever been before.

It had made me grow up. It had drawn me out of hiding and given me a chance to ask questions of my mother that I had never dared to before. It had given me hope where there had been none and love when I'd thought it most impossible...

THE TRUST FALL

I sank down into the bathtub and put my feet on the tub spout. The suds from the bubble bath made little foamy peach scented islands around me. I'd been soaking long enough for my hands to pucker and I had just about macerated the jarring echo of the flat line of my mother's heart monitor, the pain on my grandparents faces, the guilt that felled me. The deep haze of sadness had eroded my sense of who I was, and I knew that in my silence I was making things worse between Damon and me. We'd been pushed into discomposure, both imagined and real, and these last few days had been spent locked in quiet observance, the hope of peace rising in us like a current in Adam's ale, like we were empty vessels waiting for Providence.

After my bath I walked downstairs into the kitchen. Damon was working at the counter, pouring over his photographic slides with his loupe. He held the slides in his hand, sorted through them and as I approached he looked up at me.

"Hey."

"Hey."

"You okay?"

"Yeah."

He hesitated for a bit.

"Are you hungry?"

I nodded. He set down his tray of slides and walked over to the refrigerator. With his back toward me I felt more comfortable speaking up, though we'd gone too long without having a real conversation.

"Thanks, Damon."

"It's alright."

He put yesterday's primavera on the counter, kept rummaging through the fridge. Suddenly the phone was ringing. I excused myself to the living room and picked it up, slowly put it to my ear.

"Hello?"

"Samarra?"

"Yes?"

"Samarra, it's Rachel, Rachel Marsden--Damon's mum."

"Oh. Hello."

Her voice was immediately reassuring, as if my heart was transparent and she could see through.

"We were calling to let you know that we're so sorry to hear about you mum. Damon's dad and me, we'll be praying for you."

"Thank you. I'm glad that you called."

I sat down on the couch.

"Damon told me that she was very important to you. He said that you were just starting to mend things with her."

"Yeah. We never got to hammer out the rough spots, though."

A whisper light rain began to fall outside, and I could imagine it deftly washing away every footstep my mother had ever taken, leaving no traces of her in the fade.

"It's strange not having her here."

"In a way, she's with you every day."

I could hear the smile in her voice.

"Damon says that you look just like her. He speaks very highly of you both."

"Thank you."

"I am sorry that our first phone chat is under these circumstances, but we'll call and check in with you later."

"I appreciate your call."

"It's the least we could do. We'll speak to you soon."

"Okay. Goodbye."

"Goodbye."

I hung up the phone and walked back upstairs to get my jacket. Damon was standing in his bedroom at the closet looking at something on the floor. When I got closer I saw him staring at my bag, still full and unzipped sitting on the floor of the closet. He turned around, his brow arched up on one side.

"You never unpacked your things. Why not?"

I stood answerless before him.

"Where's Nathan?"

"He's sleeping. Why haven't you unpacked?"

He took a step toward me and I froze.

"One thing's just gonna lead to another and I'll wake up one morning and you won't be here--Is that it?"

"No, it's not! I wouldn't--"

"I know that you weren't keen on the idea of us under the same roof, but I need you to be here now."

"I'm trying! It's not, I'm trying! I just don't want you to be mad at me."

"Samarra, I'm not mad at you."

I looked away.

"I'm going to go check on Nate."

I turned to leave when he reached out and grabbed my arm.

"Hold on for a minute."

"What?"

I wanted to close ranks around him, but instead he put his arms around my waist, his fingers tracing along the buttons up the back of my blouse. My heart fluttered and in truth it didn't feel like a piece of unclaimed baggage anymore.

"I know I've been pushing you too hard and I'm sorry!"

I nodded.

"I didn't think it would be like this, honestly. The last thing I ever wanted to do was shut you out."

"I know you didn't mean it. It can't ever be easy. It's not supposed to be."

"A little push in the right direction never hurts, though."

He pretended to shove me and we both laughed, albeit lightly.

"Your mom's nice."

He smiled a bit.

"Yeah. She said she'd call."

Damon looked over at the door. Nathan was standing in the hallway holding his sock monkey.

"Hey buddy. What're you doing out of bed? What's wrong?"

"I can't sleep."

Nathan looked at me, his curiosity amassing.

"S'maruh?"

"Hmm?"

"Are you sad?"

I bent down next to him. I couldn't look at him and lie to him. I couldn't pretend. I couldn't patronize him or refuse him this. I nodded. Damon looked on.

"Yeah. I lost my mum because she was sick."

"Did she die?"

"Yes."

"I don't want you to be sad."

"I know. Your dad is doing a good job of helping me get better."

Nathan smiled at me.

"You're a good helper, too."

I tickled him until he dropped his sock monkey. His laughter filled the room and when he squeezed my hand I felt like he wouldn't worry anymore.

"It's gonna be alright, okay?"

"'Kay."

Damon lifted up Nate.

"It's sleepy time Nate."

The younger Marsden rested his head on the senior Marsden's shoulder. Damon leaned over and gave me a peck on the cheek. I blushed and felt the rush of warmth to my face. He went to put Nate to bed and I walked over to the closet. I looked down at my bag. This canvas duffle bag and its contents and their location and this finality I felt were the last steps in the trust fall between us. I picked up one article of clothing and a hanger until each one was neatly in place in his closet. I wondered if I would always crave the simplicity of what he and Nate had or if they were things I couldn't learn to do without. I didn't hear him come back into the room, but he was standing near the door when I looked up again. He moved closer to me and I began to realize how much I'd missed him, as if he would rescue me with the strength of his embrace or the touch of his hand. He put his arms around me and pulled me in.

"Samarra, if you need to talk to me about anything, I'm here. I can't know what you're going through, but if you wanna talk to me, I'm here."

"Okay."

"I've been thinking that maybe you don't know where you stand with me, with us, and it's my job to fix that 'cause you're not just something temporary to me, Samarra. You could never be that to me. I love you."

"I love you, too."

I was trying to uncover the origins of us, where we'd began, but I knew it did not matter and I did not move quickly to dry my teary eyes . .

THE REQUIEM

He leaned over and whispered in my ear:

"It's almost done. You're doing great."

I nodded. My eyes were shut tightly, welded closed it seemed. There were so many people here for my mother I'd be letting them down if I stormed out, but they couldn't know about our taciturn final few weeks or how it had been a challenge for me to even talk about her now. I wanted to quantify all of the things that I remembered best about her while I sat there, like how many times she'd sang to me or how many times she'd made me breakfast or our serious conversations or how many times she'd braided my hair or read to me, but I kept losing track. Suddenly, I felt Damon let go of my hand and I looked up to see him slowly rising from his seat. He straightened his jacket as he made his way to the front of the room. He stood behind the lectern and paused briefly before he began.

"Good afternoon everyone. When I think of Ms. Wells her quality as a person comes to mind first. She was kind and hard working. She was a daughter and a mother and a sister. She was a real believer with a deep, unshakable faith and she will be missed inexhaustibly by her family, her friends, and her neighbors."

He bowed his head and spoke words in Afrikaans that were a mystery to me*:

"God seen die siel van hierdie passasier as sy terug na die aarde. Veroorsaak haar sterflike vlees om te rus in vrede, totdat die dag van die opstanding. Seen die wat oorgebly het, om hulle te lei deur middel van hul smart. Gee aan hulle vrede. Hou hulle in jou ewige sorg, Here. Amen." {*God bless the soul of this passenger as she returns to the earth. Cause her mortal flesh to rest in peace until the day of resurrection. Bless those who remain, guide them through their grief. Give them peace. Keep them in your eternal care, Lord. Amen.}

Damon sat beside me and gathered my hand up in his again. He stared straight on. We'd just navigated through the most painful part of my life and he had not missed a step.

I'd hoped that the pain that she felt had lasted only a short while, if not at all, that she'd slipped away peacefully with no further designs on this earth or no concerns to linger on. I knew that if there were questions that had gone unanswered about her life that I should push them back now. Some threads were never meant to be unwound. Sed rebus (Not by words, but by things). When it was done and over with I couldn't blame her for trying to make my life better.

Grandma Camille keeping a composure that was perfectly placed with her regal, refined bearing. Grandpa Jamison stared straight ahead, his posture still and restrained, his lips trembling ever so often, somber, but steady. Uncle Mike's head was down, as if he couldn't bear her away just yet. He looked at her picture occasionally and smiled to himself.

After a co-worker sang a song, 'The Parting Glass,' and had told of remembrances of my mother and everyone had filed past her picture at the front of the chapel leaving behind flowers and sentimental tokens only the five of us remained in the front row. Grandpa James got up first. He stood looking at her portrait for a long while as if he were debating something great within himself. He approached Grandma Camille and put his hand on her shoulder. There was an unspoken solidarity that breached even this moment and brought them closer together, still. Damon turned and looked at me.

"Could you give me a minute? I need to talk to your grandparents about something."

"Okay. I'll meet you back at the car."

I hugged my uncle, grandmother and grandfather then walked outside to Damon's SUV. I got into the passenger seat and closed the door, fastened my seatbelt then unfastened it, squirmed around, carefully studied my mother's photo from the program cover, cleaned out my bag and talked to Dorian and Crystal on the phone before Damon walked back to the truck. He got in and fastened his seatbelt, hurriedly glanced at me.

"Ready?"

"Where are we going?"

"Some place neutral."

"Neutral?"

He started the truck.

"Mmm Hmm."

Everything that I thought about when I repeated the word to myself was drab, easily pacified and not committed to anyone or anything, the grayest grey. I felt woefully left out of the loop and wanted to ask more questions. Things had shifted in my world some for better, some for worse, but in the shifting I'd taken more risks, had more fun and stretched myself further than I would've ever dared to before. The requiem for my mother over, I could inch forward. I thought about Uncle Mike, Grandma Camille, and Grandpa Jamison and how they would make it over. I sighed aloud.

"I want you to be happy Samarra."

"I know. I'm trying to remember how."

He put his arm around me, turned a corner and let the steering wheel slip through his hand before docking into a parking space. He turned off the engine and we sat quietly.

"Know what?"

"What?"

"There's only a handful of people that've taught me something that I remember at least once a day every day."

"Like what?"

"One of my mum's favorite sayings is of Saint Benedict's: 'Listen and attend with the ear of your heart.'"

"Is that what we're doing now?"

"I think so."

I smiled a little.

"C'mon, I want to show you something."

"Okay."

As we got out of the truck, I surveyed my surroundings. The ornate statuary outside The Telfair Museum met my eyes. I'd always wanted to see a showing here but could never find the time. He looked at his watch as we walked down the sidewalk. The parking lot was deserted.

"Where's everyone else?"

"Hopefully sleeping."

He took a key from his jacket pocket and unlocked the door. Once inside he snapped the lock closed behind us. Damon walked closely beside me. Our shoe soles on the hardwood floor were the only noises that impeded the quiet in the massive space of plain white walls lined with canvases and sculpture. There was something alarmingly thorny about us being in a place like this with no supervision long after it had clearly closed. As we walked on he turned and looked at me.

"Close your eyes."

"Okay."

There was nothing that he could do now to cause my trust in him to disengage. I closed my eyes and he held my hand and guided me forward. I felt my heart pounding like a sledgehammer, but when we stopped walking my heart was allayed.

"You can open your eyes now."

I saw him first in his gray suit and blue bow tie, his everlasting smile. When I glanced over his shoulder I saw it: My painting hanging on a wall that was less populated by others' work. As we got closer my head swam at the possibility of how many other people had seen it, all of the feeling I'd placed upon it, and how I had yet to say anything. The card to the right of the canvas identified it as 'Soliloquy' by artist Samarra L. Wells and I knew that he thought my art was deeper and more relevant than I ever gave him credit for.

"There was a charity event here tonight. Press from the paper was here. People paid fifty dollars just to get in."

"Really?"

"Mmm Hmm. The proceeds are going to a breast cancer research charity in honor of your mum. And guess whose work got the best response?"

He was holding my hand, but it still wasn't registering.

I stood wide eyed and staring on. He didn't give away his enthusiasm and played along. I finally muttered.

"Whoa!"

He hugged me tightly.

"I am SO proud of you Samarra!"

"You did this for me?"

He shook his head.

"This is small change compared to what you've done for me."

We sat on a bench in front of my painting. He put his arm around my waist and slid me closer to him.

"What do you think you'd be doing if we hadn't met?"

"You mean if your car hadn't broken down?"

"And I hadn't been running scared."

"Or if I hadn't seen your picture in a book."

He cupped my face in his hand, his thumb marking my jawline. He shrugged slowly and all the trappings of an appositeness were in that moment.

"Who can say?"

"Do you know what it reminds me of now?"

He shook his head.

"It reminds me of that Coldplay song, 'Yellow'."

Damon tilted his head to the side.

"I can see that."

We both laughed. He stared at the painting then I caught him looking at me and when we faced each other he launched into his own rendition of the song. No matter how much I laughed, he kept right on singing, his voice echoing in the hollowness. He lifted me up over his shoulder and spun me around. I giggled as long as he twirled me. Neither of us heard the door open and when a light came on I looked up and saw someone, a security guard, standing in the doorway. I lowered my voice and whispered.

"Damon, look."

He spun around and faced the doorway, slowly lowered me back down to the ground. We looked at each other. Damon stepped forward, but before he could speak, the man responded:

"The museum's closed!"

Damon put up his hands.

"We're sorry. We didn't know!"

"Yeah, sorry officer."

Damon looked back at me and grinned. I picked up my bag and followed behind him. The guard walked quickly after us and for the second time in the same night we heard the heavy turn of the door latch. Outside on the steps, we regrouped.

I looked at him squarely.

"Damon?"

"Hmm?"

"That was crazy!"

"I didn't mean to--"

"It's okay, really."

I could tell that my smile was unexpected by the way that his brow furrowed. The lights inside the museum went out. He turned back toward me. My phone was ringing.

"Might be important."

"After the day I've had, it doesn't matter."

Damon reached for my bag. I almost willingly handed it over and watched him ramble through it in search of my phone.

"You've got a lot of stuff in here! It's like a vortex."

"I have to be prepared."

"I'll bet. That'll come in handy with Nate."

He stopped rambling and looked up at me.

"Oh no! What time is it?"

"I dunno."

Damon checked his watch. He handed me back my bag.

"Dinner starts at six thirty. C'mon, we're gonna be late!"

He took hold of my hand and we ran down the steps, through the parking lot back to the truck. We were both winded, amused as he helped me into the passenger seat then walked around to the driver's side and got in.

"It's good to see you smile."

"It's partly your fault."

A smug grin stretched across his face.

"Find me guilty, then."

He started the truck and revved the engine before we peeled out of the lot.

THE LIONS' SHARE

I was motionless in the water. The light from above made the crystalline depths like the swells of Muizenberg beach as the patterns played across my face and I sank deeper still. A current tumbled me and turned me over until I was disoriented and couldn't find my way. My whole body ached and I was left powerless to free myself and kick for the surface. Being driven into the sea was nightmarish, cold, void and hollow.

My lungs began to burn for lack of air, an aching that was deep and chronic. It felt remotely familiar, reminded me of the way I was as a kid, fearful of the ones that I loved, always worrying that something I'd say would offend or anger them, that they'd detect my artlessness and cast me away. I'd kept my own counsel for so long that my iron-like resolve had caused my atrophied heart to turn, had left me coveting some solace. I heard Damon calling me and felt what I might've imagined to be a powerful suction pulling me into the middle of the pool and then his voice, again, like oxygen frantically pursuing something or someone that was as distant as the sun. His tone and inflection rose and changed as he kept calling me, but I couldn't open my eyes. I felt hands grip my shoulders and I shuddered and finally opened my eyes. My hands were clenched.

"Samarra?"

Damon was kneeling in front of me. I was sitting on the edge of the bed with my legs over the side. He pulled my sweater up around my shoulders and I could see a prevailing fear in his face, as if there was nothing in my eyes, no spark of recognition, only emptiness. He brought his hand up to my face, hadn't needed permission to be merciful.

"Hey?"

I looked at him. His eyes were still wide as they searched my face.

"I kept on calling you, but you wouldn't answer me!"

"I couldn't. I-"

"Take your time."

I looked down at my hands.

"I was drowning! It was so real!"

"I know it was scary, but you're here with me. You're safe, honey."

His arms tightened around me as I buried my face in his shoulder and my hands against his chest.

"I'll never be normal Damon. I'm just not."

"If you were, I wouldn't be interested."

The lions' share of these days was passing. We'd spent a Christmas together and celebrated birthdays.

I'd moved my last few boxes in and settled the matter of my final exams and graduation with the UNC registrar and Dean of Admissions. My Bachelor of Arts in Art History diploma would be arriving in the mail directly. The house where I'd grown up was no longer in the family. My grandparents had sold it to the church and I had received my parent's estates a few months later. Damon had sold three of his prints (for how much he wouldn't say) and was back at work full time and we read to Nathan every other night before bed and our Bible together every Thursday. We still had dinner at my grandparents' once a week and went to church on Sundays. The circumference of the world had shrunk down to fit us, it seemed. I'd made up my mind that if I was given another chance to right my wrongs, there would be no hesitations, no more loitering. He grabbed my hand and pulled me up off the bed.

"C'mon, you owe me breakfast. I like my eggs over easy."

...Nathan was still asleep and Damon and I sat at the island in the kitchen. He was drinking from his coffee cup, looking out the window. His hair was perfect: Short back and sides, long on top. He suddenly turned to me.

"'Ya know, as long as we've known each other, I've never taken your picture."

I put my cup down.

"Do you mind?"

"No."

"Meet me in the living room in ten minutes?"

"Okay."

We both left the kitchen. I ran upstairs, thinking of what I should wear, trying to remember the last thing he'd complemented me on. Should I put on makeup or go natural? Should I wear hoop earrings or studs? Sneakers or heels? Should I pick out a dress or jeans and a t-shirt? Should I take out my nose ring? I was an expert at wasting time it seemed and ten minutes had lapsed sooner than I expected. Damon called upstairs to me.

"Samarra, you ready?"

"Yes. I'm coming!"

I'd settled on a long sleeve blue chambray button down shirt and fitted black jeans, bare feet. I imagined him picking up his camera and fitting on the lens, wiping it down, making sure his memory card was in. Damon was standing at the foot of the stairs when I finally met him near the bottom. He was holding his camera at the ready.

"Mmm!"

"What's that mean?"

"You look great!"

"Mmm!"

We both laughed.

"Do you wanna see the last pictures I took?"

"Okay."

He stood beside me and turned the camera toward me, placed it in my hand. I looked at him, back at the camera as he scrolled through.

"Oh, I got you something to wear for the picture."

I kept scanning through the photos.

"What is it?"

Damon was quiet and when I looked at him he was down on his knees in front of me. I stared him down, curious. He opened my hand and placed something in it, took the camera from me. I couldn't stop gazing at him, my effusive heart set alight. I opened my hand, inhaled sharply. There was a tiny velvet box. When I opened the box, it was as if I'd stepped outside of myself at the sight of what it held:

A breathtakingly beautiful French-set diamond band engagement ring. There were two square cut diamonds that flanked a larger center set one. He raised the camera and I heard the shutter click. Neither of us breathed, it seemed, and I felt myself leaning in.

"I've been all over the world, but I don't want to take another step without you."

He rubbed my legs just behind my knees.

"I was always sure about you Samarra. I thank God for bringing you to me. I love you and I want you to marry me."

I rushed forward and almost knocked him over. He hugged me for a long while.

"Well, is that a yes?"

I stopped to wipe my eyes (and look at the ring again) as Damon took more pictures. I nodded.

"Yes."

"Yes?"

Fade

"Yes!"

He pulled me down to where he was sitting and kissed me until we both were left breathless...

MACHINE HEARTS

One thousand ninety- eight days had melted into another summer. I ran my hand over the bluish green handira draped across the foot of the bed and thought of the handwritten letter that Damon had attached to it. It was a promise of sorts, that come what may, he would never deny me his time or his love or his patience. I'd read it again this morning as he slept and thought of how I'd never questioned myself with him a single day after we were married.

A life unordinary was what I'd always wanted, before I knew it for myself. The picture on the nightstand snared my attention and I smiled. Grandpa Jamison, Grandma Camille, Crystal and Dorian, myself, Damon, Richard and Rachel Marsden, Aaron and Nathan huddled comfortably together on the steps of the courthouse for our family wedding photo. Grandma Camille and Grandpa Jamison were my witnesses, gladly gave me away, had prayed over me and Damon.

His parents were gracious, interesting. His brother, who was his direct opposite, gregariously told me stories about when Damon was a kid and the adventures they'd had, adventures that included a backyard fort, streaking and the occasional sports related mishap. He'd brought along a picture of the two of them when they were little. Damon, who was slightly the taller of the two, was wearing an impossibly adorable smile and a Fair Isle patterned sweater.

When I examined it closer, I saw that their sweaters actually matched. I giggled aloud, overcome by their cuteness. Aaron had assured me that I was the best addition to their family to come along in a while and that he'd teach me everything I needed to know, like how to play guitar, the best words to say in Afrikaans and how to prepare a proper sosatie. Aaron said that his parents were glad that Damon wasn't going to end up a lonely, lovelorn hermit and that they'd never seen him and Nathan happier.

Now I looked over at Damon sleeping soundly and I thanked God that for as many times as I'd been written off he'd sent someone to me who would never bail on me. It was enough for me to be here now. I kissed his cheek, got up and crept across the hallway to check on Nate. I stepped over Roxy's back legs, angled over the hall. Nate was asleep, the gathers in his blanket swelling then dropping over and over.

I looked around his room at his things: His backpack, a keyboard in the corner, soccer equipment. We'd found a common bond in our mutual love of The Carolina Rail Hawks soccer team and during the regular season we would catch a few matches. It hadn't been difficult for me to learn his routines and we comfortably acclimated to one another through his soccer practices and my cooking that he thought was 'cramazing'. We painted together sometimes while we listened to Johnnyswim. My grandfather taught Nate to play chess and they got along famously.

My grandmother was his 'other nana' and she showed him how to start a vegetable garden and how to play piano. He was tall for his age with a mop of dark hair, an inexhaustible energy and a loyalty for his friends Felix and Thomas, who were in the same classes together. He was a bright student who did well in school.

I closed his door and left him to rest as I stepped back out into the hallway and absentmindedly glanced down the hallway. On a side table was a fresh bunch of dahlias in a small vase. They had been my mothers' favorite. Angelia Wells had been gone now for three years. It did not matter when I'd made landfall there was no amount of time that could have properly reconciled us to one another. There was no easy way to resign myself to the fact that our secrecy had almost destroyed us.

I'd made my own sort of peace with her fading away and bound myself to my new family and tried to cut loose the hurt and resentment and anger that I felt. I knew that the day would come when I would no longer feel an asperity at the thought of my mother, but I wasn't there yet. Damon and I prayed together (a lot) until it mattered less and less how many times I'd been wronged and turned it over and let it pass.

For a brief second, I saw the flash of Damon's face in my mind, the way he'd looked, misty eyed, at me in my patterned V-neck dress, his fresh haircut and neatly pressed suit, the white peony tucked into his lapel, afterwards. Our ceremony had been small and informal, simple and personal held in the county clerk's office in the courthouse on a Wednesday afternoon.

At first, I'd found myself repeating the words, 'Damon is my husband' just to make sure, but I knew for certain the next morning when I opened my eyes and saw him there beside me, smiling.

"Good morning, Mrs. Marsden!"

"Good morning, Mr. Marsden!"

I'd come to him almost shyly at the start of things, unsure of myself in certain ways, though he'd been a perfect and attentive gentleman. We'd effectuated a bond together and I'd become someone different with him. Today, almost a month later, I stood in the bathroom. At the back of the vanity drawer I picked up a narrow small box, peeled off the safety seal and opened it at one end. I read the instructions, re-read them then crumpled them up and turned the box over in my hands, closed the door. There was no fear in my heart, only an alacrity for us as I washed my hands and prepared the test the way the directions had read. I looked at the box again. There was a picture on the front of a woman, smiling widely, not an ounce of concern on her face, as invented as the mare's nest that it was. I mimicked her expression, laughed a little to myself, waited for the go...

A few minutes later the front door opened and I heard him put his keys on the table. He walked down the hallway and stopped at our room. I could hear him struggle out of his shoes and change clothes. He checked on Nate then circled back around to where he started.

"Samarra, I'm home."

"I'm in the bathroom."

He stood at the door.

"How was your day?"

"You'll never believe it!"

It was impossible not to smile and an incurable grin was glued to my face. There was an excitement in his voice that could not be reduced and an anxiousness that radiated through the door to me as I listened eagerly and washed my hands. He'd been working so hard, late nights editing and uploading, preparing and finishing, staying in his darkroom for infinite hours, cycling in and out of sleep to finish his editorial piece in the hopes of earning a promotion. He had submitted his final work almost a week ago and waited for his supervisor to dissect every inch of the slides, critique his work, weigh its merit. Now, it seemed, the suspense was about to be over. I clenched the test in my hand as I opened the door. He took a step forward and smiled slowly, evenly.

I thought about all the things that he and I had made together. I had broken the secret cipher of his heart and in turn he had written mine. He was holding an envelope in his hand. He drew me in and hugged me, pecked my cheek. It was wildly impossible just how much the rest of our lives would be changed by plastic and paper, their contents. His hands clenched my waist. The mechanisms of our machine hearts had not corroded. The cogs and gears and springs and wheels were sound, and I knew that the impetus that moved us would never be as strong as it was now, that God was always faithful. We both began at the same time, laughed, regrouped.

"You go first!"

THE END.